KEYNAN MASTERS

AND THE PEERLESS MAGIC CREW

KEYNAN MASTERS
AND THE PEERLESS MAGIC CREW

DAVAUN SANDERS

inkyard PRESS

ISBN-13: 978-1-335-45804-9

Keynan Masters and the Peerless Magic Crew

For questions and comments about the quality of this book, please contact us at CustomerService@Harlequin.com.

Inkyard Press
22 Adelaide St. West, 41st Floor
Toronto, Ontario M5H 4E3, Canada
www.InkyardPress.com

Printed in U.S.A.

Recycling programs
for this product may
not exist in your area.

For Azure & Dakari

CHAPTER ONE

BIZZY BLOCK

Quiet as it's kept, this summer is my most epic yet.

You see what I did there? I know you did! A year ago, that rhyme would've cost me ten pages worth of scribbles. My poems are on a whole new level now, all because I finally figured out one lesson: you can never *ever* trust your eyes. They'll lie to you. Every time.

Take today's chores in my baba's garden. Tickle leaf weeds are real slick, trying to mimic our fruits and veggies. But I knew something was up when the strawberries started giggling. Nope! Snatch 'em by their wiggling roots.

Pumping water from the creek and turning the compost used to cramp my arms into pretzels. Waste of time, right? Wrong! My hands are so strong, I can write all night.

Then…there's bug picking. Can't lie, I hate bugs. Like the three-headed caterpillar gobbling up our collard greens this morning. Big nope. But even those little monsters teach me about…dedication? Never skipping on snacks, even if a shoe is about to step on my three greedy faces?

Okay, so my chores are actually awful. But that's not important. What I meant about never trusting your eyes? Great poems get past the surface, past what your eyes show you. And that's an awesome feeling—at least, when there's time to chase the perfect lines.

Today I'm ahead of schedule, which means extra rhyme time. I sneak through the corn rows my parents planted after a storm sucked up the old Jefferson house, foundation and all, right into the sky.

That one almost got my mama when I was a baby. Baba says she's never been the same since. Sometimes she'll freeze up in the garden, hands shaking until he comes running to whisper in her ear and calm her down. We were lucky—storms can wolf down whole neighborhoods in one gulp. An old shed on the far edge of the Jefferson land survived somehow, and it's my third-favorite place to write. I perch with my notebook on an old tractor tire that's wide as my bed.

My name is Keynan Masters and I run
things on this block,
My lines will make you sit up straight like
celery stalks—

Umm, no. Let's run that back.

Friends call me Keymaster,
and poetry is what I do best,
I'm faster than pretenders,
tougher than an algebra test—

No, no, no. I'd rip the page out of my notebook and hide
the evidence, but paper is too valuable to waste. Sometimes writing starts out all hard and tough and crusty on
the outside. Like a seed. The goodness only comes with
a little soil, clean water, and bright sunshine. And lots of
love. You can't forget the love.

I stand and stretch, just in time to see my baba beelining through the stalks of corn like he knows exactly
where I am. Busted. I slide my notebook out of sight. "Hey
Dad, wassup?"

"Hey yourself. You ain't hear your mama calling you?"
He slides a chunky fist forward, solid as a brick, and mine
meets it halfway.

"Nope. Is she okay?"

"She's fine. But you're supposed to be spraying pepper soap on the tomatoes."

"I did. See?" He nods grudgingly at my half-empty spray bottle.

We look so much alike he might as well be a walking, talking mirror. Deep brown eyes, temple fades—although I've got a frohawk going while his hair is always short—and we're both lanky and lean. I finally caught Mama this summer, I'm betting I only need two more to stand eye to eye with Heck Masters. We're the exact same shade of brown in the winter, but I'm darker than him now—which is weird because he's outside twice as long as I am. But what about grown-ups isn't weird, if you stop and think about it too hard?

"Finished early," I add. "So thought I'd rest my eyes a bit."

"On this old, smelly, comfortable tire. Right. Come on, let's hear it."

The weather's perfect, but my face is suddenly extra hot. "It's um…not ready yet."

"We're waiting for this performance you promised. Along with all of Bizzy Block. Don't let great—"

"—be the enemy of good. I know, I know."

He's always ready with these little sayings that make so much sense you can't help but roll your eyes. I've pored through every faded and flaking page of my parents' poetry books, just as hungry as that caterpillar, and I still don't know how he pulls them out of nowhere like that. I squeeze my notebook a little tighter. "This one just needs a lil more spit. It's special."

"Hmm. Now if we only knew a place that could help with that. A school, maybe. With teachers who live and breathe everything you need to know about the world."

Here we go. Get comfy. My parents are mostly great, but there's this one small annoying thing: they are obsessed with the Peerless Academy. Sometime last year I received an invitation to enroll—my very first letter, even!—because of my grades in our virtual program, *Build-A-Scholar*. But I'm Keynan Masters, and I run things on this block, remember? "Everything I need is right here."

"You say that now, but Bizzy Block is too small for you. And don't you wanna make flesh-and-blood friends?"

I wince. He's actually got a point there. "Peerless just ain't for me."

Why would I need strangers to tell me my poetry is amazing? No thanks. My parents are so bummed, though. My mama's bottom lip actually poked out when I first told them I wasn't going! You would think Peerless was *their* school, like they went there when they were kids or something. They still bust out a whole lecture whenever I slip and fuss about virtual classes getting too easy.

That's the mess I'm stuck in now. All I can do is ride it out while my baba goes on and on. "...and the new stuff you'll learn! I'd bet a month's chores someone from Peerless keeps these storms from snacking on folks like—"

A sudden breeze sends the nearby stalks rippling, slicing off whatever he was about to say. He stares through the corn toward the street, forehead crinkling up. "Anyway. Since you finished chores early, you can get ahead on schoolwork." He gives me a wink. "After you polish your rhymes."

That's weird. Heck Masters never breaks from the schedule. I'm usually all for a changeup if it means more rhyme time. But he's worried, and my baba never gets worried. "Where are you going?" I ask.

"Delivery drone crashed into Old Zeph's squash patch this morning. We've gotta get it fixed before someone comes looking for it. Repair crews ain't cheap." He glances at the sky, and I realize why he's dragging his feet.

"But it's your turn to check the storm siren."

"Yup." There's no putting that off. When they don't think I'm listening, the whole neighborhood whispers about how the next storm might be the last one for Bizzy Block. It's been more than ten years since one hit us—like *forever* ago, basically—but grown-ups still watch the sky like it was yesterday. "I'll head that way first. We can't let it slide because—"

"Work undone is wasted fun," I groan.

"What, you're not gonna write that one down?"

"Dad."

"One day you'll be this talented. I believe in you! The genes alone—"

"*Dad!* Would you please go somewhere?"

He laughs, cutting across our cracked asphalt half-court, waving at neighbors on the way. Baba and his jokes. And his schedules.

Something is still tugging at me though, the same way I saw it tugging at him.

Today is Tuesday. Drones always come on Thursdays. Now I'm curious. Why is a drone here early? Good thing for me I've got some extra time to visit the shop.

I turn the opposite way down Bizzy Block. The street itself is part workshop, part farmer's market, part playground. Our co-op is named after the Bizera family, who started the first community garden back when my grandparents were kids, and people still drove cars sometimes. Eight homes set around one of the old cul-de-sacs, and not one of the families thought to have some kids my age.

I live with it, though. A wordsmith doesn't always pick

their surroundings. My rhymes will bubble up anyway, like secret ground springs.

Yeah…that's definitely going in my notebook.

I scribble and stroll past Old Zeph's house, where he's waiting on the porch for Chester from around the way. You could set a clock to when they slap the first spinner down on their game of bones.

"Hey now," Zeph croaks from the shade. "Heard you cooking up some new rhymes for the block?"

"Yes sir! About to have everyone's ears on lock!"

He cackles loudly and waves me on. Zeph's not the least bit upset about the drone squishing his squash, and that makes two of us. My mama swears on her recipe book by squash noodles, squash fries, squash pizza. All lies as far as I'm concerned. But living in a co-op means looking out for each other—sharing food, saving power, fixing things. Baba says in the old days there used to be so many drones, they blocked the blue right out of the sky. Neighborhoods like ours were squeezed so close together there wasn't any room for grass or gardens in between. He thinks people took too much for granted before the storms. Bizzy Block has my whole heart, but I can't help wondering how cool things were back then.

I pull aside the big flappy canvas door to duck inside our workshop tent. There are tools everywhere, hanging on racks or spread out on tables. If the storm siren goes off, whoever's on watch wheels everything into the Kwan family's house, next door to Old Zeph. Most days that's Yua Delmar, Bizzy Block's top gearhead. She's done with virtual school and is one of the smartest people I know. I skirt around a gutted lawn mower to join her beside the unscheduled, out-of-order drone.

"Hey, kiddo."

"Hey, Yua. Need any help?"

"Nah. Pretty easy fix." The drone looks like a big scarab beetle, wider around than I can hug, with four matching turbines paired on both wings. One of the turbines is in pieces, laid out in careful order. "You see the singed metal by the backup rotor?"

"Barely." There's a scorch mark on the disassembled turbine's blades. "That's all it took to crash it?"

"I wish." She studies me for a moment, then flips the drone over with a grunt. "Heck probably wouldn't want you to see this."

Six splintery lines cut across the drone's belly, so deep the components inside might spill out. Spiderweb cracks spread from each line, glimmering like they're still hot. A shiver shimmies up my spine. "Whoa. Did this thing fly through a storm?"

"Lightning isn't supposed to stick around afterwards,"

Yua mutters. "And the slashes are too straight. So nah. Something did this. Something with claws." She shakes her head. "I don't know why I'm telling you all that. Keep it hush, okay?"

"Okay." Why is my voice so squeaky? "Did it drop anything?"

"Whatever it was is gone." She's worried too, just like my baba. "We checked everywhere, and plenty of folks saw it fall."

"Weird."

"Yeah. Once I get this rotor spinning again, the programming should be cake." She talks things out while she works, tapping queries into a small interface on the drone's side. A golden flash lights up the turbine's hole.

"Something's sparking in there," I say, peering into the opening.

"Huh? The power's disconnected."

"I saw it. Something's stuck. I can get it out, just gimme one pluck and a little luck. Hey! Did you—"

"Yes, I saw what you did there, Keynan." Yua rolls her eyes, but I know she loves me. She hands me goggles and some needle-nose pliers with a doubtful shrug. "This isn't your shop day, you know. I don't need Heck in here fussing because I—"

Gold flashes again, and I clamp down on it with the pliers, jiggling out a piece of scrunched-up ribbon. It's the brightest thing I've ever seen, like the fancy clothes we only wear for Founder's Day or Juneteenth. I keep fishing, and a crumpled envelope wiggles loose. A beautiful seal adorns one side, like a crinkled sliver of sticky sunshine. It catches Yua's work lamp, reflecting an engraved letter *P*. The golden seal flashes like headlights on an old car. We both stare at it until Yua blinks and gives me a huge, relieved grin. "Nice! You found the package. That's one mystery solved, at least. Better go get your parents... That looks like big news."

My stomach rumbles like our compost barrel. Despite the wrinkles and creases, I've seen envelopes like this before. I'm surprised my mama doesn't have the first one framed!

Another letter from Peerless. Addressed to me.

CHAPTER TWO

THE GOLDEN SEAL

Now, don't get me wrong. Getting letters feels great! Like, am I growing up? Ascending into adulthood, the land of no rules and unlimited snacks? But it's impossible to enjoy, coming from Peerless. That's like biting into a strawberry turnover, only the inside's filled with pond gloop. I'd bury the envelope in the garden—weird, glowy seal and all— but Yua's watching me with this proud smile on her face. I hold my breath and open it on up:

> **Dear Keynan Masters,**
> **The new school year in the Peerless Academy**
> **of Movement, Art, Genealogy, Instrumenta-**
> **tion, and Composition has nearly arrived. Our**
> **faculty and staff are thrilled for you to join the**

Peerless family. To prepare all new students for this transition, Headmaster Kinder reminds your family to—

Blah blah blah. I skip down to the important parts. Uniforms provided—not my problem. Shuttle pickup is scheduled for—

Hold. On.

I'm enrolled? At Peerless?! How? *Why?*

I read it over again. Class starts in a week. Not a whole lot of prep time. How long had this drone been limping toward Bizzy Block? Whatever it ran into pushed it seriously behind schedule. The letter ends with a fancy signature. This Headmaster Kinder sure is expecting me. There must be some mistake, unless…

My parents.

They didn't. They wouldn't.

Would they?

My heart starts hopscotching around in my chest. I. Have. Questions!

"You look like you're going to pass out." Yua chuckles. "What's wrong?"

"Someone messed up. This can't be mine."

"So do what we all do when something goes wrong—get your mom!"

I race back to my house, wondering if this is why my baba was so off this morning. I find Mama working in our garden.

"Mama! I got another letter from Peerless! Acting like I'm supposed to be there."

She tucks a stray loc behind her ear, eyebrow arched. I thrust the letter out. Her dark brown eyes widen, dipping back and forth over the crinkled paper. "This doesn't make any sense… We all agreed it was best to wait another year."

"Right. Another year." Relief fills me up. I knew they wouldn't flip on me like that. Someone at the school made a mistake, and that's all there is to it.

The seal flashes again, bright enough to reflect in my mama's eyes and turn her brown skin deep gold for an instant. Hold up. Envelopes aren't supposed to do that…

A grin abruptly spreads across her face. "Heck, come out here! Our little one's headed off to Peerless!"

The screen door bangs behind me. "Say what?"

"Say *what*?" I echo.

My baba accepts the letter with a frown. The envelope flashes again, still in my mama's hands, while he reads. Doubt melts away from his face in a blink. "An…acceptance letter. Wow. Wow! This is huge, Keynan."

"But… I'm not going to Peerless," I say slowly. "You told me to trust my gut about it."

My parents exchange one of those annoying grown-up looks, like they share the same brain. My stomach clenches up. They never flip like this, change their minds from one breath to the next.

"Keynan…" Baba's voice quiets. "These online lessons are easy for you, right?"

"Yeah, only—"

"And Yua's taught you how to use everything in the shop. You could be doing so much more."

"Sure, but—"

"And friends your own age? Think on it some more. That's all we're asking."

Mama straightens from gathering up dinner veggies. "This deserves a little celebrating."

My baba nudges me. "Sounds like…tacos?"

"Or snacks?" She winks.

All I can do is stare. Who are these people? My parents are nice, maybe a pinch on the strict side—but bribing my taste buds? So they can slink out of what we all agreed was best?

Everything went left after that letter showed up. Does it just change folks' minds for them? Activate their secret shady side? My parents always do cartwheels whenever

Peerless comes up; maybe they're just excited again. But I know I didn't imagine that golden light. Either way, it's even more proof I'm better off as far away from Peerless as possible.

"Tacos," I agree reluctantly. "And I'll think about it."

"Now we're talking! The internet's actually behaving today, so knock out your lessons first, son," my baba says. "Time for tacos when they're done. Wait—did I just rhyme, again? Did I score a perfect—"

Mama and I both gag and boo until he leaves. So annoying!

"You look like you need a minute to process," she observes.

"Yeah, I kinda do. Why—"

"Well, wash up and help me process these veggies, then. You'll still have plenty of time for homework."

I chop cilantro and she does the tomatoes. It's kind of our thing. She's really pleased, but this funny sound is coming from her throat, like she swallowed a feisty bumblebee.

"What are you doing?" I ask curiously.

"Humming. It's kind of like singing, with your mouth closed."

Weird. That sounds like smelling with your nose shut. "But singing's bad luck, right? Yua's granny says so all the time... So does Dad." The humming is nice, though.

She just smiles. "You love poetry, Keynan. It sings to you. Would Peerless really be so bad?"

"Yes, actually. Why let some dusty Peerless teacher twist up something I'm already good at? Would you let Yua's granny make your turnovers?"

"If I wanted my teeth to hurt all week," she admits. "But that's how it works. I can help her ease back on the sugar. But her dumplings have taught me a thing or two about baking."

Somehow…that makes sense. "Do moms just know all the things?"

"This one does. That cilantro looks good to me. Wrap up lessons, I'll finish dinner."

I head into the office and plop down at the laptop. Lessons are dragging, and I couldn't be happier for a distraction when a game notification pings halfway through my geometry quiz:

Starbreaker wants to chat.

Every other kid in *Build-A-Scholar* uses their boring real-life names, so me and Starbreaker became instant friends. We play Mirror Maze Castle together between classes, whenever storms don't mess with our connection. It's the easiest way to chat without getting in trouble. I pull up the game window:

Starbreaker: sup u late 2day

Keymaster: its been a lot going on

Starbreaker: chores. more mutant bugs

Keymaster: nope. I got this shiny envelope by drone

Starbreaker: afvdouaewfnkoiasfdlknjsdvnjkl

Starbreaker: wait

Starbreaker: an acceptance letter right

Starbreaker: ?

Keymaster: yeah

Starbreaker: YESSSS we both going!!! happy dance break!

So Starbreaker and me? We've got rules. Don't type *lol* unless you really laugh. Don't leave friends behind in the Mirror Maze Castle dungeon. And happy dances are *not* optional. Even though this one shouldn't be happening.

Not my best moment—I trip twice on the chair—but I keep up my end. The lights flicker, along with my laptop screen. I glance out the window, but no hint of a storm. No one's sounding the siren, so we're all good. I sit again.

Starbreaker: i was SO scared to say anything. thought you didn't get in

Me? Not get in? Psshhh—I'm amazing. Of course I got in, but I'm not supposed to *be* in. So how did this Headmaster Kinder person fool my parents into the worst idea ever? They know I love Bizzy Block. They need me here, even if my mama won't admit it. No one likes to talk about how storms might drop in from nowhere—snatch *us* up by *our* roots. And all of our neighbors are like my own built-in audience for whenever I've got fresh rhymes to share. Where else will I find that? Peerless doesn't deserve my best, and I'm not gonna stress over a school I don't need to impress.

Oohhhh…lemme write that down, too!

The laptop pings again. I'm scribbling so hard I forgot about the chat.

Starbreaker: helloooooooo

Starbreaker: ur net go out? Ours been trash all day

Keymaster: here sorry. hey…i'm not going. to peerless

Starbreaker: …wait how?? if you got a letter u going. parents signed you up

Keymaster: i just gotta talk to them

Starbreaker: but they already agreed

Starbreaker: we don't get to choose

I still don't believe it. Not for a second. My baba talks so much about me finding my own way, trusting my gut about things. Why would Peerless be any different?

Keymaster: i do. sorry

Keymaster: will u still play mirror maze at least

Starbreaker: really?? welp }:(thought you would have my back

Starbreaker: there's something off about

Starbreaker: actually nvm

Starbreaker: you'll be too busy flicking bugs. g2g finish packing. c u around brick brain!

<<Starbreaker has left Mirror Maze Castle!>>

Did that just happen? Peerless is stealing my bestie from me, too! Somehow I feel guilty, like I'm letting Starbreaker down. Who knows if the school lets students play Mirror Maze Castle? But that's another day's problem. Right now, I just need my parents off Team Peerless and back on Team Keynan.

I better hurry up and figure out how before it's time for chow.

I'm so worried over what to do I forget to write that one down.

CHAPTER THREE

IF THE BRIGHTS ARE CALLING

My parents pull off a mini-feast: stuffed peppers with cheese crumbles alongside our tacos. Baba brought over some of the rainbow trout we caught last night—they glow brightest when it's pitch-black at the creek. They've been in Old Zeph's smoker all day, and the aroma has my taste buds wrestling each other for first dibs. Even a power outage can't spoil how delicious everything is. We barely need candles, thanks to the trout lighting up the walls with deep greens, reds, and gold. If this were the old days, before it was bad luck, I'd imagine we'd even sing a song or two. It'd be perfect, except for why we're feasting in the first place.

All through dinner, I can't slide in one word about Peerless.

"Trust us, Keynan," my baba urges when I try again. "We know a thing or two about a little bit."

"But y'all have been way different!" I protest. "That flashy seal did something to you, I know it!"

My parents exchange another extra long glance. Did I mention how much those bother me? "You mean to tell me," my mama says, "we've been…dazzled into wanting what's best for you? Are things so old and dusty around here that a piece of fancy mail can do all of that?"

How did she twist something I've seen with my own eyes into sounding so silly? They are really making me go. The lights flutter back on—just in time, because our fish is gone and the candles are low. Mama blows out the wicks as my baba rises and clears the table.

"That school was made for you, Keynan," he murmurs. "Not just composition classes. Science programs, too. The people who attend Peerless are the folks who make a difference. Maybe even figure out these storms one day. No reason that can't be a Masters."

"I know that's right," my mama interjects softly.

"I…I don't care." Even saying that out loud makes me cringe. My mama's seen storms up close, frets over them more than anyone on Bizzy Block. But I press on despite the disappointment on her face—because we don't lie to each other. Ever. At least, we didn't before this ridiculous school sent me that invitation. "Y'all are making me go and it isn't fair. I don't need Peerless."

There. I got it all out. The wheelbarrow finally rolls off my ribs.

The dishes stop clinking in the sink. My baba dries his hands and flips the towel over his shoulder.

"Okay," he finally says. "You don't need Peerless? Show me. Let's hear your latest. The one you were working on this morning."

I reach for my notebook, but he snatches it off the table before I can grab it.

"Hey!"

"Let's hear it," he repeats.

I freeze. Completely shook. I open my mouth, but the words won't fall out. "Dad, I just need my notebook."

He shakes his head. "No, son. Look. What you need is direction. East and west, or north and south. The very least of the best spit blind rhymes light as a feather. Their every step ignites land mines, even when they're strolling through the stormiest weather."

I can only...stare. My baba's lines are usually hopscotch-simple. Patty-cake basic. What did he just do? I've never heard anything like it before.

"You've gotta make it yours." My baba taps his chest. "In here."

The lights flicker, and my mama clears her throat. "It's been a whole day for all of us. Keynan, you need your rest. This week will go by fast."

My Peerless news turns Bizzy Block inside out the rest of the week. Neighbors drop by every two seconds to congratulate me. One night, Yua's granny brings over peanut butter honey truffles and ice-cold almond milk. The next, Old Zeph gifts me his very first set of dominoes, and the Chandler family files in with lemon tarts.

The way our neighbors act, I should be doing cartwheels down the street. I fake-smile until I can slip right back to the one thing that will get me out of this mess: my poem.

> My name is Keynan Masters and I run things on this block,
> My base lines are timeless like broken clocks—

Nope. These rhymes just aren't clicking. How did my baba do it? *Practice*, he would probably say. So I write, erase, and write some more. Especially now that I've seen him show out. He probably thinks *my* rhymes are basic.

Thankfully they go easy on chores all week—more free time than I've ever had. I slip out to write every day, and

I'm pretty sure this poem is my most epic yet. Nothing less will convince my parents that they've got it all backward. Peerless might be built for me, but I'm not built for Peerless.

The night before the school shuttle will come for me, I can hardly sleep. My parents double- and triple-checked my bags. Dried orange and mango slices, banana chips, extra salty kale chips. My mama's famous strawberry tarts, of course. Shea butter. Can't make new friends with ashy ankles looking like shredded wheat. Toothbrush. Can't share snacks with new friends if my hot breath blisters their faces. Satisfied, they kiss me good-night, and I pull out my notebook.

I've whisper-practiced my poem at least ten times before there's a soft knock, and then a sliver of light slaps away the shadows. I close my notebook and slide it on the nightstand. My mama's head pokes through my open door. "Hey you. Can't sleep?"

Seriously, she must stay up late reading an instruction manual on me. "Y'all are really gonna make me go?"

"Oh, Keynan." She sits on the covers and brushes a hand on my cheek. "This is a big moment for you. I wish it had happened the way you deserve, but me and your dad..." she smiles, just mentioning him "...other people are depending on us, too. Peerless is the best thing for you right now."

"But I can learn whatever I need right here," I protest. "You heard Dad the other night. He's been holding out on us!"

"You have no idea." Her hug is the best squeeze ever. Must be in the instruction manual. "Peerless will open doors you never knew existed. Some days you'll be so caught up with learning, you'll run through this—" she pats my notebook on the nightstand "—faster than you eat up all our snacks. You'll trick yourself into believing you don't need sleep… The poetry itself will feel like food and sleep and light, all rolled into one."

"Like my air."

"Exactly. You've got all the best parts of your daddy and me, plus some extra you made up all by yourself. We've been meaning to teach you about your grandparents, and their parents before them." Her voice is whispery as moth wings. I nestle closer so I don't miss a single word of this. "Things were never quite right after the storms got nastier… We were so wrapped up in hiding from them, we forgot to sing our songs and love on each other every single chance we get. They've picked away at things since me and your daddy were young. People were already leaving big cities back then, but these past few years have been some of the worst I can remember. You have a chance for something better. Just don't forget that our people are made of strong stuff. Do what you do best. Make us proud. And don't eat snacks in your bed." She smiles down at me and clears her throat.

"You…you're going to lullaby me?"

"Mmhmm. We can't get too busy to sing, so long as it's quiet."

She is really stuck on this! No one sings, except maybe to babies—now she's humming and singing all in the same week? Old Zeph says it's no different than daring a storm to come calling. "Mama… I'm twelve now and y'all are—"

"A whole twelve."

"—making me go to school, and I'm pretty sure that means I'm too old for—"

She hits me with the Mama Look, so I just go ahead and get comfy.

> *Baba's dancing to the castle,*
> *so hush and close your eyes.*
> *Mama's singing down the bastions,*
> *so don't you start to cry.*
> *And if the Brights are calling,*
> *hush and close your eyes.*
> *Mama and Baba love you,*
> *look to the sunrise.*

The hallway light wavers. We both tense, but no siren blares. A yawn cracks my face wide as I snuggle into the pillow. "Rest now," she says. "You finna need it." She kisses my forehead and closes the door. Parents really do love them some lectures, but Mama's exactly right: I'm made of strong stuff.

Tomorrow? I'm going to show her and my baba both. I'll show them just how much I don't need Peerless.

CHAPTER FOUR

BEST MORNING EVER

I'm up before the chickens on the big day. First things first: surprise my parents with scrambled eggs, thick toast drizzled with our leftover honey, and fresh-picked strawberries from the garden. There are just enough ripe oranges for juice—I kiss my fingertips and rest them on the tree's bark, murmuring thanks to Gran-Gran and Papa for the gift—and head inside to set the table. The eggs aren't normally brown, and a stray aphid drowned in the honey—I rewash the strawberries—but it's the thought that counts, right?

"Smells good in here," my baba comments behind me. "I'll start some coffee."

The aroma yanks my mama right out of bed, and we all tuck into breakfast like it's a Sunday dinner. No rushing off to chores or lessons at the computer. Just trading jokes and playing charades and two truths and a lie. Basically the best morning ever.

Except it isn't. But I'm about to change that.

I rise for my notebook just as Old Zeph's piercing whistle floats through the kitchen window.

"It's time," Mama murmurs.

They hustle me straight outside. My baba insists on carrying my bags. The leather is old and brown, but still oiled like my parents are always ready for a trip even though we've never left Bizzy Block.

I stop short on our porch. Balloons and streamers cover our fence, red and green and yellow and white, so many I can hardly see the wood. A loud cheer makes me jump. Yua and her grandma unfurl a huge banner that reads, *Congratulations Keynan!* They aren't the only ones here—all of Bizzy Block crowds in close to see me off! Even Old Zeph, lips twisted like he wants his dominoes back. Over three dozen people squeezed around our house, all smiling. At. Me.

This wasn't exactly part of my plan.

A gleaming blue shuttle bus glides silently up to the curb. Movement ripples behind the tinted windows in the back, probably more kids who are going to Peerless. An actual working vehicle on Bizzy Block, just for me. No one uses cars anymore. Anyplace far off isn't worth risking a random storm—especially when we have drones. I feel special and miserable all mixed up together.

The shuttle's narrow door slides open. "Heya! I'm Jocelyn." A light-skinned woman with two blue-tinted afro puffs nestled above her visor beckons me up the stairs. "Alicia and Hector? Do you release this child into the charge of the Peerless Academy?"

"I'm not going." My voice barely squeaks past my teeth, but I said it out loud. It counts!

The whole block goes silent. Jocelyn's mouth falls open. Some kids inside the shuttle open the windows just so they can stare. I feel about two inches tall. I've never gone against my parents like this. Ever. And in front of the whole neighborhood? Is it possible to be grounded until I have gray hair? I'm about to find out.

My baba drops my bags. He inhales deeply, resting his hands on his knees so we're face-to-face. "Son… I thought we settled this."

I search his face and breathe a little easier. He's not mad, only worried. "So what if I can't rhyme all that great without my notebook! I'll get better, watch."

Baba rises with a grunt.

"Listen here, Keynan Masters," Jocelyn growls down at

38

me. "The air tastes funny today, and I've got a schedule. I've never been late, not once, and today? Ain't. The. Day."

"Keynan." My mama's not happy. "Don't you trust us?"

My face is hot and my eyes are wet. My notebook is out of reach on the nightstand, but I can't go back for it with everyone staring.

It's now or never.

> My name is Keynan Masters and Bizzy Block is my home,
> the…thought…of roaming makes me dizzy, far from friends and family,
> relearning all my poetry?
> No—I…gotta trust my gut, even when it's tough,
> Because my last name is Masters and—

"We're made of strong stuff," my baba finishes.

Yua claps, then stops when no one else joins in. I forgot half the lines and messed up the other half. I might as well slink onto the shuttle right now.

My parents both blink like they just woke up from a long dream. They're sad, but…proud? My mama gives me a little nod. My baba turns to Jocelyn. "You heard him. We'll look for you again next year."

I screwed this up, I'm doomed, I— Wait, what? Did I hear that right?

"But...but..." Jocelyn's hands twitch like she's ready to snatch me inside the bus. "Check-in is *today*! Next year ain't guaranteed!"

"We'll take our chances," my baba says.

"Headmaster Kinder won't like this!"

"Then tell her come see me," my mama says, "instead of hiding behind these letters."

"Keynan, best get your bags," my baba says without taking his eyes off Jocelyn. "We're behind on chores."

I scoop them up before he changes his mind. I can hardly believe it. They've flipped back to Team Keynan? It happened so fast, just like with the golden seal. My piece actually mattered—they listened to me! Who knew one little rhyme could be so convincing?

Some of the kids headed for Peerless gawk at me as the shuttle wheels off. It crosses my mind that one of them might be Starbreaker, and I missed my chance to meet my bestie in person.

My neighbors are still standing there, staring at me while they whisper. A breeze tugs at the balloons along the fence. They put all of that love into my send-off, and I pretty much tossed it in the compost barrel. Yua and her grandma are still holding the banner they made for me,

40

like they're wondering whether to stash it for next year. I'll need to make it up to them big after this, somehow—the rest of Bizzy Block, too. They all look so…disappointed.

I got exactly what I wanted, and I know I'm right about Peerless. So why do I feel so awful?

CHAPTER FIVE

HERO STATUS: UNLOCKED

I lug my bags into my room and march right back outside. I can't just hide out for the rest of the day, as much as I'd love to pretend that strange letter with the golden seal never came to Bizzy Block. Some of our neighbors are still shuffling around, like everything was a prank and the shuttle will return any minute. So. Awkward.

My parents are dazed too, but as usual, they nudge folks into their routines.

"Late for dominoes, Zeph?" my mama calls.

"Sho' am!" He shakes his head and trundles off, clutching his straw hat against a sudden gust of wind.

She flashes me a wink that makes me feel a hundred times better. "You okay?"

"Thought I could at least help clean up after causing all this mess."

"Mess?" My baba turns away from his conversation with the Chandlers. "Boy, please. All of this…" He stretches his arms wide, as if he means more than Bizzy Block and its crops, but also the woods and creek surrounding our home. "It's for nothing if you're not good. We'll work it out. That you gotta respect, or—"

"—your name's not Heck," I finish with a grin. That sick feeling's still nibbling at my stomach, but it sure helps that I have the best parents ever. My eyes clamp on the banner, now crinkled against the fence in the wind. "I'm going to bring this over to the Delmars and thank them. And apologize? Something."

My mama beams. "I couldn't think of a better start."

I cross the street, holding the banner tight against another gust.

Something Jocelyn said hits me just then. *The air tastes funny today.* She's right. Like last summer when I left corn on the grill for too long, or when I'm helping Yua and Mama solder old circuit boards together for our solar panels. Sharp and sweet and burning.

I knock on the Delmars' front door, and Yua's granny answers. "Well look who it is. You here to waste more of my bomb truffles, or—"

43

The storm siren rakes across Bizzy Block.

Our eyes snap to the sky. Orange and gray clouds blot out the blue in a few heartbeats. The wind that had been nudging me since the shuttle arrived suddenly pushes hard enough to make Granny Delmar clutch the door-frame. I catch her and we stumble our way inside, slamming the door shut. Yua's puppy yips around our ankles.

"Quiet, Buster!" Granny Delmar scolds. Outside the window, a pinkish-purple fog clogs the air, so thick I can't even see the next house over.

"Where's Yua?" I ask breathlessly.

"The shop tent. She wanted to finish fixing the drone before lunch."

Yua can take care of herself, but moving tools from the shop is a two-person job. Would anyone remember to help after the mess I made of things this morning? I've got to check and be sure. It's on my way back home anyway. My parents will be looking for me if I'm not back soon. Granny Delmar grips my arm. "Drills say stay put!" she protests. "Don't break the routine!"

Nothing about today has been routine. "I'll be fine!"

I fling open the door and step outside. The storm siren is still blaring, a distant sound like my head is stuffed with oatmeal.

The sky erupts in a low, menacing rumble, like the storm is…growling.

Grit and leaves sweep across Granny Delmar's patio, tearing at my shirt. Something thumps into the back of my head. "Ow!" A whole clump of dirt—and lawn! Water leaks out of the grass and leaps past my ankles, heading for the clouds. Like reverse rain. A queasy feeling worms through my stomach as the storm siren suddenly cuts off.

I was wrong. I'm definitely not fine. My knees feel like sponge cake. All I want to do is hide somewhere, anywhere. But behind the wind and confused rain, a tiny voice urges me to put one foot in front of the other.

"Granny Delmar! Grab Buster! It's not safe here."

"But the drills say—"

I loop my arm through hers and trot us toward the street. We're taught to shelter in place during storms. Get under a table. Find a bathtub. We practice all the time, but now, I barely remember what to do. The sidewalk is quivering beneath our feet, like it's alive. A string of lights crackles through the sky, a thousand Peerless acceptance letters caught fire. If I didn't know any better, I'd swear the thickest clouds are following me. Not exactly moving, but extra bubbly right overhead. Stalking me down the block.

The shop tent is just ahead, and we duck inside. Yua isn't there. The tools are still scattered around the clawed-up drone. Wind batters the canvas, like a hundred paws grasping for us. Then in a blink, it's still—so still that our own panting sounds extra loud. I remember that the biggest storms have a quiet hole in the middle. Maybe we're in it?

I risk a peek outside.

The Delmars' house is *gone*. Fence, sidewalk, patio, garden, foundation—there's just a bare patch of earth where a whole home used to be. I can't believe it—we were just there! I gape, craning my neck to peer into the sky. If their house is up there, the clouds gobbled it up.

"We need to be off the street," I murmur. "Over by the creek. Something. We can't wait to be snatched!"

"If you're just now figuring that out, maybe that fancy school isn't such a bad idea," Granny Delmar observes. Buster yips in agreement.

I grit my teeth. "We'll head for my house, okay?"

She nods nervously. "If it's still there."

My mouth dries at the thought. Where would we even live if the storm snatched up all of Bizzy Block? I lean into the wind and help her forward, trying not to panic. My parents will know what to do. Just get inside. Then we'll be safe. That thought is the only thing that keeps my legs moving, even if I know it's not true. Between shielding my face from dust and the murky purple-pink fog, I can barely see two steps in front of us. But I hear something whipping around just ahead. "The balloons are still on the fence! Just a little farther!"

"Okay! Thank goodness!"

We reach my gate. Thunder rumbles in the sky. Buster wriggles free of Granny Delmar's arm and tears off across the street. Granny Delmar cries out, but he's named Buster for a reason. In seconds, we can't see him. My heart sinks as I tug her toward my house—I'm too scared to chase him! "I'm so sorry!"

She chokes down a sob as I pull her away.

A sudden yip turns us both around. Yua emerges from the storm, wearing a dust mask and goggles. She's cradling Buster. "Gran! Keynan! You're okay!"

"Yua, your house—"

"I know. We lost the siren, too." She loops an arm over Granny Delmar's shoulders. "No one's hurt, thank goodness. Just get inside. The worst of it has blown past, but I need to go check on Old Zeph. I'll tell Heck you're here, before he tears the block apart. And Keynan? Good job, kid! This was hero stuff."

"Let's not get ahead of ourselves," Granny Delmar sniffs as they hustle down the street.

I trudge inside my house. The storm feels like it's moving on, and my breath finally comes a little easier. My knees are still wobbly—along with everything else. I knew storms were scary, but I didn't *know*. I barely remembered half of the checklist from our drills, and did half of what I *actually* remembered all wrong. But we're okay, and I helped! Hero status: unlocked. No one can argue against me staying home now!

"Mama, you here?" She's probably outside helping my baba hold Bizzy Block together. The windows are all closed up in the dining room. Kitchen's empty, too. Out back, our vegetable garden took a beating. Bedroom, nope. Office…

That's where I find her.

My mama's still as a stalk of corn. She sways just a little, like she got touched early in a game of freeze tag and her legs are getting tired. It would make sense if she was watching out for our neighbors, but she's not in front of a window. Her nose is close enough to brush the blank wall. I can't tell if she's breathing.

"Mama?" A lump rises in my throat. "Mama! Wake up!"

I yank urgently on her sleeve. Nothing. Squeeze her hand. She turns, and I immediately regret it. My mama's face is lifeless. The crinkly laugh lines around her eyes are gone. I'm so scared my legs are shaking again.

But in the next instant, her eyes fall on me, and a huge smile tugs her cheeks high. "Keynan, I missed you so much!" I'm so relieved when she drapes me in a hug, I can't choke out words. "Tell me everything about Peerless! Favorite classes, all of it. Is your roommate cool? And clean?"

Something's still wrong. "Mama…"

"Did you meet anyone special? I know you love poetry, but—"

"I didn't go to Peerless!" I exclaim, trying not to flip out. "What happened to you? It's like you were frozen!"

Something cracks in my mama's expression, confusion bubbling through her cheerful glaze. "That's not funny. Stop playing."

"Mama, I'm not lying, I promise!"

The screen door bangs open behind me. Baba sweeps past, gathering her up. "I got you, baby." He guides her toward their bedroom with an ache in his eyes I've never noticed before. "Keynan, she's not feeling well. It's clear outside. Go wait on the porch."

This is way, *way* beyond not feeling well.

The few minutes stretch out like years until my baba joins me on the steps. "I'm sorry you had to see that. She just needs some rest."

"What's up with her though?"

My baba glares at the horizon. "Your mama's always been…sensitive to storms. Feels them before anyone else since…" He looks away, gazing out at the corn patch.

"The Jeffersons," I breathe. "Did she see it happen?"

"More than that. She tried to stop it, with her stubborn self. She's been closer to a storm than any of us. Experiences like that leave scars. Change the way you wired. There's nothing we can do except help her rest. She'll be okay."

I can't even look down the block at the…hole where Yua's house used to be. Next season, the space will just be more crops. Where are they going to stay? Where will any of us stay if houses keep getting plucked up into the sky? "Baba, I was so scared."

"You and me both. Thought these storms were done with us. We've had some close calls, but nothing straight-on since you were still toddling around. But now you've seen one for yourself."

"Maybe other co-ops could help if we—"

My baba shakes his head. "We've tried, son. Too far away. And they've got their own storms to worry about. At Peerless they might be able to…" He clears his throat, and I know he's changing what he meant to say. "No need to worry about that now. What's done is done. Next year, though."

"Next year." I look away so he doesn't see my face crumple. How can Bizzy Block last like this?

My baba offers an outstretched fist as he rises. Even our dap doesn't feel as solid as before. "Fix yourself something to eat. We've got work to do. This was a tough day, but we're Masters, right?"

"We're made of strong stuff," I say numbly.

"That's right. We'll be ready for the next one."

Fog must be trapped in my ears. I did *not* just hear him say that. The old Jefferson house, I barely remember—but the Delmars are here and now. Yua is my friend. If any of us can get yanked away, just like that, what are we supposed to do? A fading gust tugs at my shirt, like the storm is calling me out. Like it knows Bizzy Block can prepare all we want, but there's nothing we can do. I remember what my baba thought about Peerless, what he almost said again just now.

Not just composition classes. Science programs, too. The people who attend Peerless are the folks who make a difference. Maybe even figure out these storms one day.

I'd do anything to make sure I never, ever see my mama's face like that again. Dig holes in the yard for no reason and fill them back up. Run the paradox gauntlet level on Mirror Maze Castle by myself. Watch and wait for new corn seeds to sprout. *Anything.*

Build-A-Scholar teaches exactly zero lessons about storms, and I blew my chance to go to the one place that does!

CHAPTER SIX

UNFAMILIAR STREETS

So the question is: What am I gonna do about it? Strong stuff doesn't go cry over a sandwich. I can't wait around for another year to go to Peerless, not now. But work needs doing, all up and down the street. I help my neighbors and family as we pull the cul-de-sac back together, one mess at a time. Deep down, though? I know I could be doing way more…away from Bizzy Block.

Yua and Granny Delmar move into Old Zeph's spare room. They even join his morning game of bones, although they fuss about his house rules at first. Some days between chores I find Granny Delmar just standing where her house used to be, like a new one will spring out of the dirt.

My mama's acting like herself again, guiding folks

through repair schedules and offering a ready smile for anyone who needs it. But my baba has been different since we lost the storm siren. Every night he stands on the porch, watching the sky until after sundown.

Bizzy Block heals because we take care of our own. Everyone gets used to the changes over time.

Everyone except me.

Sure, I do my chores. Crack open lessons in *Build-A-Scholar*. Play Mirror Maze Castle, which doesn't feel right without Starbreaker. I help everywhere I can, even fixing up the busted drone with Yua. There's no patching the claw marks without better tools, but we challenge ourselves to get the thing flying again.

Bizzy Block stays busy. But I find myself staring at the Delmars' empty yard like it was a piece of *me* stolen away forever, not just a house. Other days I'm watching the sky like my baba. His words about Peerless won't leave me be.

No reason that can't be a Masters.

Buckling down for the next storm isn't enough. My parents won't take me to Peerless—not after a storm like that. I don't even need to ask, I can see the answer on my baba's face every night he's studying the clouds. I've got to make it happen somehow. On my own.

Two weeks after the storm, I finally get a decent idea. My bags are still ready, stuffed under my bed and never unpacked. My baba's old rusty bike is in the toolshed be-hind our vegetable garden, right where I remember it. I air up the tires and make sure they don't leak out.

I've got wheels!

I stash the bike behind the shop tent—it needs some more tuning. On my way back to start morning chores, I run into Old Zeph, ambling down the sidewalk. Time for my next move.

"A map? To go where?" He eyes me suspiciously when I ask. "You lost your mind? Storm already took a nibble out of us, Keynan. You really want to risk more?"

I make a hasty excuse and hustle off. Hopefully he won't snitch. I hate hiding stuff from my parents, but I can't stay here. Not anymore. Bizzy Block isn't safe, not unless I make it safe.

But how will I get to Peerless without help?

The problem bothers me all through morning chores. Knocking on neighbors' doors one at a time asking about a map is gonna get me caught faster than fast. Still no fresh ideas after virtual lessons wrap for the day. I take my lunch back to the workshop tent to tinker with the bike. Some grease on the chain solves the squeaking. That still leaves directions—I can't just ride around until I bump into Peerless. If I find Yua, maybe I can make it all sound like a homework problem. She's always trying to teach, just like with—

That's it! I don't need anyone to take me to Peerless. The drone! If it's fixed, I'll have my own personal escort!

The drone is ported to Yua's tablet, glossy and black and big as my laptop screen. The turbine that ate my letter is put back together. My eyes slide away from the claw marks. The circuitry still looks ready to spill out. It will hold up. Nothing to worry about. I scroll through menus and code on the tablet until my eyes water, and finally find something that looks like a map. Success!

Only…it's the weirdest looking map I've ever seen.

Bizzy Block is there, right down to the roof tiles and cracks in the asphalt. A bright blue dot shows the drone. But blotchy orange and purple swirls blur out the cul-de-sac at the edges, and the houses past our co-op completely fade away into…what? Clouds?

My whole stomach lurches. This isn't just a map—those weird blobs of color must show where storms might hit. Bizzy Block is practically surrounded by them. The sky is clear though, so I don't know what to believe. Maybe the map is busted.

"What you doing, Keynan?"

I spin around with a yelp. "Yua!" Her head is poked just inside the tent flap. "Me? Nothing!"

She arches an eyebrow. "Well…don't waste any more time on that drone. It barely flies. I got the okay to scrap it for parts."

"When?"

"Now. Right after I feed Buster." She ducks back out.

So much for my big plan—it's over before it started! Even if the drone is falling apart, I've gotta try. A year until Peerless is a year too long. And if I get even the tiniest hint that a storm is smacking its lips over my head? I'll ride straight home to Bizzy Block.

The drone's turbine is put together, but the rotor is still busted. I disconnect the power supply to its twin on the opposite wing. Hopefully it stays balanced and doesn't crash again. I tether a whole spool of fishing line to the drone, braiding it so it won't snap.

Moment of truth: a final tweak to the code and I reset the operating system. The screen. Takes. For. Ever. But it finally blinks back on: *Delivery Complete*.

Yes! I did it!

The front rotors spin to life. Sawdust swirls around inside the tent, sending me into a coughing fit. The drone rises straight up into the tent's canvas.

No! Not like that!

The drone twists and turns like an annoyed kite. It's ready to go *now*. No time to run back for my bags. I scribble out a note to my baba—Yua will see it—tear the page out of my notebook, and pounce on my DIY leash. I barely wrangle it through the door flap and knot it around my handlebars. I tuck my notebook away just as the drone zips east, pulling the string taut. I hop on Baba's bike and race after it.

I've never actually left Bizzy Block. Now it's all behind me in a flash. But there's a slight problem. My front tire skids against a curb, and I almost go over the handlebars. The bike swerves back to the right, and I just miss getting the leash tangled in a tree.

This thing is flying *straight* back to Peerless! It may not need roads or sidewalks, but I do!

I grab the leash with both hands, ghost riding the bike while I zigzag through unfamiliar streets. The houses here feel off. Like if I peeked through a window randomly, there'd be no furniture or food cooking. Just bare white walls, or something worse.

Neighborhoods that have outlasted storms figured out co-ops like my grandparents did. Warning bells. Shelter plans. Community gardens. That's what my mama and baba always say—and that's exactly why this all seems wrong. Where's the crops, the soccer goals, or barbecue pits? Worst of all: not one person outside. Either they're hiding or left everything behind. Maybe they had everything Bizzy Block does, but it still wasn't enough. Is this what's ahead of us?

Actually? Worry about that later. Right now?

Just. Don't. Crash.

Wind drives grit into my eyes and sends goose bumps up my arms. It's silly to even admit this…but ever since helping Granny Delmar, I can't shake this weird feeling that the storm didn't just happen to slide up to Bizzy Block— that it wanted me for a snack.

The drone's path straightens, following a long winding road with fewer houses between lots of overgrown weeds. I decide the drone deserves a name for getting me to Peerless.

Hmm. Sturdy? Chrome-Skillet? Reliable? Reliable!

"That's perfect. You're Eli from now on!"

A fog rises, worse than the stuff we get back home that makes people across the street look a little fuzzy. This mess is thick as gumbo. Silver clots the air until I can't see the glowing claw marks on Eli's belly anymore. The leash just trails off into nothingness, my knuckles purple from gripping it.

Am I halfway there or half a day away? Maybe I should turn back. My legs are burning, and I can't stop thinking about Old Zeph's muttering: *Storm already took a nibble out of us, Keynan. You really want to risk more?*

A streak of red lightning slices the sky in half. Eli's silhouette is visible for an instant—it's okay! A deafening boom scares me into clapping my hands over my ears, before I remember that I'm holding on to something important. My bike veers, and I crash into a wall of branches and leaves. The leash slithers free of my fingers, disappearing into the soupiness.

Fat tears slide down my cheeks. The wind softens, like the whole sky is holding its breath. Waiting to see what I'll do next. I stumble to my feet. Thin scratches from the bushes line my forearms. I'm okay, but I've got bigger problems. Eli's gone—my whole plan is busted!

Panic squeezes around my ribs as the storm starts churning on every side. I thought it was passing, but the worst of it found me!

I just want to go home. Snuggle into bed and pretend this never happened. How am I even supposed to find my way? Fog drowns my vision. Squeezing my eyes shut only brings back the afterimage of the lightning. But instead of one ugly streak, I see six long crimson gashes.

Six. Just like the marks on Eli's belly.

No way can I stick around and find out what did that. I heft my bike up, leaning into the surging wind. Everything aches. Bits of broken branches swirl by, tugging at my clothes like little teeth. At least, I think they're branches until something tries wriggling down my shirt! The storm is more than wind and rain and fog. It's hungry and sneaky and *after me*. I get why storms have twisted my mama up now—I'm so scared I can't see straight. I don't trust my own eyes.

Distant lights pierce the fog, too high to be streetlights. I wonder if Eli's somehow brought friends to show the way. I trudge forward nervously, too shaky for more riding. The road ends in a long covered bridge. It's sturdy, but I don't trust it to protect me from the storm—not after what happened on Bizzy Block. I've got to keep moving.

The lights aren't more drones—they're *letters*! Perched on the biggest building I've ever seen, they read, *PEER-LESS Academy*.

I'm here… I made it!

I wasn't worried for a second.

CHAPTER SEVEN

STORM AND ALL

A gleaming double door beckons me up a curving drive toward Peerless. Enormous granite columns frame the entry, four on each side. The building must be three whole stories, and I've never imagined such sturdy brick. These walls probably laugh off a little wind, and the fog stops nipping at my ankles with every step closer. I'm so relieved I could bust into a happy dance all by myself!

As I edge toward the stairs, a woman appears, pacing before the entrance. She's wearing a fancy black suit with frills along the sleeves and a bright red scarf around her neck. Her slim fingers churn over a tablet like an orb weaver wrapping its dinner in silk. Her legs are long like her arms, and her face is deep brown tinged with rose by the tablet's glow. Her eyes latch on to mine, glittering and wide and relieved to see me. Even if she's clearly big mad.

"Hey, hi! Headmaster Kinder? You sent me an acceptance letter and…well, here I am. I'm Keynan!"

Her lips twitch like she's repeating my words. Or…talking to herself? Probably just impressed I made it here alone. "I thought things over," I tell her, "and Jocelyn said Peerless might not let me in next year, but I'm here now and mostly fine and I'll catch up on all of my homework. Promise. So anyway, surprise! Could you tell my parents—"

She steps forward. Her eyes never leave mine as she reaches around my back and plucks my notebook from my waist. Neat trick, how did she know it was there?

The headmaster's eyes flick down to the pages. I take a moment to smooth out my shirt and pick stray leaves from my hair. She's not just reading. She's taking my rhymes apart and putting them back together, like Yua did with Eli's busted turbine.

"Do you have the slightest idea of the danger you've exposed us all to with this stunt?" She closes my notebook with a *slap*.

"But I'm here by myself! I even brought in a broken drone."

"A thousand drones aren't worth one student."

"But it was just me," I insist.

"Peerless is a family, Keynan. Your actions never affect just you. Didn't Heck teach you that?"

She nods toward the curving drive. Distant lights curl through the fog—headlights. "Your father messaged us once he found out what you did. I sent Jocelyn to search for you."

"She's been looking for me this whole time?" I squeak. "In the storm and all?"

"Storm and all. And not just her, Keynan. An emergency like this called for recruiting some of our third-years to help."

The shuttle pulls up before the entrance. My shoulders hunch a little lower with every student that steps off. They're all older, taller. What if they got hurt, looking for me? They form a weary, nervous half circle around the steps.

"You've all failed a very simple task," Headmaster Kinder announces. Eyes narrow and mouths tighten. No one lets out a single peep or glares at me, but I'm ready to hide under the shuttle. Headmaster Kinder thrusts a crimson-varnished fingernail at Jocelyn. "This child found his way here, alone, without seeing a single trace of you. His parents trust us to do better. Am I understood?"

"Clear as crystal." Jocelyn's gaze never leaves her shoes.

"That isn't fair!" a voice rings out. Other kids inch away from one of the students, a short brown-skinned girl with her locs tied back. "We were driving everywhere, trying to find this dough head!"

Headmaster Kinder presses a hand to her middle. Her voice goes shadow-soft. "Leah Jamison."

The girl blinks. "The one and only."

"You've been enrolled for *less than two weeks* and decided—without permission—to join these third-year students?" Kinder erupts. "All of you. Inside!"

Yikes. This is bad. Really, really bad. Everyone here risked themselves for me, and now they're in trouble for it. The older students shuffle through the doors, faces downcast.

Headmaster Kinder's eyes narrow when Leah lingers. "I'm sorry." Leah sounds like she means it. "I only went because…it sounded like something my sister would do. I haven't seen her since I got here."

Exhaustion melts through Headmaster Kinder's glower for an instant, along with something else…sadness. "Yolanda's got more important things to do than chase around misbehaving first-years. If you intend to achieve half of her success at Peerless, you'll follow my rules.

"Some of us had high hopes for your class, but judging from tonight—" Kinder glares at me and Leah "—they may be misplaced. Your parents will be informed you've arrived safely, Keynan. Dinner will be sent to your dormitory. I expect nothing but your best from this point onward."

The headmaster glides for the double doors, a step behind the third-years, who skitter inside like crickets chased into a jar by a wolf spider. Leah scowls at me as she hurries after. "Better get your life together, brick brain!"

Jocelyn spins around to wag a finger under my nose. "You. Already on everyone's last nerve!"

"I know I messed up, okay? I just need—"

"A chance?" Jocelyn thrusts a tablet into my hands with an angry snort. "Headmaster Kinder's all out of chances, breaks, do-overs, and oopsies! Keynan. Forreal. Do you even want to be here?"

"I...well, I kinda need to be, because—"

"Real convincing. Figure out your story, kid. And stick to her rules. We all end up doing what she says, whether we know it or not."

Yikes. So not the best start.

The important thing is that I made it. This latest storm is fading away, like Peerless scared it off. My hands finally stopped shaking. My parents know I'm safe. I can still figure out what's behind these storms, help my mama and Bizzy Block. A shiver of excitement sweeps over me as I step through the doors. The only way to go from here is up!

CHAPTER EIGHT

CALL ME KEYMASTER

I try not to gawk in amazement at the entryway. The ceiling stretches overhead, high enough to fit the flagpole our storm siren was mounted on with room to spare. If the rest of Peerless is anywhere near this big, we could squeeze in every home at Bizzy Block!

Dimmed chandeliers lead me farther down a hallway lined with more columns and tall windows. I turn a corner to find couches and reading nooks and unlit fireplaces lining both sides of a corridor. The white walls and polished wood floors all feel built to last, extra plain, and very old. Peerless seems like a big empty cave so far.

My new tablet chirps to life in my hands. Nice, built-in navigation! *Straight ahead and up the stairs.*

Stairs. Of course there are stairs.

I prop my bike beside the grand staircase and trudge up. Another empty hall lined with doors on both sides greets me. I remember that Starbreaker could be on the other side of any one of them. The tablet chirps before the second door to my right, and I rest my palm on its touch pad. The hinges squeak open.

There are two comfy-looking beds, two desks, and two closets—identical, like one half of the room is a big mirror. It's way bigger than my room at home. The only difference is the tray on one bed and the boy who's just replacing its lid.

"Oh. Hi, roomie!" His voice is muffled. Cheeks puffed. We're about the same shade of brown, but he's taller than me; probably older, too. He tries to smile and lets out a little cough. A single crumb torpedoes from his mouth, and both of our eyes follow it to the floor. "So...this is awkward."

"You're...eating my dinner?"

He winces, and finally swallows.

"You *are*!"

"Not all of it!" he splutters. "I'm real sorry. Can you blame me though? I didn't even know I had a roommate. When they brought the tray up, I didn't ask questions. I just thought to myself: *Self, we don't let good food go to waste.* The empanadas are especially tasty—"

He gives me a hundred more apologies as I peer around the room, and I decide he's okay. "I'm not real hungry, it's cool. I'm Keynan, by the way."

"Ian," he says, still looking guilty.

"Seriously, you can have the rest...only, can you help me get my bike up here?"

Ian's hand freezes over my tray. "You rode a bike here?"

"Yeah, the headmaster was hot about it. And I basically got everyone who went looking for me yelled at."

Ian whistles as we trot down the stairs. "Everyone? That was mean."

"I know, right? It's gonna be hard enough catching up, I don't need a bunch of folks hating me too!"

"Won't happen. Anyway, whoever shares food after a day like that can't be all bad. Besides, you're here now. That's all that matters."

Aww, that was nice. A right-on-time reminder that I'm made of strong stuff. I also shared my food with him, so we're basically best friends now. Maybe my parents were actually a tiny bit right about the whole flesh-and-blood friends part of Peerless.

"So...where's your bike?"

I stop short. "I left it right here!" Did someone snatch it? My heart starts to thud as I hurry toward the entry.

"Keynan, wait!" Ian points at one of the columns. The

bike is stuck behind it like someone nailed the wheels to the stone.

Not stuck…the wheels are creeping toward the ceiling! We both gawk up at it as it floats higher and higher. "What is happening?"

The bike shudders and drops. Ian and I pull each other back with a shout as it clatters to the floor. I kneel beside it, checking for damage.

"Pranks," Ian announces. "Everyone loves to scare first-years."

"Pssh. Is that all they got?" I scoff nervously, hefting it up. Nothing's broken. We stash it in our room, then compare schedules on our tablets, munching on the cold empanadas from my tray.

"No classes together," I observe. Nothing about storms on my schedule, either. What would the class even be called? Bad Weatherology? Physics is the only science class I see. That's a start. "What else did I miss for orientation?"

"Meeting all the professors, the headmaster's big fancy tour—I almost fell asleep on my feet. You won't need to worry about that with Ian's Extra Exclusive Hall Hop. You're my first customer and—" Ian pats his belly "—you've already paid in advance."

"But you just got here yourself!"

"Details. Feels like I've been around for years." He looks

me up and down. "Can you get to places without being…
seen?"

"Come on. I sneak with the sneakiest. My middle name
is Sneak."

"Can you even run after pedaling on that old beast? You
might be too tired for the Extra Exclusive."

"I'm down, but only if we check out the library first. I
wanna see if this place is really as epic as folks are acting."

Ian's face scrunches up. "Epic? At the library? I don't
think that word means what you think it means."

I barely hold in a laugh. "Let's just go!"

We leave our tablets behind and slip out. The hall is
empty. Conversations and laughter leak through the other
first-years' closed doors. If Peerless turns out to be as awful
as I'm expecting, at least I have someone fun to suffer
with me.

Opposite the stairs, the hallway splits two ways. One
side holds a common room with tables and lamps, perfect for playing dominoes and spades. It reminds me so
much of Old Zeph's summer game tournaments that my
eyes sting a little bit, homesick already. The right leads to
our restroom, with long rows of shower and bathroom
stalls beyond the sinks.

"Hot water's gonna go quick if we're all getting ready
at the same time," I murmur.

"Seriously. Imagine how much Peerless uses!" Ian flushes a bit. "I wonder about stuff like that all the time. I want to be an engineer."

"Sounds fun," I offer. Welp. I can cross Ian off my list. Starbreaker always talked about being a search and rescue pilot. But it's all good! That just means I get two best friends.

Another long hall sweeps us away from the dorms and straight for the library. I barely hold in my excitement, imagining rows of books full of everything I need to know about storms. I tug on one of the tall double doors and find the room locked up tight. "Dang. Tomorrow, then," I sigh.

"I can't have you giving the Hall Hop a bad review! If you want to study that bad, check this out." We double back and turn left to find more study space, glass-enclosed desks and tables. "Soundproof. Cool, right?"

"Umm…" Made so the whole world can walk by and watch you do homework, like a giant square fishbowl? No thanks.

A huge courtyard lies beyond the study area. Stone benches snuggle into quiet nooks beneath the smaller trees, footpaths meander around a patchwork of well-tended flowers, and an oak tree in the middle of it all is crowned with massive twisted branches perfect for climbing. Roots thicker than my legs poke through the soil before they sink deep. It's old, definitely older than anything on Bizzy Block. Somehow, I feel safe around it, same as the school walls. If a storm tried to flex on us, I'll bet this tree would just yawn at the wind. The open sky makes my whole body itch, but I'd do homework here over a glass box every time.

Ian leads me to a tucked-away staircase just past the courtyard. His eagerness is making me nervous, like he wants to redeem himself because the library was closed or something.

"Here's the good stuff," he declares. We stop before a set of double doors on the third floor. It's locked up tight like the library—with heavy chain looped over the handles, too. Ian tugs on it wistfully. "Supposed to be closed for repairs, but I don't believe it. A whole wing? Some of the other first-years said things get weird past this door."

"Like what?" I'm doubtful, but still a little curious.

"A stray cat named Ratchet that no one can catch. Professor Touré's smelly sock collection. The bones of every professor who made Headmaster Kinder mad. All kinds of stuff."

"Nice!" My heartbeat wobbles at mention of Kinder, especially remembering how mean she was to Jocelyn. "How about we finish exploring tomorrow?"

"You're dipping out? Aww... I thought you weren't going to be boring."

I flounder for an excuse, but something completely different happens:

> *Don't call me boring,*
> *I'll never leave you snoring.*
> *But sneaking in here might set off a disaster*
> *Put that on my name, just call me Keymaster.*

Ian stares like I just sprouted horns. "You just made that up? On the spot?"

"I guess so." I'm just as stunned. Where did that come from? "My written stuff is way better, most of the—"

"Awesome! I can barely get a book report right. Do you have any more?" The lights overhead suddenly flare bright and flicker. My shoulders tense up like I'm back on my baba's bike, pedaling through the storm. "Okay, that's twice since we got here." Ian's not smiling anymore. "You're right. Tomorrow."

My legs are shaking as we hurry to our dorm. I'm glad Ian knows he should be scared, too. Power surges mean storms. I thought they wouldn't bother us here, but it looks like I was wrong. I've had more than my fill after today.

Back at our room, a surprise waits outside our door. "My bags! How…?"

Ian shrugs. "Jocelyn probably scooped them for you. She's nice like that. Why are they so…lumpy?"

I haul them inside, wincing. I'm grateful for all of my stuff, but there's no mistaking the tragic sound of crunched snacks. Jocelyn must have kicked my bags up the stairs!

Ian helps me unpack once he discovers my ruined snacks. Afterwards we chatter nervously as we walk down the hall to the bathroom to scrub our teeth and wash our faces. Today started out rough—didn't end so great, either—but I'm already bouncing back. I even made a new friend…who starts snoring the instant his head hits the pillow.

Uh-oh. What's this deep pain in my soul? I need my sleep, but this boy's nose rattles whole windows! We're friends by day—but at night? Utter foes!

Oooooh! Where's my notebook?

I scribble that down and set out clothes for my first day. My closet's full of uniforms: dark pants and red or green shirts. They fit perfectly. My parents must have sent the school my sizes anyway, like they always knew I would end up at Peerless. They thought of everything. Now it's my turn to think about them.

CHAPTER NINE

SETUP FOR A COMEBACK

I'm awake before my tablet's alarm pings, already show-ered and shea-buttered up while Ian's still snoring. I scrub my teeth and throw on my uniform, then head downstairs to breakfast as the sun rises. Only a few kids are awake, giving me odd looks like…well, like I'm new here.

The cafeteria is the next room after the courtyard. Re-cessed overhead lights give the rows of rich wood tables and benches a cozy glow. Gleaming, spotless buffet lines with steaming breakfast are set to either side, though only one is open. A whiteboard behind it shows the day's menu in messy handwriting. On the far wall, twin doors lead back to the kitchen, and living greenery covers the rest of the wall between them. Some herbs I recognize and others I don't.

The strawberries and cantaloupe came straight from the garden and taste delicious. Along with a slice of honeyed bread sprinkled with cinnamon and a small mug of tea, I am full and ready to go. I've got two things to do today: find Starbreaker for our first face-to-face happy dance, and climb to the top of Headmaster Kinder's Favoritest Student List.

Cake, right?

I'm the first one seated in my homeroom, front of the class, there even before Professor Wiley. Part of me is excited, but mostly I'm just nervous that it will take me forever to catch up. I can't be stuck doing homework when I'm here to become a storm expert. My tablet makes everything easy: the built-in class schedule with navigation even shows my professors' pictures. I'm so busy trying to find Mirror Maze Castle that I don't realize I'm not alone.

Another first-year sits in the next desk over, leaning close enough to touch. She's smiling extra hard. "Hi! I'm Lacretia. Looks like you finally figured out where you're supposed to be."

I smile back, a little creeped out. "Umm…yeah? It's all laid out."

"You feeling good? Refreshed? Confident?"

Is she forreal with all these questions? "I can't wait to learn more about…" I almost say storms, but stop myself.

"…poetry. That's my thing. You umm…ever play Mirror Maze Castle?"

"I'm studying dance." She beams. "We won't have many classes together, then. Too bad."

"Too bad," I agree faintly. Okay, I can definitely cross Lacretia off my Starbreaker search. More students enter, eyeing me curiously. I'm surprised that some are older and others are my age, but decide it's no big deal. My roommate's older than me and that's fine, except for his snoring.

Professor Wiley strolls in, and the class stills—including Lacretia, thankfully. A neat beard and thick-rimmed glasses don't hide the twinkle in his brown eyes, like he's a prankster just pretending to be a grown-up. His pale skin is pink around the cheeks as if he just got done wheezing over someone's joke. His white collar is unbuttoned and his sleeves are rolled up, and I halfway wonder if Kinder made him wear nice clothes but he sidestepped the rules later. A folded blue tie peeks out of his pocket.

"Morning," he says. "You all can see our cohort grew today." He winks at me. "I'm a firm believer that home-room is like a little family inside a bigger one. Let's reintroduce ourselves. Lacretia, start us off?"

Lacretia stands, sharing her name and pronouns as she

nervously twirls her braided ponytail. "I love to dance and that's why I'm here," she finishes.

Professor Wiley's eyes narrow after I go next. "Poetry? Interesting. I heard about you, but I didn't hear that."

I sink back in my desk. There are stories about me already? I just got here! I swallow down my embarrassment and listen to the rest of the introductions for clues, any scrap that might sound like something Starbreaker would say.

"I'm Desmond, everyone calls me Dez. *He* and *him* are my pronouns." Dez is light-skinned with the sharpest fade I've ever seen. His curly, cinnamon-brown hair is the same color as his eyes. For some reason, he's scowling at me. "I'm not sure what I want to study. I'm just glad to meet new friends my age—so long as they have each other's back and aren't jerks."

Okay. What is his problem?

"Keynan, you have Dez to thank for bringing your belongings up to your room last night," Professor Wiley supplies.

"So you're the reason they're full of crumbs," I grumble.

"My bad," he smirks, sitting down. "Must have dropped them on accident."

Unbelievable. The kid who vaporized my snacks is in my cohort? A horrible thought comes to mind: Dez couldn't be Starbreaker, could he? He's stubborn enough—Starbreaker hates giving up on Mirror Maze Castle. How am I even going to ask? *Hey, you crushed my neighborhood's care package, but I think we're best friends?* Would I even *want* to be friends anymore?

As Professor Wiley makes announcements, one thing is obvious: everything I dreaded about Peerless is coming true. So boring, I'll have snoring battles with Ian! Tears pouring from my eyes when—

Stop that! Now isn't the time to write new rhymes! Wiley's studying me. I slide my notebook back under my tablet. I'll scribble that down later. A kid two rows behind me raises a hand. "Yes, Amari?"

"Can you skip to the part about the recital?"

Professor Wiley gives him a withering look. "Is there somewhere else you'd rather be?"

Everyone in the class shifts to stare at Amari. I didn't see him before, he had his face buried in his tablet. Amari's got a low-cut afro that could use a pick, and a carefree calm about him, like he could take a nap, wake up, and finish a math problem on the spot. Umm, wow. I like him already. He just smiles quietly and waits.

"The all-school recital at the end of term confirms that Headmaster Kinder is making the most of your natural talent. You kids are the future of Peerless." Professor Wiley's tone grows serious. "So I'm not pleased to share that Wiley Squad is starting off this week with negative points."

Lacretia's face screws up in confusion. "We're *last*? It's only been two weeks!"

"Thank Keynan!" Dez blurts out. "It's his fault."

My throat dries up as I scan my tablet. It's true. The co-horts' point system counts excellent behavior, grades, kindness—and professors can award or deduct points whenever they want. My mouth bobs open and closed like a fish. Headmaster Kinder plopped a mountain of nega-tive points on my cohort!

Everyone's giving me the stink eye—except Amari. I sink even further in my chair.

Professor Wiley raises an eyebrow. "The funny thing about family is that they don't stop being family when they mess up. *Especially* when they mess up. We'll earn back the points, together. And I'm sure Keynan will catch on quick."

"Yes, Professor!" I squeak.

Our tablets chirp, alerting us that homeroom is over. I feel awful but a little relieved, too. Yeah, I got some bad news, but Professor Wiley was cool about it. Encourag-ing, even. Amari doesn't get up as everyone else hurries off to their first class. "I've never seen anyone squirm as bad as you just now."

I give a small shrug. "Could've been worse!"

"*Kinder* worse." He nods sympathetically. "Heard you rode through a storm to get here. Was it worth it?"

"Definitely." I'd ride through another one too, if it means clear skies for Bizzy Block.

"Wanna see something?" He flips his tablet around. I choke down a laugh at a drawing of Dez with goofy ears and teeth twice the size of his face.

"Artist track for sure," I say. "Those teeth want all the cheese, please hide the kitchen keys!"

Amari chuckles. "Composition track for sure. I think I like you. You might be the realest person I've met these past two weeks. I'm betting you're about to have an amazing story."

"What makes you say that?"

"Your name's mud here. But my granny says a setback is a setup for a comeback."

"Thanks." I think Amari is my second official real-life best friend, after Ian. He's different, but I like him anyway. "I didn't know our tablets can do that."

"They can if you're not afraid to…tinker."

Innocent expression but a tricksy twinkle in the eyes? This is the kind of rule-breaker energy I expect from Starbreaker! But when I hint about Mirror Maze Castle, he gives me a blank look. I ask another question to hide my disappointment. "Could I get a first-year into a chat with these? I'm trying to find someone."

"Probably. Kinder might see it, though. That will definitely tank Wiley Squad."

I frown. I hadn't thought of that. Our tablets ping again for the next class, but the chirp sounds different somehow. Warped, like an inside out silver finch. The lights flicker. Amari shivers. Hair on my arms stands straight up.

"Where I'm from," Amari murmurs, "we'd be looking for a good place to hide right about now."

"Same," I whisper back. "Professor? We good?"

Wiley peeks up at the ceiling from his desk. "Peerless is sturdy enough to handle a little wind. Get moving, you two. I want my points back, Keynan."

I can't help but notice he didn't answer my question.

In the hall, we compare tablets. "Nothing together," Amari mopes. "See you at lunch?"

"Bet!" We hurry off in opposite directions. My tablet's navigation flickers, but Professor Wiley isn't worried, so I won't either. Besides, not even a blackout could hold down my excitement. Next class is my best class: Creative Writing. I'll earn back Wiley Squad points, easy. I finally get to show Peerless what I'm made of!

CHAPTER TEN

I'VE GOT BARS

I hustle down the hall, eyes glued to my tablet so I don't miss any turns. Left ahead. I barely sidestep as a student darts past.

"Sorry, first-year!"

"It's cool, I…" The words die on my lips as I look up. The older student is already sprinting into another classroom. I catch a flash of dark pants where shoulders should be, sneakers slapping the door closed behind them. A…handstand? Gotta be. My eyes insist their arms and legs were swapped around, and that can't be true. Dance classes must assign weird homework.

I trot toward my class so I'm not late. Someone pops out in front of me at the last instant: Leah, from the shuttle. Her dark brown eyes jerk from her tablet, examining my face before her eyebrows plunge into a scowl. "Watch it, brick brain!" The tips of her locs are gold as woven rays of sunshine; she gives them an irritated shake as she brushes past and disappears behind a closed door.

My tablet pings. She's in composition too? Perfect.

I need a minute. This is no time to worry about Leah Jamison right now—not Dez, power outages, or anything else. I'm made of strong stuff. And if I'm going to earn back those lost Wiley Squad points, here is where I'll make it happen.

So. Let's. Go!

The class is already full of buzzing students. I barely hold in a smile. Writing is my jam. I can recite quotes from my favorite poets, and even my not-so-favorite poets.

I know:

Iambic pentameter.

Acrostic.

Haiku.

Epic.

Limerick.

Basically, I've got bars, as my baba says. Whatever that means.

And I also have my notebook.

The only seat left is closer to the back than I'd like. Everyone chatters away while our professor taps at her tablet, squinting at the screen over her sleek glasses. I stop my foot from tapping with impatience. Leah's in the front row—that should have been my seat. I triple-check to make sure I'm in the right place, but my schedule confirms Introduction to Creative Writing with Professor Mendoza.

My shoulders prickle like someone's staring at me, and I turn.

Lacretia tilts her head at me and flashes her teeth. "Hi! I'm Lacretia. Looks like you finally figured out where you're supposed to be."

I blink and try to play along. "Yep…uh, it's all laid out for me."

"You feeling good? Refreshed? Confident?"

Okay…huh? "We already met! Why are you messing with me?"

She gives me a confused look. "I'm studying dance. We won't have any classes—"

Professor Mendoza stands so abruptly the whole class falls silent. A laugh hides in her dimples like she knows a secret and won't share it. Wavy dark hair trails from the messy bun teetering fearlessly atop her head. Her amber-gold skin has a touch of red at the cheekbones. She hunches over like Old Zeph does when his back aches in the winter, as if her amethyst-blue blazer is a size too small. "Suppose I better teach you something today."

She pauses, glancing through the rows before her gaze stops on me. "Keynan, is it? The one who thought he was too good for this place. How fascinating. Stand, please. Come on now, don't be shy. Up, up! There's nothing I love better than a fresh new voice to mentor. Let's see what you're made of."

I practically float out of my chair. It's my time! Murmurs and giggles break out around me, but I don't care. I flip open my notebook, searching for a rhyme that will impress. Professor Mendoza glides down the row, brushing past my shoulder. "Recite today's reading. Class, follow along on your tablets."

Say huh? Tablets? I set my notebook aside and blink at the new file in our class portal. My eyebrows climb up my forehead as I scan the poem and recite.

I'm already apologizing to my brain by the time I sit down. What in the daydreamiest slumber party did I just read? These weren't even my rhymes and I'm still embarrassed.

A glance around confirms…yep. Naptime. Lacretia frowns at Professor Mendoza. Leah glares at her tablet like it just slapped her. "What does any of that even mean?" she blurts.

"Indeed." Professor Mendoza nods thoughtfully. "Poetry speaks on many levels. Your assignment today is to find them. Memorization! Repetition! And most importantly, regurgitation! The Peerless way." She returns to her desk and tablet as though none of us exist.

Wait, is that it? Everyone pretends to read for a while, but pretty soon the occasional whisper turns into all-out jabbering. A peek at Professor Mendoza shows she couldn't care less.

I'm not just disappointed. I am heartbroken.

This was supposed to be my one bright spot at Peerless. Lacretia offers me a sympathetic shrug. "No one takes it serious, not even her." She glares at Mendoza, who is popping blueberries into her mouth one at a time, chewing blissfully with her eyes closed. "Don't feel bad. You're the first person she's called on since school started."

Only memories keep me seated: my mama staring at that wall, face spooky-smooth like she'd never smiled before. My baba, afraid like I've never seen him, guiding her to lay down. I could never look them in the eye again if I quit. I decide to poke through my tablet settings—there's got to be a chat app, a list of students, something!

"This might be hard for you," Professor Mendoza murmurs beside me.

I almost jump out of my shoes—when did she leave her desk?

"It's not hard," I say. "Just...easy." I'm proud of myself

for changing what I meant to say. *Boring* fits better. "My parents taught me…a lot of different stuff. Zora. Langston. Saul."

"Ah. A young scholar." She's holding in a giggle. But why? Grown-ups are so hard to figure out. She leans in, whispering for me only. A splotch of blueberry juice stains her cheek. "I don't normally take on mentees, but maybe you'll change my mind. You know Peerless is…off. Yes?"

"I think so," I say uncertainly.

"Splendid. You need points?"

I nod sheepishly.

"A clever boy like you knows how to procure snacks." Her brow furrows. "That vile cook actually smacked my hand with a ladle. But I like my desk stocked with whatever's in season and such. That's worth some points."

The professor gives me a wink, smiling so hard I can see all of her teeth. I wink back, uncertainty bubbling in my stomach.

"All right, now." She nods, satisfied. "Keep your head down and practice for this dreadful recital. You'll do great things here, no matter what anyone says. And I mean anyone…even your headmaster."

Hold on now, is she bad-mouthing Kinder? "I'll do my best," I manage.

"I know you will. Your parents trusted you to. So see to it."

She moves to Leah next, murmuring in her ear while students laugh and gossip all around. Before long, Leah's nodding. I wonder if she's getting the same lecture. Maybe I need to be more patient. It's only my first day.

I zero in on the most boring poetry I've ever read.

"Why are you so salty?" Lacretia asks.

"Memorized it already." Her face rumples a bit, and I want to kick myself. She's nice—weird, but nice—and poetry isn't everyone's thing. "You want to practice together? Reading it to a friend helps."

A kid with pale skin in front of her turns, blue eyes narrowed. "First-years," he snorts. "Think they got Peerless all figured out but barely know their tablets!"

"Oh fall back, Joey!" Lacretia growls. "Every day it's some new mess from you!"

Leah suddenly spins around in her seat. "Isn't this your second year taking this class?" she hisses. "Maybe we'll help you pass!"

I clap back too—first-year slander will not be tolerated! "I'll trade you lessons for snacks if you ask me nice." I guess it's not really a clapback if I mean it, though.

Joey's face turns bright red. "If you snots think for one second that I'll—"

"What? Move us to tears with your sleepy rhymes?"

"Keynan! Leah!" Professor Mendoza puts down her tablet, brown eyes flashing like she's mad enough to catch fire. Uh-oh. "Oh no, scribes. None of that. You're about to make me look bad."

"But he started—" Leah begins. Mendoza cuts her off with a disgusted gesture.

"I am not the one for foolishness! Points docked for…" She scowls at her tablet. "Valiant's Victors and Wiley Squad."

Every student holds their breath as Professor Mendoza taps briskly. Why is she just calling out me and Leah? Everyone was talking! The whole class! Joey shoots us a smug leer. Leah's tablet chirps, and mine follows an instant later. I stare numbly at a new alert. This is *not* happening.

> Report to Headmaster Kinder's office immediately after class.

"Oh my." Professor Mendoza shakes her head regretfully. "The headmaster's not happy."

CHAPTER ELEVEN

YOUR PROBLEM NOW

I numbly shuffle into the hall when class is over. My tablet chirps with the route to Kinder's office. Great. Sent to the headmaster on my first day!

How do I explain what had *really* happened, how I tried to *help* Joey? I offered to share some of my vast poetic talent, for the good of Peerless. If anything, Wiley Squad deserves points for my—

"That's your plan?" a voice behind me moans.

Dang, was I talking out loud?

I spin to see Leah, shaking her head. "We're so done. If I get sent home…"

"We're fine! Kinder loves me, she just doesn't know it yet." No way I'm leaving Peerless until I find out how to help Bizzy Block outlast these storms. "They're not even ready for my poems, and—"

Our tablets chirp. The headmaster's office is straight ahead.

An assistant with strands of gray in her short purple ringlets doesn't even bother looking up from her monitor, she just points to an open glass door on her right. We slide into two chairs in front of a huge desk made of dark, lavish wood. No windows, not even a monitor, and worst of all? No snacks. There's no way Headmaster Kinder gets work done here, unless this is some special torture chamber for lecturing first-years? A huge painting of Peerless surrounded by blue skies swallows up the wall behind her desk. The whole piece is kinda ordinary, except for a hawk with viper-red wings perched on the school's wall. It peers at me, spreads its wings, and swoops off into the canvas sky.

I blink. This is a *painting,* not a monitor. Did that just happen?

I turn to ask Leah, but she's glaring at me. "If your poetry's so good, you'd be in writing classes with the second-years."

"They don't even do that," I retort.

"Then why am I the only first-year in my dance class?" she snaps. "Help Joey? You'll probably *be* Joey if you last more than a month. Why don't you do us all a favor and go back to *Build-A-Scholar*, brick brain?"

My face flushes. Dang. I didn't know first-years took higher classes. She ain't gotta rub my nose in it! "You really need to stop calling me outside my—"

A sudden realization smacks me. Only one person I've ever known calls me brick brain. I shoot my shot. "If you're such a boss, why can't you beat your sister's record on Mirror Maze Castle?"

Leah gapes at me. "No way. You? *You're* Keymaster?"

"You're Starbreaker."

We both groan.

"I don't believe it," she says. "Your parents must be worried sick about you! Who does that, biking straight into a storm to get here?"

"I didn't mean for that to happen, okay?" *This* is supposed to be my BFF, my homie, my ace beaucoup? Of course she is. Stubborn? Check. Rule breaker? Check. I'm kicking myself for even thinking Dez or Amari could live up to this buster. Nothing is working out right, but I still want to fix it. "Anyway, my bad I got you on Kinder's grumpy side," I offer. "Do-over?"

"So you can get me in more trouble? Nope. I never should've got on that shuttle looking for you. Do you know how many points that cost my cohort? Professor Valiant made me apologize to everyone thanks to you—"

Leah's mouth snaps shut so fast her teeth click. Headmaster Kinder strides into the office, expression troubled and shoulders slumped. I've never seen someone need a hug so bad.

Do headmasters hug? Is that a thing?

Another grown-up glides in right behind her, so close I'm scared she'll lose an ankle when the headmaster slams the door shut. Kinder gives an irritated shake of her head and sits. The other woman settles in beside the headmaster's chair. Freckles dust her brown cheeks, and her fluffy twist-out brushes her shoulders. Her plain dark slacks and faded white blouse are nothing like Headmaster Kinder's lime-green pantsuit and pink heels.

The headmaster takes a whole extra breath and turns to me. This is gonna set records on the Epic Lecture scale. "Why do you two chuckleheads insist on working my nerves so hard? Shuttle pick up: disaster. First day of class: disaster. At this rate, Professor Wiley will need to wash dishes and mop floors to get these points back, Keynan."

Leah's smug smile melts away when the headmaster gives her the stink eye, too. "If your behavior doesn't change drastically, *immediately*, you won't like the consequences. I'm responsible for two things—keeping this school running smoothly, and the safety of my students. Even if it means tying you both up until your parents come gather you. Understood?"

"Yes," I squeak.

Leah bobs her head.

"I'm sure it won't come to that," the other woman says thoughtfully. "First-year jitters. They'll sort themselves out before the recital."

Headmaster Kinder snorts. "That's optimistic, even for you, Professor Touré."

"We'll have the best recital Peerless has ever seen," I jump in, nudging Leah. "Right?" She just sits there with an unconvincing scowl. "*Right...?* The best—"

"—Peerless has ever seen," she finishes stonily.

Touré's lips twitch. "See?"

The headmaster's smile could cut glass. "I hope so. They're your problem now."

They both go silent, staring like they spotted a piece of lettuce in my teeth at the same time. Leah and I share an uneasy look.

An instant later, thunder rumbles somewhere above Peerless.

"You deal with them." Kinder rubs her temples. "I'll check the grounds."

"Be careful," Professor Touré says softly. She bustles us

out of the office and down the hall. I'd be relieved, but we walk straight past my next class.

"We missed my turn."

"Mine, too," Leah adds anxiously.

"Glad you're both getting familiar with the halls." She flashes me an unreadable look that makes me nervous all over again. "I'm Professor Touré."

"Umm, what subject do you teach?" I ask.

"Mostly I keep the school running, or teach whenever professors are…out sick. I also deal with bigger problems for the headmaster. Today, that means overseeing your detention."

"*Detention?*" Leah shrieks. "But our classes—"

"Will still be there tomorrow."

Two hours with Professor Touré makes my schedule on Bizzy Block feel like a holiday. Across the grounds, we change light bulbs that won't stop glowing when the switch is flicked off, or even after we unscrew them with thick leather gloves. We eat a quick lunch, then peel yams for dinner. Set buckets under drips in the teacher's lounge. I swear something's crying behind the ceiling panels, nasally and blubbering. Leah stays fixed on her mopping, pretending she can't hear it, but her jaw is clenched the whole time. I don't say anything either and finally remember to breathe when we finish.

Kinder's voice pops out of nowhere during our water break. *"Proceed indoors immediately. A storm is approaching the school grounds. This is not a drill."*

Come on, intercom! Scaring me half to death! Wiley assured us that Peerless is sturdy, but I don't know if I'll ever feel all the way safe with a storm close by, chunky school walls or not. "Did you notice how Kinder and Touré acted back in the office?" I ask Leah, hoping she didn't see me just shoot water out my nose. "Got all quiet, like they knew the storm was coming."

"Grown-ups have been around them longer," Leah replies with a shrug. She sounds calm, but her eyes dart nervously at every little echo. "They get funny feelings about weather—joints aching or whatever."

"Yeah, that's weird." We're not quite talking about the same thing, but I leave it. Me and Leah are a long way from becoming besties again, but we share a relieved grin when Kinder's voice announces the storm danger has passed. That counts for something.

Touré doesn't say much besides announcing our next chore, and she's always studying me as if she's waiting for something—or can't wait to snitch on us to Kinder. I keep my mouth shut so she won't get one scrap. There's no way I'll turn things around at Peerless if I get in trouble while already in actual detention.

We untangle knotted extension cords. Check old garden hoses for leaks. Finally, we finish and lug our supplies down a wing that passes the second-year classrooms. Leah's feet drag beside an open door. There's no desks in the room, and mirrors cover every wall. "It's like the dungeon level in Mirror Maze Castle," I remark.

Leah rolls her eyes. "It's a dance studio. *My* studio. I've been waiting to learn something new for weeks, but the classes have all been super boring... The way things have been going since I met you, I probably missed out on it today."

She sounds like Amari, complaining about his art courses. Detention's been way harder than my first writing class, now that I think about it. If Peerless is supposed to be everything my parents said, why are our courses so simple?

"Been awhile since I had any help," Touré says as we return mops, buckets, and wide push brooms to a closet near the first-year classes. She taps her tablet. Ours chirp on the shelf where she's kept them during our detention. "Here's y'all's homework. The dining hall's closed, but I made sure Soup set something aside."

Leah's brow creases. "What is it?" Professor Touré asks.

"I was hoping to finally eat with my sister tonight. Yolanda. It's like she's been avoiding me ever since I got here."

Touré nods slowly, rearranging containers that are already straight. "Third year is pretty demanding. Not much free time."

That's how we wrap the worst day ever. Leah and I are silent the whole walk back to the first-year dorms. I can't take it anymore. I've got to get us right somehow. "Let's not do that again, deal?"

Leah nods.

"Wanna eat together? We—"

But she's already closing the door to her room. I go inside mine to find a tray of cold, limp salad waiting for me. Ian's nowhere in sight. I munch my sorry dinner and try to do some homework, but I'm so tired I can barely see straight.

Tired…and sad. Leah and I were supposed to be forever friends. That's not looking too good right now. I wouldn't have lasted through *Build-A-Scholar* without Starbreaker's jokes. I'd let Joey run his mouth every day if it meant starting over from scratch.

Just as bad, I've not had one single spark of a rhyme the entire day—not since this morning. It's like Peerless is sucking poetry right out of me, exactly like I was afraid of. But I've still got to dig myself out of trouble and stay that way. If I'm stuck in detention so much I can't learn about storms, I'll have no one to blame but myself.

Some first day.

CHAPTER TWELVE

RATCHET THE CAT

Lucky for me, my new friends don't let me mope very long. Ian has a joke for everything, and Amari's facial expressions make it hard not to crack up in homeroom. I finally settle into the rest of my classes too, but every day for a week, my professors all give me the exact same funny look when I plop down in my seat. A look that means: watch out for Keynan Masters, he's a whole problem!

The best part of my days usually involves food, especially lunchtime, when the three of us can complain about our classes. I beeline straight for the dining hall after Physics lets out. Other first-years cluster at the long wooden tables or wait in line for the day's lunch options. Ian's grinning at me from the other side of the room, and I meander over to where he stands with Amari.

"Would you please tell him to cheer up?" Ian asks me.

"Stick figures, Keynan!" Amari exclaims. "For the third straight week! If my drawing class were any more basic, we'd be using crayons! At least tell me writing went better?"

"Things will look up. They have to," I say, trying to believe my own words.

"That's what I said!" Ian declares. "The professors will fuss about recital for weeks and weeks. Who cares? Make your own fun—it's not like we'll get to do any of this over. Come on y'all. I'm starving, and we need to hurry."

"For what?" I ask.

Ian and Amari share a secretive grin. "Food first. Then we'll talk."

I don't bug them about it, not with the savory goodness from the buffet line teasing my nose. The school chef is decked out in his usual white uniform and apron, greeting us with a broad smile, the kind you can't help but give back. The cornrows beneath his hairnet are braided in a cool maze pattern. "There they are! I asked myself this morning: *Soup, which one of my first-years will have a hollow leg today?*" He directs his spatula at the three of us. "Y'all gonna strip our whole garden bare if we're not careful."

I laugh—that sounds exactly like something my baba would say. "We're all pretty hungry."

"I've been wondering," Ian says. "Is your name really Soup?"

"Why? You got a problem with it?"

That sends Ian spluttering. "No! I just—"

"Well, that makes one of us. I'm Andre." His dark eyes crinkle like they're holding in a lifetime supply of jokes. He's a grown-up I'd actually talk with more if it didn't mean getting a ton of free advice. On cue, he leans closer. "Don't ever let a nickname stick, or it'll screw all kinds of things up. Best to name yourselves. I would've liked Scoop. Smoother, you know?"

"At least it's not Bloop," Amari offers.

"Or Droop," I add. "And definitely not—"

"Smart guys, huh? I ain't got time to shoot the breeze, go get some food in ya."

My stomach is so ready. There's roasted veggies and rice stuffed in open-ended burritos, next to a spicy salsa with cilantro so fresh the aroma dances in my nose, barbecued jackfruit sliders, sweet potato fries, a salad bar, steaming rolls, and a simmering pot with a little chalkboard sign beside it that reads, *Soup's Soup of the Day*.

This stuff smells like happiness. I inhale deeply, mystified by this delicious mystery. Potatoes. Corn. Basil. Spices I don't recognize. Loads of peppers, between the bubbles. Some kind of chowder?

Only one of the bubbles…isn't a bubble.

A round, brown, gooey eye winks at me from behind a sprig of thyme just before it pops.

I flinch back with a yelp. "Did y'all see that?" I splutter. "There was an eye—"

"So you got jokes?" Soup gives me an offended look. "Potatoes have eyes, you know."

"Not like that they don't!"

"Keynan…you're yelling," Ian moans. He's right. The whole cafeteria is staring at me. "Don't get on the grown-ups' bad side. Especially the ones who feed us!"

"Who's holding up the line?" I jump at Professor Mendoza's voice farther behind us. "Move it, you three. This is the best part of my day!"

Amari and I grab burritos, while Ian gets a bit of everything.

"For science," he explains with a smirk that promises more clowning.

We pour lemonades and claim an empty table. I hold my breath when Ian spoons right into his soup. Nothing happens, at least not until Ian and Amari bust into howls at my expense. I'm never gonna live this down.

"Eyeball soup," Amari chuckles. "You couldn't have picked a worse school for an imagination like that."

"So what are we hurrying for?" I ask, eager to change the subject.

"Not until we're alone," Ian answers mysteriously.

Dozens of students pack the hall, chattering breathlessly or poking at tablets. I remember some of the older kids from the shuttle and worry they're laughing about me. I glance around for Leah, hopeful to see her and also relieved when I don't. My stomach goes all twisty when I think about what to say with her.

Amari chews his burrito thoughtfully. "Almost as good as my granny's."

"Finish up quick," Ian says. Me and Amari stare; he's half my size but halfway done already!

They won't peep one word until we're done and away from nosy folks, pulling me into an alcove of trophies just off the main hallway. "We're redoing your Hall Hop."

"Thanks to me," Amari cuts in.

"What good is a tour now?"

"He found a way into the locked wing!" Ian exclaims. "Don't you want to explore?"

"I've seen plenty of the school with Touré—"

"I told you he would be down." Ian rubs his hands together.

Dang it. I'd hoped to finally study up on storms in the library. The doors aren't locked anymore—I checked before cohort. But what will they think if I whine my way out of exploring? I'm already down one friend. I don't want to lose Ian and Amari, too.

I sigh as Amari disappears behind a case holding a golden plate and old medals. A door is hidden in the space just behind it. Beyond is a flight of musty stairs. The others don't notice that the stairway leading downwards goes on and on and on. I can't even see the bottom, just a gloomy abyss. My chest grows tight as we trudge upward, the floor crunching like gravel beneath our shoes as if the concrete itself is…rotting. We finally spill into a hallway just like the rest of Peerless, but so quiet and still and clean that our footsteps echo both ways. If I didn't know any better, I'd guess no one's walked it in twenty years.

"This is it?" Ian's bottom lip pokes out.

I check the time on my tablet, but the display is funky. Colors swirl across the screen for an instant before my menu and map come back up. Amari and Ian notice the same thing when I ask about theirs.

"We'll be fine!" Ian insists. "How about first to find something spooky makes the others do a dare?"

"Okay, bet," I agree. Amari and I join in as Ian starts opening random doors, mostly empty classrooms. He's so fixed on finding something bizarre, he's missing what's right in front of his face. Peerless must have been meant for more kids, a lot more. But where are they?

After the sixth classroom of empty desks, Amari's had enough. "Lunch is almost over," he calls out. "I don't want to lose Wiley points for being late."

Ian reluctantly gives up the hunt. We retrace our steps back to the stairwell. Amari opens the door and stops. Stacks of old yellowing papers are piled to the ceiling. "I swear this is the right door."

"I thought it was too," Ian groans. "We're lost!"

How did I let myself get talked into this? I'm going to end up back in detention thanks to these busters! "Check your tablets for—" I stop, listening. "Wait. That sounds like someone. Come on!"

We hustle around a corner. At the end of this new hall, a group of older students jokes and laughs as they disappear through a door.

"First third-years I've seen," Amari says thoughtfully. "Where've they been hiding?"

Maybe off on more of Kinder's field trips, but right now, who cares? "They'll know the way back. Come on!"

I take off, ignoring Ian's protests. I fling open the door to a student lounge filled with couches and comfy pillows, reading nooks. Just one problem: no students. The hair on the back of my neck stands up. "Like, forreal?" I ask the empty room.

"Okay, that's just freaky," Amari murmurs behind me.

"I know…it's almost like I can hear their echoes."

"Quit acting scary." Ian shudders. "Probably just another hidden door in here."

"*Where*, bro? Or maybe you mean a ghost door, for ghost third-years?"

"That's not funny, Amari!"

"We better keep looking," I say quickly, "unless this means I won the bet?"

The distraction works, keeps them moving.

Amari tries another door on the opposite side of the hall. "Y'all look at this."

We don't step one foot inside. There's nothing off about the room itself, but the window is getting pelted with sleet. I swallow a sudden tightness in my throat. "Are the storm sirens broken?"

None of us are happy about that possibility.

"It's sticking to the window," Amari says with a frown. "But it's not cold enough to be freezing. Wrong time of year."

"Let's just go," I say, pulling the door closed. "We can't tell anyone we saw it, anyway." He's right about it being too warm for sleet. I refuse to say it out loud, but the little pellets clinging to the glass looked more like clumps of pale, silken spider eggs.

I peek into the next classroom, empty rows of desks, same as all the others. Only...not. A whiff of something familiar twists my nose, a knot of stank foulness, like compost when it's rotting. It smells old and wrong, so faint it's more like a memory or a dream. I follow it to the professor's desk and nearly sprint back out of the room.

"Keynan! Ian found the stairs. What are you—"

Amari falls quiet when he sees it. Strange gouges dig trenches across the professor's desk, lines burned so deep into the wood the whole thing might snap in half. "You definitely win the bet," he whispers. "You going to tell Ian we found Ratchet?"

I swallow. "Cats don't have six claws."

"How does it look burned and melted at the same time? Like lightning hit it."

Something clicks into place. My brain tried to hide it from me, but I know exactly what it smells like in here.

The air before a storm.

CHAPTER THIRTEEN

GET AHEAD OR GET LEFT

We argue about the closed-off wing for days. I want to tell someone—anyone—about the melted desk. Amari's convinced older kids made it somehow and insists he saw hundreds of kid-sized handprints in the ruined wood. No way it's a prank! Ian and Amari remind me that telling is a no-brainer road to losing Wiley Squad points, not to mention detention or another headmaster visit. So I keep my lips sealed and head down, worming my way out of any more exploring for now. The library keeps calling, and I can practically feel all of Bizzy Block cringing in disappointment. But where is the time? I've still got plenty of homework to catch up on, and good study spots are hard to find.

My room is usually out—when Ian's not crunching, he's

snoring. The study nooks off the entry hall are perfect, at least until a couple of third-years started crashing the space, laughing and whispering fiercely. I finally work up enough courage to ask them to keep it down one night, only to find that their palms are *stuck together*, drippy fingers intertwined like melted string cheese!

One sees my horrified face.

"Prank's on you, first-year!"

They crack up as I hurry off. I'm no snitch, but I know scared when I see it—they were frantic, and that wasn't glue. I cross those nooks off my list of study spots.

Most of my days are worse than pulling weeds and doing *Build-A-Scholar* at the same time, but I don't cost Wiley Squad any more points.

Not that any of it matters.

Every single class, except for morning cohort and writing, my professors all eyeball me. Like...there's no one else in the room. Or I might put garden slugs in their coffee— me, lover of snacks and all delicious things! Really? Their stares remind me of Headmaster Kinder so much it's like she found a way to borrow their eyes. Professor Okoro, my Physics teacher, actually stands in the hallway scratching his colossal beard, until I'm in the room and seated. Dez is in that class too—lucky me. He was late yesterday, without a single word about points from Okoro! Class after class is like that, Peerless professors waiting for any excuse to send me back to detention.

I know why I'm here though, so I don't give them one. Not even when Ian and Amari try to pull me into their latest clowning. Which is pretty much every day at lunch.

"Keynan, I'm telling you," Amari insists over his bowl of Soup's Soup, which is a tasty gumbo today. "The rooms keep changing."

"They're locking off different spaces for repairs? How is that weird?"

"No, the rooms are *gone*. The one with, you know…the paw print? It's just a closet now."

"Maybe you got lost."

"Lost?" Ian rolls his eyes. "We weren't lost. I've probably been down that hall a hundred times."

"A hundred times," I say dryly. "Not even done with your first year."

"Whatever, I know this place, okay? Besides, he—"

"I drew a map." Amari flicks on his tablet and thrusts it out.

I pick out lots of lines and boxes with arrows and scribbled notes, calling out hallways, windows, classrooms. "Well, maybe your drawing was…"

One glance at Amari's face warns me not to finish that

sentence. He's super touchy about his art. He swipes the screen. "Here's two days ago."

My breath catches. Hmm. The hallway is the same, but with half as many doors. He's drawn huge question marks in the blank spaces where whole rooms used to be.

"Here's yesterday."

Now the hallway is…twisted, like a snake just starting to slither.

Their eyes are on me, waiting for me to say something. That Amari's tablet is busted. Or he's drawing with his eyes closed. Anything except for what it looks like: Peerless is eating itself.

"Maybe Professor Wiley will take a look…without, you know, snitching?" I suggest, surprised when they both seem relieved.

"Good call." Amari stares at his hands for a moment. "Thanks for listening. Forreal. We've been trying to tell the other first-years about this stuff, and they just keep changing the subject."

"I got you," I say, standing. "But I gotta go. Professor Mendoza finally gave me some new reading."

I'm up and out, but still catch Ian's muttered whisper. "Change the subject, huh? Didn't he just do that to us?"

Ouch. That stings. I'm probably lucky we all still eat together. I'm not the most fun roommate or cohort homie right now, catching up on my first two weeks. It's hard to make more friends. I probably still smell like trouble to the other first-years—especially Dez. Not to mention Leah, my former bestie. Real-life friends beat the pants off *Build-A-Scholar,* my parents definitely called that part. But right now, for me? It's either get ahead or get left.

The courtyard has been turning into my new favorite place to do homework, but no one really uses the weird glass study rooms, so I decide to try one of them instead today. I finally get to do more poetry. Professor Mendoza assigned me extra credit after bringing her a napkin stuffed with cherries.

> *Can a thousand worlds spring from one?*
> *forests rise from a single seed*
> *if the hand guiding the fire is bold*

No author, again. Sometimes I wonder if Mendoza makes them up on the spot. I explain why the poem isn't haiku, then rewrite it to fit a traditional pattern. It's different, but at least it's interesting, and a little challenging.

The best part? I'm finally creating my own verses again! Writing this piece feels like curses lifted, fresh soil sifted into dry clay, new life meshed with my wordplay. Come what may, I'm going to get through this, make my way out of Peerless and beyond, then—

Whoa. Did that just come out of me? I need to write that—

Down down downdown*downdowndown*

The air shudders, like a thousand invisible palms are drumming the glass-walled study room, trying to break free. I clap my hands over my ears, but the echoing increases until I grab my stuff and rush out.

So… I'm pretty sure that's not what soundproof means!

Besides… I didn't say anything out loud.

I knew I hated those study rooms for a reason. It all makes about as much sense as…well, classrooms playing peekaboo or third-years with taffy fingers. Ian and Amari are right…something is seriously off about Peerless, and I can't keep ignoring it.

I hurry back to my room. The whole thing was spooky, but at least something good came out of it. I got my rhymes back!

I'm still cheesing about it the next morning—at least until Professor Wiley gestures for me to stand during cohort.

Oh, shoot. What now? Did I lose more points? The whole homeroom goes silent. Lacretia sighs. Amari's face pinches in sympathy. Dez shakes his head. Am I ever going to start winning in this place?

"New homeroom point totals were updated today," Professor Wiley intones. He taps in his tablet, all of ours chirp. "I'm delighted to share that we're now tied for second place and that our very own Keynan Masters made up his personal point deficit—and then some."

Our cohort bursts into excited whoops as we read our announcements. It's true! Valiant is in the lead, followed by Wiley and Osana, then Qadira and Guerrero tying for last.

I sit in dazed disbelief. Wow. Professor Mendoza really delivered on the extra credit. I owe her snacks for sure!

"I told you," Amari says proudly. "A comeback."

Professor Wiley claps my shoulder. "You slipped up, but you never let up."

"Thanks, Professor." I can't help but grin. That sounded like something my baba would say. Wiley even gives me a fist bump.

Lacretia beams. "You feeling—"

"Better than good. Great!"

Other classmates acknowledge me with dap or nods— even Dez is barely keeping his stank face strong. "He's right, you never let up," he mumbles. "Now just don't let us down."

In my next few classes, it's like a cloud lifted. The doubt

so many of my professors have been holding just evaporated with the points update. Professor Mendoza murmurs her approval as I carefully unfold a napkin of raspberries on her desk. Other first-years aren't smirking at me when they think I'm not looking. I'm not a whole problem anymore. Which means I can relax a little more, dive into figuring out this Peerless weirdness with my friends, and finally start inhaling everything I can learn about storms.

Amari waves at me impatiently from our table once I enter the dining hall. For lunch, Soup's serving up some bubbly enchiladas—one of my favorites. "Just for you, kid. You earned 'em." He slips a string of melty cheese onto my plate. "Keep at it!"

I'm so pleased and famished that by the time I weave over to our table, I don't even realize we're not alone until my cheeks are puffed with food.

Leah's sitting straight across from me.

"You've been holding out," Amari pouts. "You knew each other, before Peerless?"

My mouth is still overflowing, but Leah speaks up. "Yeah, we were best friends."

"How cool is that?" Ian says around a mouthful of rice and beans. "I wish I'd had real friends back home."

"Me too." Amari sighs. "All these other first-years start

to look the same after a while. And she's on two tracks already, in her first year? Writing and dance. Whew."

Leah cringes. Is she…embarrassed? No way.

"Twice the talent," I offer.

"You mean twice the homework," she says, but gives me a quick, grateful glance.

Hold on. Are we back? I think we're back!

Ian blinks, frowning between us. "Wait…you said you two *were* best friends? Did y'all—"

"So Leah's who showed me Mirror Maze Castle," I interrupt hastily. "Last summer, we spent two weeks mapping out the paradox gauntlet together."

"Almost beat it, too," Leah adds, chasing a lone bean around her tray with her spoon.

"I like maps," Amari remarks as he and Ian lean in eagerly. Leah shows them how to pull up the game on their tablets. I add in a few pointers on how to switch back to homework without losing all of your progress—the Mirror Maze doesn't let you save, and it's never built the same way twice.

Pretty soon we're all laughing, and it's not so awkward anymore. Why didn't I show them this a long time ago? Or invite Leah to sit with us? After detention, I was pretty sure any hope of Keymaster and Starbreaker as besties was cooked. But I didn't even try. And I should have—best friends are worth fighting for, even if things get messy. Despite me being awful—and thanks to Amari and Ian—we could still actually be okay.

Ian's already guiding himself through the maze like he's played it before. "I'll have this beat in a day," he declares. "What else you got?"

I roll my eyes. "You dream. No one will ever beat Yolanda's score."

Leah stiffens. I forgot she's really competitive.

"Why does that name sound familiar?" Ian murmurs thoughtfully. He misses a turn and drops down a hidden chute that plops him back at the beginning. "Dang it! So who is she?"

"Leah's big sis. How's she doing, anyway?" I ask, but Leah's eyes are fixed on her tray. "Did she finally get through all of her third-year assignments?"

"Another homework fanatic?" Amari grumbles. "Y'all are the worst!"

"Seek cover immediately," Kinder's voice drones overhead. *"This is a test of our storm warning system. Shelter in place and await instructions."*

Groans ring out around the dining hall as we all bring our trays under the tables. "I'm getting tired of eating like this," Ian complains. "That's how many this week?"

"Too many," Amari agrees. "But better than not being ready."

Leah stands. "I'm gonna finish up in my room."

"But—will you eat with us again?" I blurt out. Her dark brown eyes swing to mine. I can't just let her go. I don't wanna go back to ignoring each other.

"She's not—" Ian starts, but Amari nudges him quiet.

"At dinner?" I ask. "I'd—we'd, uh…it'd be really cool if you…and your sister could come too—"

"Yeah. Sure." She strides for the door, but not before I see her face crumple.

Amari and Ian exchange a mystified look. "What's up with her?" Amari asks. "She didn't even take her food."

I have no idea, but I'm going to help, somehow. No matter how messy it gets.

CHAPTER FOURTEEN

THROUGH THE BREAK

Next time I see Leah in Writing, she stays fixed on her tablet, even with our class throwing grapes at each other and playing slapjack while Professor Mendoza naps. When class is over, Leah's up and out the door before I can say anything. There's no sign of her at dinner either—I even check Mirror Maze Castle, just in case.

"It's obvious something's up with her sister," Amari says.

"Maybe we can help?" I say hopefully. "She's my best friend, and this isn't like her at all."

"If she wants help," he replies.

"Right," I agree. Nothing worse than someone bugging you so *they* can feel better, when you just need some space.

"I was so sure we were all going to be cool," Ian grumbles. "We even got the same food for lunch. That *never* happens!"

The three of us go our separate ways after dinner. Amari's been teaching Ian and some other first-years how to play spades this past week, but tonight he wants to draw. Ian's still stuck repeating the first level of Mirror Maze Castle, so he's busy.

Me? I can finally just do my homework and not feel so sick about it. Then dig every single book about storms out of the library, finally! The courtyard is the perfect place to knock out assignments. I hear sniffling closer to the old oak tree and tiptoe closer. It's Leah. She's leaning against Professor Mendoza, who pats her shoulder and whispers in her ear. My feet pull me forward before I even decide if it's a good idea. I'm not sure we're all the way okay yet, but my friend needs a hug.

Mendoza's eyes glint when she spots me. Uh-oh. Her head jerks slightly, and I take the hint and go.

I feel awful that Leah's still upset. Somehow I'll be Starbreaker's friend again, but it's gonna take a lot more than Mirror Maze Castle and snacks.

My tablet chirps at me while I'm trying to find a good study nook. A new message? I bite my lip and open it up:

The start of a new semester can be a lot to take in.
You've got this.
Love you and miss you!
—Mama & Baba

Not exactly my mama's perfect advice or my baba's crushing hugs, but it sure does make me feel better.

I remember seeing benches tucked between the basketball courts and soccer field while we were following Touré around for detention. Since the courtyard is out and I'm never stepping foot in one of those weird glass study boxes again, that's my best bet for some space to focus. My tablet guides the way.

A tingle scampers up my spine as I step outside. It's a little chilly, and fireflies wink in and out over the grass. The setting sun paints everything golden and beautiful, and I've got the whole space to myself. An idea for a new rhyme pops into my head, and I grab a pen to jot it down:

Detention first day,
throw the whole thing away.
What would Mama say?
Found my homie Starbreaker,
but Leah don't know me.
Can the Keymaster start over and—

And…that's going nowhere fast. I pull up my Physics homework instead, something about soundwaves. It's not so bad, so I read ahead. It can't hurt to be ready for what's coming up. What would my baba say? *If you stay ready, you ain't gotta get ready.*

The next chapter talks about rhythm and time, four counts and three counts.

Too easy.

Maybe I can change it up, show Professor Okoro how creative I am? Get on his good side, if he has one. There's rhythm everywhere, after all. Crickets at dusk. Rainbow trout pulsing in the creek. My heartbeat. Old Zeph drumming his fingers on the dominoes table when he thinks folks are moving too slow.

"Study long, study wrong," I murmur to myself.

So I just try something…maybe not new, but different. The bench makes it louder, left-hand knuckles smacking the wood and right palm slapping it. *Bump. Slap.* I like that.

On the soccer field, the fireflies all wink with every bump. Cool! I didn't know they could do that.

BUMP. SLAP. BUMP. SLAP.

This is actually really fun. What if I change it up again?

BUMP. SLAP. BUMP BUMP. SLAP!

This beat wiggles my bones, like I've heard it before.

The only other thing that gives me this feeling is starting a new poem. When the words snatch straight past my ribs and won't let my heart go until—

Wait a minute.

Wait.

A.

Minute.

This must be…what music feels like? No wonder my parents get so sad whenever I ask why no one makes room for it anymore. How could our neighbors call something so cool a waste of time, or bad luck? Poetry and beats go together like peanut butter and jelly.

If I get this right, my professors will love it! I might even be able to use it for the recital! I flip through my notebook for an old poem that's easy to say while I try and make my hands cooperate with this beat. I got this.

Morning started great, knocked out all my chores,
Since I'm finished early, it's time to go explore.
What's in the hills and valleys, far beyond the corn?
I love Bizzy Block, but there's got to be—

Dazzling blue and purple light suddenly flashes beneath my hands, the bench's wood peeling apart like a blooming flower. I yelp and scramble away, clutching my notebook and tablet. What is happening? The light pulses, shooting brilliant cracks across the field. The bench sinks as I turn to run. "Help! Somebody—"

The grass and sidewalk beneath my feet melt away. The sky overhead churns as wind rushes in on every side. I'm… falling! Before I can even let out a wail, I flop onto something soft and spongy and sticky.

Peerless is gone. A lumpy, multicolored plain stretches off in every direction. Bubbles rise out of the ground like pancakes that need flipped—some as small as me, others the size of a whole house. A stone's throw away, one as big as my dorm room swells and bursts. Ripples sweep over the ground and bowl me over. Their color shifts with each new wave, like a chameleon that can't make up its mind.

I'm so scared, I can hardly think. "Where am I? Where is everybody?"

Another bubble swells up. I almost run, but then I notice there are people trapped inside.

My parents.

Huh? They smile, but their faces are sad, like when I ask about music.

"Keynan," my baba calls. "Make it yours." He taps his chest. "In here."

"Baba, what is this place!" I cry.

"Don't eat snacks in your bed," my mama adds just before the bubble bursts. The spongy ground quakes again. My arms windmill as I fight to keep my balance. When I look up, they're gone.

It felt so real. But how? They're safe at home now… aren't they?

I back away, my whole body shaking, avoiding any expanding bubbles. Some rise into the hazy pink not-sky, full of translucent shapes like oil floating on simmering water. More bubbles hover just above the sponge, bouncing off each other. Big nope on seeing what kind of mess might be inside those.

My eyes fix on the one thing not bubbling: a brilliant point of light at the crest of a distant hill. Its shape reminds me of the oak tree in the Peerless courtyard, but even older. Bigger. All of its leaves shimmer like a thousand shards of fire. The most beautiful thing I've ever seen—if only this place weren't so scary.

Then I hear the roar.

A shadow stalks around the tree, a glimmer of stained turquoise and bruised violet dimming its golden glow. Shapes are hard to make out. Wings, maybe? A lashing tail or two? Three? The only thing my eyes agree on is that the monster moves like a cat. The scribbles of mucky light shift. Two glowing red points pierce right through me. Eyes.

I freeze, terrified. The gashes on Eli the drone's belly, the six slices of lightning in the storm sky. Along with the charred claw marks we found on the old desk in Peerless? There's no explaining any of that away now. This monster has stalked around Bizzy Block, lurking in the storms, after me this whole time... Ratchet. Ian was right.

Maybe it can't see me yet. If one of these bubbles pops, I can slip away. Just gotta hold still. Another set of eyes—green this time—peels open beneath the first.

Seriously? How is that not cheating!

Another horrible roar rumbles out. Even the goopy ground is terrified—it turns pasty yellow and stays that way! Now I'm definitely seen. When the monster roars again and lopes toward me, my ears agree on something, too. The monster is hungry.

CHAPTER FIFTEEN

NEVER COMBINE ART FORMS

A small, sad whimper leaks from my throat. I'm over. Done. Cooked. But I still have to try, so I take off. If I'm going down, it'll be as the worst snack in the history of monster snacks. I barely make it two steps before something loops around my shoulders. Is it a monster tongue? Again with the cheating!

"Get off me!" I squeal.

A flash of light blinds me. Is this it? Am I swallowed whole? I blink and my eyes come into focus again. Green grass. Bleachers. Soccer goals. Basketball court. Along with two worried faces, Amari—and Leah! They yanked me out with some of Touré's old extension cord.

"Keynan, what did you do?" Leah cries. "Are you okay?"

"Nothing! I was doing homework, then—bam!"

"How about we talk later?" A flash lights up Amari's face.

I spin to see the…hole. It's getting bigger, a vibrant sphere that's swallowing grass and concrete with each pulse. Like it's breathing.

We take off across the soccer field for the nearest building. Wind howls at my heels, trying to suck me backward. Could the monster fit through? The hole is Keynan-sized for now, but how long will that last? Could it swallow up Peerless like it did that bench?

We burst inside the school's double doors. "Wait!" Leah wheezes behind me. "What's happening? Why is there a storm on the ground?"

"It's not a storm, it's a hole! It took me someplace."

"Like…a tunnel?" Amari asks.

"I don't know, but we've got to tell somebody!" I wave at them to keep going, forgetting the first rule of running for your life: watch where you're going.

I crash straight into Joey, the jerk bucket who got me and Leah detention in Mendoza's class. He scowls as we untangle. "Get out of my way!" He edges past Amari and Leah with a threatening look. "First-years. So annoying."

He's holding a soccer ball. "You can't go out there!" I splutter.

His hand hesitates over the door handle. "You're too old to be scared of the *darrkkkkk*—"

The door flies open, and wind roars into the corridor. The hole has eaten away half the soccer field—and it sucks Joey right in!

130

All three of us tear off again, shouting at the top of our lungs. But a familiar voice is even louder. "You finally get yourself together, just to pull this mess?"

Professor Touré strides straight for us, clenching and unclenching her fists.

"Professor! There's—"

"A storm. I have eyes, Keynan." She passes us without stopping, face grim.

"But it swallowed up Joey!" Leah cries.

"I'll save him if he can be saved. Back to the dorms. Go. Now."

Before I can protest, she sweeps directly into the light.

"You heard her, let's go!" Amari yanks on my arm.

"No! She didn't see what I did. There's a monster in there!"

Amari and Leah don't come any closer, but they won't leave me behind, either. Another blast of air swipes for my legs as I inch forward, and the double doors peel off the hinges in a shriek of metal! I freeze. A silhouette is just a few steps away, but it feels like an impossible distance. Professor Touré's voice rises above the roar:

...no repast for outcasts, from this day to the last one...

...my ancestors speak with one voice, get some...

My mouth falls open. She's rhyming!

"Keynan!" Leah's practically shouting in my ear. "Don't you leave us!"

"But I can help her!"

Amari's still dragging me back. "She doesn't need help!"

He's right. The fractured blue and purple swirls filling the air retreat toward the strange hole. It's collapsing in on itself. No uprooted trees or chunks of scattered brick. Touré stands beside the bench as the wind dies.

A distant door slams behind us. Running footsteps ring out down the hall, followed by a frantic shout. "I'm here! I'm coming!"

Headmaster Kinder. Scared as I am, I'm even more scared of being the first person she sees when she turns that corner.

We scatter. Leah ducks into a bathroom. Amari and I dive behind the ruined door an instant before Kinder sweeps straight out to the field, where Professor Touré is…fine. She's holding Joey's soccer ball.

"Are you hurt?" Kinder cries. "Did the walls hold?"

"Shouldn't the grass at least be on fire or something?" Amari whispers.

"Quiet!" I snap. I can *just* hear their voices. Kinder doesn't stop running until she's face-to-face with Touré. She squeezes the professor's palms and arms like she fears bones are broken. She clasps Touré's face in both hands, peering into her eyes until the professor shrugs away.

An urgent hiss turns us around. Leah beckons, and we abandon the crumpled door to hide beside her. "Where's Joey?" she whispers.

"I don't know." No one deserves to be lost in that awful place. Amari and Leah are ready to bolt, but I can't—the professor and headmaster are arguing loud enough to overhear.

"…let me do my job," Touré is saying. "Detention got them back in line. But if you overdo it—"

"The Breaks are getting worse," Kinder declares. "You're *sure* they're not experimenting? If they figure out the truth before they're ready…"

"Breaks are storms as far as they know. They have no idea—probably slept through the whole thing. Peerless held strong like I knew it would. You should have more faith in the walls."

I share a confused look with Leah and Amari. Storms… aren't storms? And why did Touré just lie for us? She could've called us out, but hasn't even glanced back at the hall. Leah tugs at my sleeve.

Kinder shakes her head, studying the night sky above the field. "Peerless won't work if you keep tinkering with it." Her voice grows so soft I can barely hear it. "I gave up everything for…this school. To make sure it's safe for these children. Everything."

"And you keep *throwing* it in my face," Touré snaps.

"Because you're naive! Peerless won't survive these attacks. We both know it."

"I know no such thing. Where's your fight?"

"Just…do your job," Kinder growls. "And stay out of my way when I do mine. This must be them."

She turns back toward Peerless, and us. A whimper escapes Leah, and Amari squeezes his eyes shut. My whole throat dries out—we should've dipped by now! The headmaster's scowl doesn't make her scarier than that monster, but she's a close second.

Touré snatches her arm and wheels her around. "They're all fast asleep. I'd bet the whole school on it." She's loud. Extra loud. "When's the last time you rested in the courtyard?"

A realization jolts some juice back into my legs. "She's stalling for us," I hiss. "Move!"

The three of us lurch into a tiptoe, triple-time, down the hall. We turn a corner and break for the dorm. Amari's heaving by the time we reach the courtyard and pass the glass study rooms. My legs are burning on the stairs leading up to our dorm, but we can't stop.

Leah reaches her room first. "Good luck!"

I slip inside, dive into bed, yank the covers up and squeeze my eyes shut. My legs won't stop shaking, I probably still stink like that nightmare place, I'm breathing too loud—

A shard of light slices through the night's shroud. I hold my breath. Nothing to see here. Relaxed, sleepy face—good dreams. Good, boring student having good, boring dreams!

"Well, look at you," the headmaster mutters. "Seems we finally outgrew that snoring."

The door clicks shut.

Whew.

I count out twenty more excruciating seconds before I take in a deep gasp. Another minute goes by before I risk a peek in the dark.

Headmaster Kinder's not waiting for me. All is quiet. My eyes adjust. I groan—my shoes are poking out from the bottom of my blanket. Either Kinder's not surprised when Peerless students collapse into bed with all their clothes on, or Ian distracted her just enough.

A low whimper flutters over from his bed.

"Ian? You okay?"

I shuffle over to check on him. My roommate's not snoring…not moving. My throat tightens like it's suddenly clogged with spiderwebs. I can't hear him breathing.

I tear the blanket away.

Pillows.

A blubbering sob breaks the silence. I lean down, heart pounding all over again, cheek brushing the floor. "Ian? Why are you under the bed, bro?"

"I followed y'all," he whispers. Lanky as he is, he squeezes even farther under his bed. "To the field. You combined art forms. You *never* combine art forms."

"But…why?" I ask hoarsely.

"That's when the bad stuff happens. The magic. You let it in. The walls ripple like eels are playing tug-of-war with the bricks, your uniform squeezes you tight if you're late for class, the professors swap voices with each other at night—"

"Ian, what are you talking about? You're freaking me out!"

"Me? *You* opened the *Break*!" He puts some oomph in the word, just like Kinder and Touré did. "Why'd you do it?"

"I don't know what I did! You're not making any sense!"

"I…I know." He tucks his knees under his chin and hugs them tight like he's trying to fold himself into a turtle shell, and starts crying forreal. "I'm sorry, Keynan. You shouldn't have come to Peerless."

CHAPTER SIXTEEN

NOT REALLY STORMS

It takes a minute to coax Ian out from under his bed. Even then, he cocoons himself in his sheets and twists away from me. He won't say another peep. I don't know what else to do but just be there for him, patting his shoulder until he calms. Finally, deep breathing replaces his snuffles.

My whole brain is spinning after everything that just happened. A storm swallowed me whole, whisked me off to some nightmare place. The monster is real, and the only reason it didn't get me is because my friends pulled me back to Peerless. Then Professor Touré stopped the entire thing somehow, with better rhymes than my baba's.

And it all started with my old poem and a beat I drummed out on the bench.

The magic. You let it in.

I've got a hundred questions, but I've got to check on my friends. I peek into the hall. Leah's sitting cross-legged across from my door. She rises silently, finger to her lips. I follow her to our common room, blocky gray couches lit by dim lamps. Amari's at one of the game tables, stacking a pyramid out of chess pawns.

"Thank goodness!" he exclaims. "I thought she caught you."

Leah shudders. "She sat next to me for a while—about scared my roommate out of her sleeping cap. I'm surprised she didn't see sweat through my sheets. What happened with you, Keynan?"

They still when I share that Ian followed us. I try to explain everything he told me, and the impossible things I saw in that…hole. Leah and Amari are just as stunned at the words falling out of my face as I am. Magic. Not magic like wishing my chores would mysteriously disappear. The real deal. Words that change weather. Portals to an impossible land. Monsters.

I shiver when I'm finished, and the three of us just sit there, numb. Why didn't anyone tell us before now? Is this why my parents wanted me to come to Peerless so bad? If that's true, why didn't they give me a hint? If Amari and Leah's faces are any clue, they're asking themselves the same questions.

"He really said magic?" Leah finally asks. "I mean…that's just silly. Right?"

"Ian likes to clown, but this wasn't it. He was scared."

"And we're not?" Amari asks.

"I'm just saying." I shrug helplessly. "What if he's right? In Mirror Maze Castle, we can walk on the ceiling and turn night into day. What if it's been around us all along, and we just didn't know it?"

"But that's a game!" Leah crosses her arms.

"My granny used to say magic is just stuff we don't know the rules for yet. We've all seen things at Peerless that don't make sense."

"You mean the stories about your mystery cat that walks through walls and burns claw marks on the furniture?" Leah scoffs, but her heart's not in it.

"Well, we all just saw that mess outside." Amari's hand twitches, and the pawns topple. "You *can* admit you saw it!"

"I don't know what I saw!" Leah says.

"They called it a Break," I cut in, fighting the urge to panic. If we all start shouting, we'll wake up the whole school. "So did Ian."

"And Kinder said something about attacks," Leah admits. "So there's…a monster trying to bust into Peerless? What's up with that?"

"Busted in already," Amari corrects her. "It must have been smaller before. Maybe it likes Soup's Soup."

Leah shudders. "That would explain why the headmaster's so grouchy."

Peerless is the complete opposite of the grown-ups back on Bizzy Block—they would never with all of these secrets! I miss my parents. Answers are all dangling just out of reach, ever since I saw those claw marks on the drone's belly. A magic monster that's behind the storms... and after me. I drop my head into my hands.

"Let's pretend magic is a thing. If I didn't want people to know it was real..." Amari purses his lips in thought as he sets the chess pieces back on the board. "I'd hide it somewhere they were afraid to look. Somewhere...they were taught to run from? Somewhere—"

"—that Keynan opened up," Leah finishes. "What if storms are not really storms at all?"

They both turn to me expectantly.

Now, I've got no problem admitting I'm scared. There's been plenty to go around. Like pulling Granny Delmar through the storm on Bizzy Block. Or that monster chasing me away from that fiery tree. Or finally figuring out Leah is Starbreaker, but we weren't gonna be friends. Or my mama, not acting like herself because of the storm.

Correction: the magic.

But my fear right now? It's bigger than all of that put together. Because I'm scared of myself. I should be hiding under my bed like Ian. Or better yet, back on a shuttle to Bizzy Block in time to help with harvest.

But I'm *excited,* and I shouldn't be.

All of Bizzy Block is built to outlast one thing: storms. If Leah's right, and magic is tangled up in them somehow—and I can learn it—what might be possible? I'm here to keep my neighborhood safe, my family safe. Somehow I know that won't happen churning through dusty pages in a library. Not after tonight! Maybe I could—

Wait. Pause. Breathe.

I don't want to get my hopes up *too* much. I know less than zero about what I'm doing. But the whole reason I came to Peerless is finally right in front of me—if I ignore the part about the monster looking for a Keynan snack!

I stand straight up. I should be scared to death, but my mouth slaps together words that don't even belong in the same sentence, saying stuff like, "I am *here* for this! Touré's rhymes stopped a whole storm, so why can't mine?"

"Do you remember your poem?" Amari asks eagerly.

"Or what Touré rhymed?" Leah adds.

"My notebook!" I groan. I completely forgot I left it out there! I'm lost without it. "Great. It had all of my poems. My tablet's gone, too." They both look crestfallen, but I wave it off, like I'm not freaking out in my mind. "I'll get another tablet somehow." But there's no replacing all of my lost rhymes—years of my life. Years of me.

"Let's get to bed." Leah nods, a determined glimmer in her eye. "We can't let Touré know what we know, or we'll end up living in detention."

"You're right," I agree. "She and Kinder are homies. They need to think we're…as scared as Ian."

"That won't be hard." Amari scowls. "She acted like Joey didn't even matter, and that could've been us! For all we know he's…"

We're quiet for a long time after that. I'm still scared of how badly I want this, but knowing my friends are right here with me makes all the difference. "So it's agreed, there's no way we're trusting Kinder. Right, Starbreaker?"

The biggest grin spreads over Leah's face. "Right, Keymaster."

I can't help but cheese a little—I've got my best friend back. We gonna be all right. We laugh and trade dap; it's easy like we had practiced.

Amari gives us a miffed look. "Hey, when were we passing out nicknames? Where's mine?"

"Pretty sure Goop is available," I offer, and Amari groans. The lights flicker. We all hold our breath, but the intercom stays silent. Storms were bad enough before, but after tonight I'll never look at them the same way again. "We'll think on it. We need something else, too. A promise we'll watch each other's backs."

He gives me the screw face. "Like a pinkie promise? That's baby stuff."

"A pact," Leah says quietly. "That's the word you're looking for."

It's perfect.

"Peerless Pact," I declare. "We'll find out what's really going on with Peerless—magic, all of it—no matter what Touré or Kinder says."

CHAPTER SEVENTEEN

NOW IS NOT THE TIME

The next morning, Ian's gone.

I can only stare at his crisply folded blanket and fluffed pillow. There's not even a hint of snack crumbs. It's like I imagined him this whole time. I barely believe yesterday happened, and it doesn't help that the one person who warned us about magic has vanished. I didn't even get to ask how he figured it out before us.

Nightmares ruined my sleep, of the monster biting and clawing its way through Bizzy Block, hunting for me, every house it touched in flames. Or chasing me through Peerless with Headmaster Kinder perched on its back, cackling wildly.

Your actions never affect just you, she shrieks. *Didn't Heck teach you that?*

A knock at the door comes when I'm getting dressed. "We're gonna be late," grumbles Amari's muffled voice. "No time for breakfast."

We're both groggy and grouchy as we hurry for cohort through strangely empty halls. Amari's eyes widen when I bring up Ian's disappearance. "But why would he leave like that?" he asks worriedly.

"I don't know." I shrug helplessly. "He's definitely not okay."

"Does all of this feel..." Amari gestures vaguely at the halls.

"Pointless?"

"Yes! Classes and points. It's so distracting."

"The last thing we should be worried about," I agree with a frown. Do routines and schedules really matter when my words might accidentally punch holes in the air?

Professor Wiley's waiting for us outside of the class-room. "You two look awful," he pronounces. "Make a habit of checking your tablets first thing. Or having it in the first place, Keynan." He hands me a familiar-looking tablet and...my notebook! "Professor Touré asked me to give these to you. No points lost. This time."

"Thanks," I say nervously.

"Where is everyone?" Amari asks.

"An assembly's been called."

We exchange a worried look. No question it's about last night.

"Professor Wiley," I begin, "my roommate—"

"Ian's with the nurse and doing much better. I understand he's…homesick. Did he say anything strange?"

"Umm, no stranger than usual." I try to laugh, but it comes out squeaky. Lying takes serious practice!

Wiley nods, but doesn't seem convinced. "I'm here if you two ever need to talk." He hides a frown of uncertainty with a smile. "Let's find out what this assembly is all about."

The auditorium lies in the next building over, separated from the school by a walkway lined with messy rows of tulips, the same way my mama plants them. We file in, gawking at the size of the space. This is where our recital will happen. Dozens of rows ripple out from the stage. Leah waves us to where she's saved two seats at the front, close enough to the stage to see up Kinder's nose. Leah's scowling up at the balcony behind us.

"Second- and third-years?" Amari whistles softly, gazing at the shadows shifting among the seats. "Wow. I've never seen them all in one place. Think they heard…what happened last night?"

"They must be used to storms nipping at the walls. If Peerless couldn't take it, they'd all be freaking out." Amari

146

and Leah nod, just as relieved as I am that the school is tough. "I wonder how many of them know about…the other part? Rhymes with *tragic*?"

Amari rolls his eyes. "Thanks for the hint, Keynan."

"My sister's up there somewhere," Leah grumbles. "Yolanda still hasn't come to see me. Not one time!"

"You could go see her?" I suggest carefully.

"We're not allowed on their side of school grounds. Could lose a week's worth of points if I'm caught."

The auditorium quiets as a dozen Peerless professors line up behind Kinder. Professor Touré is with them, hiding a yawn behind her fist. She squints at us, like she knows all about our Peerless Pact. Maybe she does. Who knows what magic lets her do?

"As many of you have learned, Joey Geiger decided that Peerless wasn't the best fit for his learning goals and has transferred to another school." My mouth falls open. Leah's tablet hits the ground. Kinder waits until the murmurs finish drifting through the auditorium. "Peerless is a bit dimmer today, but I'm confident this won't impact our focus as we prepare for fall recital. Just remember… attendance here is a privilege."

A different professor replaces Kinder at the podium, droning about more storm drills and outdoor spaces being off-limits. I can barely believe my ears. "They're lying!"

"This is so messed up," Leah whispers furiously. She nods at the stage. "That's Professor Guerrero, my sister's cohort teacher. I bet he's in on it, too!"

"We don't know what happened," Amari points out. "Maybe Touré found Joey and he's fine."

I glance back at the stage. Dark circles ring Professor Touré's eyes. Is that why she's so tired? Would she tell us? I catch Professor Mendoza watching me before her gaze snaps back to the podium. Her face is still tight when we're all dismissed. Unlike Touré, she's scared.

Amari lopes off, promising to talk more during lunch, but Leah grabs my arm. Her hand is shaking. "Peerless Pact?"

"You know this! Are you okay?"

"I…" She takes a deep breath. "What if I haven't seen my sister because she *isn't here*? I can't get what happened to Joey out of my head."

"Not the highest scorer in Mirror Maze Castle! If Yolanda's half as smart as you, imagine everything she's dug up about Peerless. I'll bet Kinder assigns her extra homework. Personally. For sneezing too loud."

"You're right. Yo's probably been stuck in more detention than you and I could be if we tried." She wraps me in a quick hug before we part ways. I'm glad she's feeling better, and hope we find Yolanda soon.

For Leah, and for me.

Even after everything that's happened, my hands still itch to try out another beat. My notebook? Back where it belongs, although I'm surprised Professor Touré returned it. I don't know if just writing down my rhymes will be enough again. Even though Ian said the storm is my fault somehow, every line I've ever written is nipping at the tip of my tongue, begging to be heard while I'm still young!

Ooooh! I should write that—

Actually, nope. Now isn't the time. I'm supposed to stay low-key, do my part as a good student. But why trust in grown-ups who've lied to us from the start? Hiding all of the answers out of reach, up on the top shelf! If they won't teach—fine! I'll find a way to learn magic all by myself.

CHAPTER EIGHTEEN

SLOW FEET DON'T EAT

For a whole week after the assembly, Headmaster Kinder is inescapable. When Soup dishes up blueberry muffins, she's there to scoop up the biggest, fluffiest one. She's sipping tea on top of the rock wall in Orienteering when Professor Valiant makes my class race our best climbing times. I couldn't fall asleep that night, wondering how she got up there in chocolate-colored heels and a matching pantsuit.

Professor Tapscott in Geometry is serious as a storm drill and wears all black for some reason, but they turn sweet as pie when Kinder slides into the back of their class. In Horticulture, Professor LaRue botches a pruning demonstration so bad that the headmaster sets down her coffee and takes over.

She pops up in hallways, watches from the bleachers when cohorts challenge each other in obstacle courses for extra points. She walks the courtyard at night, sometimes with Touré but mostly alone.

With everything happening it's hard to believe I've only been at Peerless for a month; back home, Bizzy Block families are hosting jam parties to jar up the pickings from our berry patches and marmalade from our orange tree. What I'm doing at Peerless is just as important though— more important, now that we know what the headmaster is hiding from us.

If we don't see Kinder, we hear her on the intercom. Storm drills happen so often now they might as well be an extra class. I know they're just drills, but my heart climbs into my throat every single time the intercom crackles on. One afternoon, we get a drill during PE. The headmaster just happens to be there, spinning a basketball on one rose-tipped fingernail like she's daring me to play one-on-one.

Amari and Leah get into an argument about Kinder over dinner that night, zucchini lasagna with steaming slabs of garlic bread slathered in melted cheese. Ian would already be on his third helping by now. I worry about him every day and hope he's okay. He should be with us.

Over by the buffet tables, Professor Touré pretends to

chat with Soup, but she's watching us the entire time. I fight down the urge to stick out my tongue at her.

"Kinder couldn't have passed you by the trophy case," Leah insists. "She was coming out of dance class that hour!"

"I'm surprised she's not here right now," I say gloomily. How can I experiment with my rhymes without Kinder catching me? "She knows we know about magic by now. She's waiting for us to slip up."

"I saw what I saw," Amari growls.

"She can't be in two places at the same—" Leah stops abruptly, definitely thinking what I'm thinking. *Can* Kinder be in two places at the same time?

No one wants to say it out loud.

"Can we not?" Amari shudders. "Anyway, I drew a picture of her. Butterfly pattern sundress with the jangly silver earrings! See?"

He holds up his tablet.

Leah's eyes widen, and I choke on my bread.

"What?" he asks. "You can just say it's amazing."

"You did great," I cough. "Um, really lifelike."

"Amazing," Leah croaks.

"Glad someone can appreciate it," he mutters. "I'll lose points if I don't delete it before class."

"Too bad," I offer faintly, trying not to sound relieved.

Amari chatters about what he'll draw next while I try to hold my food down. Leah saw what I did, I know it.

Amari's picture of Kinder *smiled* at us. Then gave us the scissor-fingers eye-stab, as if to say, *I'm watching you*.

Like I said: she's everywhere.

Another night alone in my dorm room is unbearable without knowing how Ian's doing. My tablet guides me through quiet halls to Nurse Manny's office. Their door is halfway open, and voices trickle from inside.

"I don't care how good Soup's curry is! Chew your food longer unless you want bubble guts for...oh!" Nurse Manny opens the door wide, peering me up and down. Cool tattoos cover the brown skin of their forearms from the wrist up; the patterns remind me of a maze. Their goatee and extra clean fade remind me I'm overdue for a haircut. "Can I help you?"

"I'm...here to check on my friend. Ian?"

"Sorry, no visitors." Someone stirs behind the nurse. I crane my neck to see, but it's not Ian. Dez sits in a chair with a glass of water. His face looks so hot, he's about to melt through the floor. "Peerless policy."

"Can you at least tell me if he's all right?" I ask, trying to ignore Dez and whatever is going on between his dinner and his stomach.

Nurse Manny's eyes narrow. "And who should I tell the

headmaster is keeping me from my patients, and probably losing points for their cohort?"

I cringe. "Never mind."

"Indeed. Good night."

Motion behind the nurse catches my eye as the door closes—Dez flashing a thumbs-up. I'm pretty sure he mouths, *Ian's okay*.

Nurse Manny's already shut the door before I can say thanks. Dez is probably worried I'm going to spread whispers about his visit here—but I could only tease good friends about something that embarrassing. Besides, he helped me feel a little better.

The next day in Creative Writing, Professor Mendoza assigns us another sleepy poem to memorize—then just plops down at her desk. Does she take anything serious? Her snoring is so ferocious her mouth is fluttering!

Before long, light chattering ripples through the class. My tablet pings. Leah's pretending to work, but she's in Mirror Maze Castle. I jump in, too.

Starbreaker: talk to her

Keymaster: srsly? she SLEEP sleep

Starbreaker: wake her up then! creative *writing* teacher, helloooo

Starbreaker: she has 2 know somethinggggg

Keymaster: i saw her face at assembly. she'll go straight to Kinder. she's scared

Starbreaker: yeah…you're probably right

I risk a peek across at Leah. Her face crumples, hardens into a scowl, then crumples all over again. She's staring at Joey's empty desk. We need to track down Yo straight-away, for Leah's sake. I wouldn't be surprised if the head-master's kept them apart on purpose.

What would my baba say? *Slow feet don't eat.*

I tap some lines in my tablet, erase the whole thing, and try again—but this time with my notebook. I tear the page out carefully and shuffle forward.

"Professor? Thought I could turn in some extra credit early this week."

The snoring ceases immediately, and Mendoza's brown eyes fly open, citrine-sharp. I slip the folded paper in front of her.

"Keynan, what is that?" Mendoza recoils like I just dropped a spitting scorpion on her desk!

I gawk before I remember myself. "A…limerick?"

She unfolds it, delicately, and reads, whisper-soft.

A student once searched for a Break,
His professor called it a mistake.
"Nap and snack, never fear!
There's no monsters in here!"
But he knows her excuses are fake.

Professor Mendoza slips the paper into her pocket and stands. "This is too much. I cannot. Not one more day."

"But class isn't even half over," Leah squeaks.

Professor Mendoza glances around like she's forgotten the other students, all murmuring curiously. "You'll scurry along just fine without me. The two of you are playing a dangerous game, and I refuse to be dragged into it!"

CHAPTER NINETEEN

A REAL ONE

Leah and I share a disbelieving look as Mendoza sweeps out of the classroom. "Did she just…quit?" I screech.

"Come on!" Leah bolts after the professor. I catch up to her in the empty hall. "She's faster than she looks. Which way?"

That's easy. Follow the snacks. We creep for the dining hall, but lunch hasn't been served yet. We spot Professor Touré muttering over an enormous ring of keys on our way to the courtyard. We back away, and fast-walk down a side hall toward the courtyard. Touré doesn't see us.

We finally find Mendoza muttering over the green strawberries in the garden. She sees us and sighs. It's a perfect day of sapphire sky, the kind of glorious weather that might get chores called off early back on Bizzy Block.

Dappled sunlight glimmers through the branches overhead, playing hide-and-seek with Professor Mendoza's azure-tipped fingernails as she gestures us toward the old oak.

"Sit," Mendoza whispers. "What have you done?"

Leah gives me an encouraging nod. I spill, from the moment my hand slapped out a beat on the bench, that night I called up a storm. When I get to the fiery tree, Mendoza plops herself between us. After I bring up Joey, she buries her face in her palms. "Oh dear. Oh my."

Leah clears her throat when I finish. "You know about magic, too. Same as Touré and Kinder."

Mendoza stiffens. "I wouldn't dare presume to share the same grasp of it as the headmaster. Or Touré."

"Can you teach us?" I plead. "Please don't leave Peerless."

"Let's see." Her gaze darts around the courtyard nervously. "Follow Kinder's instructions precisely. There. That's your lesson."

"Oh, come on!" Leah bursts out. "Why won't you help us?"

"I'm trying, please believe! The…place you described? Beyond the storm? It affects everyone differently. Some people think magic is bad because they're afraid of it."

"I knew it," I breathe.

She nods at the oak tree behind us. "Stout trees repel invasive magic, keep it from hooking into you. Changing you. Any flora will help—even a dandelion is better than nothing—but trees most of all. Remember that."

Leah and I can't help but shiver. "How would we know?" she asks. "If magic is messing with us?"

"Or with Peerless?" I add.

Mendoza takes in our faces. "Oh, children, children, children. You can't afford to be this naive." She laughs so softly, I almost think she's crying. "You'll know if it's inside you. You'll feel it. Like a color you've never seen before, or—"

Our tablets chirp. Class is over. Professor Mendoza leaps up. "This…was a mistake. If you find yourself in the radiant waste again, come straight here if you want to keep Peerless safe. Say you understand!"

"We will," I reply quickly. But my brain is tangled around her disturbing words. *Invasive magic. Radiant waste.*

She hurries off, panic rising in her voice. "I've said too much already. No more extra credit. I'm sorry. Touré will know, and if she knows, so will the headmaster."

"But—"

"No more!"

She scampers over a stone bridge and disappears. "I…I

didn't even get to ask her about rhymes!" A lump rises in my throat. "This was a terrible idea!"

Leah pats my arm. "We know more than we did before. Amari's always good at thinking things through. Come on."

She's right, again. We hustle off before we're late for class. At lunch, Amari nods along with our whispered suspicions when we catch him up.

"The radiant waste," he murmurs thoughtfully. "So that's what it's called? Sounds way different from what you told us, Keynan."

"I know, right?" I say around a mouthful of Soup's Soup. "But listen…we need to leave it alone for now."

"She was pretty spooked," Leah admits bleakly.

"She's not talking again until the tangerines are ripe," I agree. "And probably the strawberries, too. Not one professor will help us without Kinder's say-so."

"And Ian's out, so you know who that leaves."

Amari's eyes light up. "Yolanda!"

Leah stands suddenly. "I need to show y'all something." We polish off lunch and hustle for the dorms. Leah's room is spotless except for a worn-out stuffed lion and an old photo pinned to the wall beside the bottom bunk. There's no mistaking Yolanda with her matching locs and the same radiant brown skin, like rainbows play behind their cheekbones. She's like a more cheerful version of her sister—but that might also be because she has Leah in a headlock. "Look what's written over the bed."

A message is scratched into the wood:

something's wrong with them not you

"I found this snagged around a bedpost." Leah fishes a necklace from her pocket, like the small hand-hammered golden hearts Yua makes back at Bizzy Block. "It's Yo's."

Amari and I share a perplexed look. "They put you in her first-year room?"

"The same freaking bed! Professor Touré keeps saying third year is busy, but something's up. I know it." We throw out ideas the rest of the afternoon on how to get to Yolanda. I'm still not sure she can help us, honestly. I hope I'm wrong, or this will be a nice big waste of time— and Bizzy Block can't afford wasted anything right now. But at least Leah's back to her determined self, and Amari has a new puzzle to solve.

Me? I'm just glad we're bonding, and for the distraction. I've avoided cracking open my notebook since Professor Mendoza's reaction to my limerick. Too tempting. More and more, my thoughts wander to new beats.

Is this what Mendoza meant? Is magic inside me already?

A new heartbeat in my chest is unlocked, a real one. The old stuff was just pretending this whole time. And the one thing that I know will bring my magic to the surface? My rhymes. It's all I can do not to say them out loud.

CHAPTER TWENTY

A DOZEN LARGE RINGS

We spit out ideas over a few more nights before finally settling on our plan. Third-year classes and dorms are in a whole different wing. They eat with us, but Soup let slip that there's a smaller, private dining hall meant for studying, which explains why we never see Yo at meals. Soup always welcomes volunteers in the kitchen, so what if we accidentally wind up in the small hall and bump into Yolanda? Leah's extra excited, like we're on a rescue mission.

The day our plan is about to go down, the lights flicker out in cohort, right during Wiley's morning points review. A long-suffering sigh escapes him when the power doesn't return. "Nothing we haven't seen before—"

My tablet winks out. This is new. I share a questioning glance with Lacretia, her screen is black, too. "Umm, Professor…?"

Headmaster Kinder's voice grates over the intercom. *"Proceed indoors immediately. This is an emergency drill—"*

The recording cuts off. The hair on the back of my neck stands up. I'm about to crawl under my desk! Peerless doesn't seem so sturdy this morning.

"Doesn't feel like a drill," Dez mutters.

"I know that's…" Oof. Things are bad if I'm agreeing with Dez.

Professor Wiley rubs his beard thoughtfully. "A little wind shouldn't stop us from learning. How about a homework day until things are running again?" There's no way Wiley knows about magic; he's more irritated than worried. "Head back to the dorms. Recital practice, practice, practice!"

Dez slides up beside me and Amari. "Hey…hi."

Amari and I exchange a look. "Hi…"

"I'm pretty sure Soup has some leftover cinnamon rolls. Wanna snatch some before the professors finish them off?"

"Couldn't hurt," Amari offers.

"Umm, maybe later?" I'm starting to think Dez is actually not terrible. Right now just isn't the greatest time to find out. "We've got…umm, writing track stuff to catch up on." I nod down the hall to where Leah's waiting for us, bouncing on her toes.

Dez hides a disappointed look. "Oh. Okay, then."

"Sorry," Amari adds. "Next time?"

Leah can barely wait for Dez to shuffle off. "I think we should go find her now," she blurts out. "Everyone's gonna be in the dorms."

Amari and I glance around anxiously, but no other students heard. "We already worked out the dinner schedule with Soup!" I protest.

"But there won't be a more perfect time!"

"She's right," Amari murmurs uneasily. "Emptier halls."

I swallow. The halls will be empty for a good reason. This blackout means the storms—my brain still calls them storms, even with everything we know—aren't messing around today. "How do we get there, without our kitchen excuse?"

"The closed-off wing must have shortcuts," Leah answers immediately. "And we just happen to have an expert mapmaker to find the way."

Amari flinches. "Who, me?"

It's bold. Dangerous. Probably a bad call.

I love it!

"We got you! Right, Amari? Peerless Pact!" The tightness behind Leah's eyes melts away as we bump fists. "Better get moving. Last thing we need is for classes to restart."

We head for the trophy room, Amari dragging his feet

the whole way. I ask Leah to be lookout while we check the door for surprises. "What's with the face?" I whisper to Amari. "You okay?"

"No. I'm telling you…these halls are seriously messed up." He grabs the door's handle, exhaling like he's relieved it's still there. "What if we can't get out? Our tablets are still off. My map—"

"Don't need it. We've got you!"

"Doesn't it bother you that we don't know *why* it's happening?"

"Not as much as seeing Leah miserable." He still looks doubtful, so I try something else. "When we pull this off, we'll have found someone who can finally answer some questions."

He perks up, and we wave Leah over. Peerless Pact, holding strong thanks to me! Amari takes the lead up the musty, dusty stairs. Grit crumbles away beneath our feet, bouncing down the stairwell. Leah's eyes nearly fall out of her face when she sees where it falls.

"My bad. Should've warned you about the whole bottomless stairs part," I say.

"It's just my eyes messing with me," she mutters. "Right?"

"Yeah… Ian's never gone down to check it out, and I don't blame him," Amari calls over his shoulder. "I wish he was here."

"Me too!"

We reach the door to the hidden wing, and I sigh in relief, peering anxiously down the silent hallway. "Mostly how I remember. That's good, right?"

"Y'all had me worried the ceiling and floor would be tied in knots or something." Leah laughs nervously.

Amari's eyes narrow as he inspects the hall. "We joked too, but you'll see. Let's try this way first."

The chandeliers overhead glow brilliantly, tinkling like hidden breezes are brushing the dangling crystals. There's still no power in Peerless, no cool air blowing from the vents. So how? As we pass beneath, prismatic slivers of light stretch toward the edge of my vision. My eyes snap up to the ceiling—I'm ready to run or scream at the top of my lungs. There's nothing. Just chandeliers. Not the glimmering crystal pincers I imagined.

Leah tilts her head. "Y'all hear that?"

Voices echo and beckon us around another corner. Laughing, arguing, pleading. Before long, we're all walking so close together our shoulders are brushing. A buzzing near my waistband makes me jump halfway out of my shoes. Our tablets are back on, I give mine a glance. "Classes are still canceled."

Leah eyes the chandeliers. "I was kind of hoping the power would stay off."

"Same." Amari stops beside a door that's no different from the others. He takes a deep breath and cracks it open a sliver. "No stairs. Third-year dorms are one floor down."

"So we're close?" Leah strides to the next door.

Amari's jaw drops. "No, don't!"

We clutch each other as she flings it open and disappears inside.

"You two should come see this!"

Amari and I untangle our arms sheepishly and hurry after her. He's got me nervous enough to jump out of my own skin! Inside, there's no desks, no chairs. Not a classroom. Leah's marching toward a door on the far side, angling through maybe a dozen large rings, spaced out evenly on the polished wood floor. A bead of sweat trickles down my spine.

Of course, Amari peers at one curiously like he's about to pick it up. "Never seen these before."

"They look like they were made for hoop dancing," Leah says, rocking her hips side to side to demonstrate.

"Aren't they kinda heavy for that?" I fish a pencil out of my pocket and tap it on a ring.

Ping!

"See? Metal."

The hoop vaults into the air, thumping into my chest! I scramble away with a yelp. It hovers at eye level, then blurs back down, so fast it whistles. Instead of splintering the wood, it stops perfectly on the floorboards, still as if it never moved.

"Can we *please* not touch anything else?" Amari pleads, gripping his fro with both fists.

"My bad! At least it's—"

Ping! The hoop shoots up again, then back down. Faster this time. Amari makes a strangled sound as Leah's hand closes on the far door. "Not that way!"

She opens it wide. "Am I lucky or just good?" She points triumphantly at a narrow, curving stairwell.

"Success!" This feels happy dance worthy. "We did that! Yeah? No? Amari?"

"That's impossible." *Ping!* We all jump as the hoop flies up and down again, like invisible hands heft it. "Have you ever seen a tower on Peerless when we're outside? We're on the top floor, and those stairs are going up, not down. It doesn't feel right...trust me!"

Leah relents with a nod and picks her way back around the rings. *Ping!* My feet should be moving, too—why aren't they? There's something off about the space inside the hoop. The air shimmers with a bruised blue-purple hue, like other colors are avoiding the metal. I can't look away.

"Y'all, come *on*." Amari is almost hopping himself.

Ping!

Leah nudges me, gazing at the strangely familiar, see-through shape forming inside the hoop. Peerless uniform. Lanky loose arms. Hair that *really* needs trimmed up. "Don't be mad," she says, "but it kinda—"

"Don't even say it! I'm way better-looking than—"

The…silhouette turns to me. Those eyes are my eyes, but a hungry-hollow blue instead of my dark brown, and thirsty—like it's trying to drink all of me in.

With a shout, we break for the door. Amari's foot hits another hoop. *Ping!* We all freeze as it zips upward. Leah cries out in alarm and bumps at least three more as she flees the room, me and Amari hot on her tail.

Ping!

Ping! Ping! Ping!

I slam the door shut behind us.

"That thing," she gasps. "It tried to copy you!"

"I know, right? Weird." There's only one Keymaster. Snatching my good looks? Or even worse, my rhymes? The rudeness! "So who's opening our next door? Not it."

"Are you forreal?" Amari snaps. "This is serious!"

"He's in shock." Leah shakes her head. "I'm sure your rhymes are safe, Keynan."

"Right…safe. Totally safe." That's my Starbreaker. She just…gets me.

"Do y'all hear that?" Amari lets out a strangled moan.

I hold my breath, listening. Muffled words creep from the room we just escaped.

"See? Metal."

"Can we please not touch anything else?"

"Am I lucky or just good?"

No. *Nooo.* My ears must be lying. It sounds like us. Beyond creepy. I crane my neck to press an ear to the door, and that's why I see the talons snaking around Amari's waist. "Look out!"

Sharp crystals wrench Amari off his feet. He screeches, flailing wildly. Leah and I both grab a leg, shouting. A terrible hissing rattles from the chandelier, crystal talons grasping like a glimmering praying mantis.

"Do something!" he cries, inching higher.

A sudden thought seizes me. Could I…rhyme at the thing? The way Touré stopped the storm? A loud thump shakes the door behind us. I grab the handle before it twists open. More voices clamor behind it. A lot more! Leah's tugging with all of her strength, but Amari still rises steadily—pulling me with him! My hand's about to slip off the door!

Okay, Keymaster. We need to rhyme a way out of this mess. Now or never!

CHAPTER TWENTY-ONE

THE WARS OF ILLUSION

I open my mouth...and nothing comes out. The school is trying to gobble up my friend, bizarre copies of us are pounding down the door—and my rhymes are in hiding!

Leah growls, grabbing Amari's belt, then his arm—using him like a ladder!

"Watch the face!" he yells. Leah flips up and twists in midair, the back of her heel whirling into a light bulb. It shatters and the chandelier creature screeches. Amari's free! They both tumble down—but neither busts their head on the floor. Shoutout to my face and ribs for breaking their fall!

I groan, and Leah drags me to my feet. "You okay?"

"Eeeero shtatus...un...un..." I can't breathe. Worse, I can't talk!

"He got the wind knocked out of him. Which way, Amari?"

"I don't know!"

The door behind us flies open. Purple-blue, see-through hands reach for us.

"Run!" Leah yells. My friends haul me down the hall. Angry crystal echoes from every side. More chandeliers sway furiously overhead. The first one must have called for reinforcements!

"The hallway changed again!" Amari shouts. He's right— there's so many doors! Some are just inches apart from each other!

If some luck worked for Leah, I can take a chance, too. I stagger to my left and peek inside one of the rooms. "Y'all, in here!" I croak. Air is finally working back into my lungs. "Hurry!"

We slide into a dim room and slam the door shut. New voices sprout in the hallway.

"*Metal? See.*"

"*Touch not anything please else can we?*"

"*Or lucky just I good am?*"

The words make zero sense!

"*Bad* copies." Leah shudders.

A thunderous rattling of crystal almost shakes the door from its hinges. The strange voices shout and squeal. Then

173

everything is silent, faster than it began. We all remember to breathe again. "Sounds like they…ate each other?" I venture.

Leah squeezes herself tight. "Every *single* time I try to find Yolanda, something goes wrong! Sorry, y'all. I should've stuck with the plan."

I pat her shoulder. "We're in this together, don't worry."

"Are you two seeing all of this? Maybe we can still find something useful." Amari peers around curiously. I'm starting to dread that thoughtful expression on his face—it's never a good sign. This room's definitely better than Leah's so far. No rings on the floor, for starters, and— actually, nope. Take that back.

Bookshelves line the far wall, which would normally be nice. But the rest of the room is filled with display cases of bizarre stuff. One is a beautiful, iridescent moth's wing longer than my arm, dark green with glowing violet spots. Another object is an alligator's skull, huge and milky smooth, only with extra eye sockets parading all the way down its snout. Beyond the cases, a full set of gleaming metallic clothes rests in one of the alcoves nestled between tall windows. The word for it pops into my head: armor. I palm the helmet, big as a bucket but sleek like a river snake with two wicked slits for eyeholes. The metal is light as steam and warm to the touch.

Instead of books, the shelves hold crates stuffed with unmarked square sleeves of paper. I peek inside one of the sleeves, revealing a round thing bigger than a dinner plate, with a pinky-sized hole in the center. It is flat and black and smooth as a beetle's shell.

Leah rubs her chin. "There must be thousands of these things."

"Yeah, but what are they?" I put the helmet back with its armor set, noticing the matching alcove beside it is empty. I wonder what it held.

"Y'all, look at this." Amari's rummaging under a wide table past the shelves. He hefts another crate, full of old tablets. Leah snatches one, turning it over in her hands. There's a crack across the screen. Some letters are scratched into a corner: *YOLOJ*.

"That's my sister's. I know it. Why wouldn't Yo have it?" Leah asks anxiously.

"These are old," Amari offers. "Touré doesn't seem like someone who wastes parts."

"You think you can get it working again?" I ask.

"One way to find out."

"To do what, check her grades?" Leah grumbles, handing it back.

We watch interestedly while Amari sets his tablet down next to Yo's, then produces a bunch of cables he's stashed in his pocket. One of them connects the two tablets together. "Her screen's hopeless, but if I switch up the display…"

Yolanda's home screen flickers on Amari's tablet. We both give him dap, but part of me feels…icky somehow. I wouldn't like anyone thumbing through my notebook this way.

"Old homework." Leah's eyes widen as Amari swipes through the files. "Wait. Keynan, look at the name of that course!"

"Magic in History!" I exclaim. "Open it!"

Yolanda's face fills the screen. Her nose is a little rounder, and her dark eyes are more intense—which is saying a lot—but she resembles Leah enough to pass for her twin. Her voice is pitched higher than I expected. *"Anyway, I'm supposed to be a teacher assistant or something to help the first-years…adjust."* She lets out a bitter laugh.

Leah covers a sudden grin with her hand. "Always such a buster." She sounds proud.

We lean in breathlessly, soaking up every word.

"Back in the day, there was a war over magic, so long ago it doesn't matter. Magic made the impossible, well…possible, I guess? One side wanted to use it to fix every little problem, but they thought they were better than everyone else…umm—"

"Elite is the word you're looking for," Headmaster Kinder's voice interrupts. *"Continue."*

We exchange wide-eyed glances. A quaky fear burrows in my stomach.

Yolanda rolls her eyes. *"Fine. Whatever. Elite. The other side believed magic was meant for everyone, and I guess a third side was everyone else caught in the middle. The elites won the war but lost it, too. Their weapons jacked up everything—broke magic. Shattered it."*

Amari hits Pause. *"Shattered* magic? What does that even mean?"

"Good question! Maybe, I don't know, finish the freaking video so we can find out?" Leah growls.

"Okay, okay!"

"That was the last big fight of the Wars of Illusion," Yolanda says, *"and—"*

"The Failing," Kinder interrupts again. *"Please get it right. If they don't understand the next part—"*

"But we could just tell them about Peerless, forreal!" Yolanda says.

A new voice breaks in—Professor Touré! *"Yolanda. We've tried that. You know the risk. You wouldn't want that for Leah."*

Yo grits her teeth and wipes a palm over her eyes.

"Tag-teaming her," Amari says uncomfortably.

"Not fair," Leah whispers.

This is really messed up. Yo's voice is so quiet I barely catch it. *"She can handle it. If you just—"*

"Enough." Kinder's one word cuts like glass. *"A year isn't nearly enough time to prepare for a new cohort, but it's what we have. Continue."*

Yolanda flinches, but her scowl returns. *"So…people didn't understand what happened at first. They were just glad the war was over. Most sorcerers—that's magic users—got their brains cooked by the Failing. Folks hid away anything to do with magic so it wouldn't happen again. But nobody understood how badly it was messed up. Weird stuff happened when people sang or instruments were played. When the radiant waste started—"* She stands up suddenly, and the screen tilts wildly, showing a classroom ceiling. *"No. I won't lie to them! They deserve to know the truth! They deserve to hear why Peerless—"*

The recording freezes. Amari whistles softly.

Leah snatches the tablet and wordlessly pulls open other files. Amari and I wait in silence. What could we even say? She finally sets it down with a dejected sigh. "The rest is all homework. The Peerless kind. I think I hate it here."

"That's a year old." Amari muses, tapping his lip. "I'll bet she knows even more now."

"We've been gone long enough," I say carefully. "Sorry we didn't find her Leah, but this counts for something."

"We can still try our first plan," Amari chimes in.

I nod in agreement. Yolanda *did* help us. Sort of. But an

old book might have told us more. We need to track her down, for Leah, but that's time I could be messing with my own rhymes. I'm twitching to get back to my room so I can—

"The halls," I groan. All the bruises around my middle groan, too.

"I...I don't know if I can get us back," Amari whispers.

Leah swallows. "We should probably get ready to run again."

We trudge to the door. My heart is booming through my ribs. We didn't uncover this ancient history just so we couldn't solve the mystery. Can busted magic help our feet take flight, if I find the right—

"Keynan?" Amari gives me a strange look. "You gonna open the door?"

"Oh! My bad."

Where did my head just go? I'm standing here holding the handle. I take a deep breath and twist—

—and step into the trophy room. The other two follow, gawking just like me.

"Not that I'm complaining," Leah breathes, "but is any part of today going to make sense?"

My voice almost sounds unbothered. "About time something goes our way! Let's not waste it getting caught."

We make for our rooms, wondering about busted magic

and relieved that at least here, it's not trying to snack on us. Amari's got that thoughtful look again, no matter how much I try to distract him. He's going to figure out what just happened. What I *think* just happened.

Somehow… Peerless peeked at my thoughts and bailed us out. Professor Mendoza's right. There's magic inside me. But from what Yolanda said, it's busted. Dangerous. The scariest part is that I don't even care. Whether we find her or not, I just wanna keep rhyming.

CHAPTER TWENTY-TWO

LIGHT TO SHINE

From then on, we avoid anything that hints at the slightest trouble. I keep things simple. Teeth scrubbed. Showered. Shea-buttered up. Dressed and downstairs with the sun. Wherever my tablet says to go next, I'm there early. Whatever homework I'm assigned is turned in before dinner. I'm the first one in class, for every class. I don't cost Wiley Squad any points. I don't even raise a fuss when Professor Okoro pairs me with Dez for our physics project, making light bulbs shine with water somehow.

During the day, me and Leah and Amari are model students. But at night? We replay Yolanda's video in the study lounge, arguing about what it means and what to do next. Magic is busted. We've seen that ourselves. So how is it *really* supposed to work? Headmaster Kinder and the professors are hiding more stuff from us—big surprise!—but whatever made Yo so upset feels way worse. We all know that we need answers, but we can't agree on how to get them.

One good thing happens after a week of going in circles, at least. Ian comes back! I'm so relieved to see him I can't help but crush him in a hug. He's still about his snacks, but he's different somehow. When I bring up what he said that night, about magic, he just shrugs.

"A nightmare was probably just my brain's way of spicing this place up." He yawns.

"But you saw it, out on the field," I press. "You called it a—"

"Storm, Keynan." A sudden tightness to his face is there and gone. "We get them everywhere else. Why not here?" He goes back to playing Mirror Maze Castle on his tablet. "Ugh, this game!"

"Still on the first level? I thought you were going to beat it in a day!"

"I never said that." He gives me a puzzled look. "Anyway. Speaking of nightmares, how's it going with Dez?"

"Maybe okay, actually," I say, remembering Dez's offer to snag those extra cinnamon rolls with us. Ian arches an eyebrow at me, and I add, "Well, kinda."

"You could just invite him to eat with us," he points out. "It worked with Leah."

I shrug and he goes back to Mirror Maze, keeping to

182

himself for the rest of the night. As the week goes on, I feel like I barely see him. He's so different. I really miss the old Ian. He should be planning a new Hall Hop, or another new scheme. I can't make myself ask him about magic again. Not after what happened to Joey. And definitely not after what we found in the closed wing.

The worst part about magic? Now that I know it exists, I realize it sneaks in everywhere. Waits for me around every corner. Every day I'm doubting what's real and what's not. One morning in the bathroom, my own reflection *winked* at me while I was brushing my teeth. I spluttered so hard I had to change my shirt! There's no pretending like magic isn't there.

On Wednesday night, Ian's already snoring by the time I'm back from dinner. I'm glad at first to hear the sound— at least that hasn't changed—but before long, I can't concentrate on my writing. I give up and bail for the courtyard. But I'm still not focused. Pesky guilt keeps slinking into my head—I should be thinking up a way to find Yolanda, or finding the key to shrinking the storms, but I'm focused on my own writing and magic instead.

"Keynan?" Professor Touré's question startles me.

"Hi, Professor." I slide my notebook under my tablet. I was so wrapped up in my thoughts, I didn't even hear her walk up.

"You good?"

"Yeah, you know. Homework."

"Ah. Plenty of that going around." Her pants are covered with white stains—plaster, I'm guessing—and she's holding an old rusty trowel and a small bucket. "I've been meaning to talk with you since the storm. But this school's old bones fall apart the second I turn my back."

I want to spill about finding Yo's tablet. I want to ask about Ian, or Joey—not to mention Breaks, storms, magic hiding inside of storms, everything! Maybe even magic hiding inside of me. Touré is...steadier than Mendoza—definitely not about to quit Peerless over a limerick—but who knows if I'll get a straight answer? And it's hard not to imagine her whispering everything I say in Kinder's ear. "I guess we're lucky you were there to take care of it," I say instead.

Touré's brown eyes twinkle. "You're not wrong there. You remind me so much of—" A tight smile lops off whatever she was about to say. "You remind me of why we believe so deeply in Peerless. You and your friends."

Then why are you lying to us? I howl inside my brain. "Does 'we' mean Headmaster Kinder?"

"Always, even when it doesn't feel right." The professor hefts her bucket and turns back to the path. "I promise you that Peerless will click. Her rules will make it all make sense."

I can't quite stop myself from sounding salty. "I'll do my best not to *break* any more of them."

Touré stops in her tracks. Her shoulders stiffen.

Okay, yeah—that was petty. I couldn't help myself.

She doesn't look at me when she speaks. "I hope I meet your parents. I truly do." She's not angry. Just…tired, like she's been plastering for so long that there's more patch than there is crack. "I can only imagine what they'll say when I tell them stories about you."

Somehow, I'm guessing her stories will leave out the most amazing parts, but I stop myself from getting too saucy before it earns me more trouble. I trudge back to my room, not really feeling like studying, or writing. Truth be told, I'm not feeling like myself. Sleep won't come easy, and not just because Ian's snoring is louder than ever.

On Bizzy Block, I held down my parents' schedules. Mostly. Here at Peerless, I kept to the rules. Tried my best, anyway. But they make zero sense.

"Time to make my own rules," I whisper.

I dress quietly, grab my notebook—along with the light bulb I borrowed from my Physics project with Dez—and slip off. The halls are still. It's a nice night, but a shiver still tickles my spine when I sneak out of Peerless through a door past the second-year classrooms. This time I make for the covered bridge, where Touré made us change light bulbs during that very first detention. It feels like a hundred years ago, but I still remember that one of the sockets wouldn't work, no matter how many times she swapped out wires and tried different bulbs.

It's so obvious to me now. Magic was the problem. Which means that magic should be the solution.

The bridge is twice as far from Peerless as the soccer field, in case something goes wrong. It's the farthest I can go and still be on school grounds.

The wood underfoot is creaky like Old Zeph's bones, and the creek's water below groans through the boulders and rocks. I should be afraid, but I'm excited from my fade down through my shoulders and my socks. Goose bumps prickle my forearms as I flip through my notebook. I'm pretty sure I get why the old rhyme that formed the Break went left. Poetry is about crystal clear words. Even if the poem ends up meaning different things to different people. Beautifully intentional, my baba would say. I've been thinking how to make this new rhyme just right.

"Here goes everything," I mutter. I screw my bulb into the socket. Take a deep breath. Drum a beat on the bridge's old wood…and speak:

> Sometimes we need light to shine,
> Without it we can't see.
> Today I'm here to get what's mine,
> so I need this light to be.

Baby blues and lavender hues fizzle to life inside the glass. Oh no. This doesn't look right, not at all. A mini-Break? Ratchet's eyeball staring at me? My legs tense to flee, but the swirling magic fades. The metal filament inside the bulb turns blinding bright.

I step back, waiting. But the light just shines. Doing its job, exactly like I willed it.

With.

Magic.

Headmaster Kinder's voice drifts from Peerless. *"Proceed indoors immediately. A storm is approaching the school grounds. This is not a drill."*

Only…there's no storm. No Break. No radiant waste. Just me.

I remember to breathe again. I can do this. I can *do* this! I'm tingling all over with excitement. Who needs Yolanda? No way she can even rhyme like me. When I get good, a lot more is going to change than some light bulbs. My mama will never need to worry about power outages or snatched up houses on Bizzy Block—all with a little wordsmithing in my notebook. If I give these rhymes everything I've got, no one can slow me down!

CHAPTER TWENTY-THREE

OUR LITTLE SECRET

The next morning in homeroom, Amari knows that something's up. I manage to keep my lips zipped until after, when I can pull him and Leah aside in the trophy room. It seems only fair that I tell them together.

"Y'all, guess what?"

"You're more cheerful than usual," Leah observes. "New poem we've gotta hear?"

"You could say that." I grin, flipping through my notebook.

"Look at the time. Can't be late for class." I love the way Amari jokes, like my poems aren't the best part of his day.

"I…I made magic. With a rhyme and a beat. Last night."

Amari looks up from his tablet. Leah's face goes very still.

"No Break, nothing terrible," I add hastily, explaining the light bulb. "If I get my rhymes just right, I can handle magic."

"What happened to Peerless Pact?" Amari asks, voice pinched.

Leah folds her arms. "We're supposed to work together."

"I...didn't want you to get in trouble. Besides, it worked! I don't think magic is busted like they told Yo. I can go even bigger if I—" Leah's eyebrows climb up her forehead, and I fix what I'm saying "—if *we* try again."

Their eyes shift from me to each other, and practically a whole year passes, which is really inconsiderate with me not breathing and all.

Finally Leah nods, and I exhale in relief. "We've figured out another way to link up with my sister. You down?"

"For sure!" I stuff just enough excitement into my voice to convince them I mean it. "Like you said...together."

"Together." Amari offers his dap. We've worked hard on it, and it's basically perfect—*slap, bump, snap hook fly and dab*—before Amari heads off to his next class. "Spill it all at lunch!"

Leah giggles. "I should've recorded all the practice that took y'all."

"Jealous ain't cute!" Amari calls over his shoulder.

I'm relieved as Leah and I set off for the auditorium—

189

Mendoza's having us meet there today for recital prep. Why was I worried my friends would be mad at me? That's silly. They're—

We both slow. Professor Mendoza is standing below the auditorium stage, letting the steam from her giant mug of tea tease through her fingers. "Keynan, finally!" she exclaims. "You've got some explaining to do."

"'No Break,' you said," Leah hisses. "'Nothing terrible.' And I believed you!"

My whole body freezes as Mendoza sips her tea. "Leah? Shoo." Leah heads for the stage worriedly as the professor eyes me over the top of her foggy glasses. "So delicious. Listen. I'm concerned that you're not adjusting to Peerless well. We need to address it."

I'm so busted. "I should've gone to the courtyard last night after—"

"Keynan," she interrupts, suspiciously pleasant. "I don't care where you study."

"But you said the oak tree helps with—"

"*Keynan*. Focus, please! Is your recital poem ready?"

Headmaster Kinder appears on the stage just then, slowing to listen. I almost jump out of my socks, but still manage to bob my head. "Umm, yes? I have it memorized."

Kinder peers down at us, giving Mendoza a tight nod before glancing back at her tablet.

Professor Mendoza's gaze latches on to me. "So creative writing isn't too challenging?"

Just be cool! Don't mention magic! "Kinda…? My dad said Peerless would be different, but sometimes I just wish we were doing…more. I'm…uh…looking forward to the recital."

That's mostly true—even if my poem is trash, the idea of taking that stage in front of the school is exciting. More of my classmates mill around uncertainly now, and the headmaster finally strides backstage.

Professor Mendoza lets out a sigh like a deflated balloon. "Always with her little check-ins for this recital," Mendoza mutters. "What to think, what to say, when to blink!"

"You were…covering for me!" I wasn't sure before, but I am now. Her eyes glitter innocently as we take the side stairs for the stage. "I…I owe you one!"

"Indeed."

An argument bursts out between two classmates on the stage. "My poem is before yours." Tasha waggles a finger under Akil's nose. "So you stand behind me!"

"You're so dang tall, I can't see past your fro!"

Professor Mendoza spins toward them. Irritation crackles through her voice. *"Still and silent you will achieve, or loud and screaming, best believe."*

The two jerk like she slapped them. "Yes, Professor." They speak in unison, sending a shiver up my spine. Sweat beads under Akil's fro as he lines up where he belongs. Tasha's lips wriggle as she rehearses her recital piece, beaming like it was written with soft hugs and sunshine.

Wait.

A.

Whole.

Minute.

I know rhymes when I hear 'em! "Did you just—"

Professor Mendoza winces. "That was a no-no. Our little secret, okay?" She bites her lip nervously. "Headmaster Kinder doesn't like it when promising students get the attention they deserve. Just ask Yolanda." I barely keep my jaw from hitting my shoes. She winces again. "There goes me and my mouth. What did they tell you about her? Big, juicy, nothing-sandwich? I shouldn't be surprised. But I've still got a good feeling about you. You're sneakier. Show me that I'm right. And keep my snacks flowing."

I take my place on stage beside Leah, completely dazed. Our tablets chirp, and recital prep begins. There's nothing to it; we'll wait our turn, say our piece, get off stage. But I can't believe no one else saw. Mendoza—sleepy, snack-loving, scatterbrained Professor Mendoza—just pulled magic out of nowhere!

Leah elbows me. "That bad? Tell me you're not packing your bags!"

"She just said she expects a lot out of me," I mumble. How do I even tell her the part about her sister?

"Oh." Leah lets out a relieved sigh. "Why was that so hard to spit out?"

I shrug and mutter an excuse as we wait for our turn to recite, trying not to yawn like everyone else. Everyone except Tasha and Akil, anyway. Mendoza used magic on them. I feel wrong for keeping this from Leah. But if I'm picking up what Mendoza's putting down, she's *this* close to slipping me more magic secrets—even if it's by accident. She's got serious skills. So why is she afraid of Headmaster Kinder?

CHAPTER TWENTY-FOUR

AN OBVIOUS SOLUTION

I thought I had my next move ready to go. A whole plan, even. But these grown-ups are really bothering me. Touré? Knows magic, pretends like she doesn't. Mendoza? Also knows magic, might actually teach me. When she's not napping, or about to run from Peerless, that is. Headmaster Kinder is behind it all, keeping everyone nice and nervous.

I'm sure she used magic on my parents. That flashing golden seal changed their minds about Peerless. We can use magic for good things, I know it! I just need to prove it.

Every fresh power outage is another reminder of all my questions. I've used magic on my own once—twice, if I count the Break on the soccer field, even though that was an accident. When I lit the bulb, Kinder's storm warning sounded. Because of me, my magic.

So what's causing the rest of them?

I remember how afraid I was racing that storm to Peerless—like it was chasing me. Every time a blackout hits, I feel that way again. I can't help but believe the monster is behind it.

"Make it make sense," Leah says when I bring up my suspicion in PE. Did I mention how much I hate this class? Especially on days like today, when we play dodgeball? "One monster in the radiant waste is doing all of that? How?"

"Maybe there's something in our neighborhoods the monster wants."

"Like what?"

I stare at my feet. "I don't know. Us?"

"But why?"

"Haven't figured that part out yet. But it's trying to get into Peerless. *Back* into Peerless."

"Choose your weapons!" Coach Maluchi bellows.

Panic surges through my veins. Leah and I were too busy talking to see the older kids come in the gym. We're a step behind the mad dash to grab the red balls set up on the center line of the court. Of course, Leah takes off anyway! What kind of friend would just let her go get clobbered?

I rush after, but Leah freezes in her tracks. I just avoid crashing into her.

"What are you doing?" I wail. We're so dead!

Then I see someone who makes me stare, too. Yolanda Jamison. Her hair isn't locced up like Leah's anymore—she's rocking a pixie cut with violet-dyed bangs that flop in her eyes as she scans for a target. Her eyes zero in on her little sister.

Red dodgeballs ricochet across the gym. First-years somersault all around us, howling for their lives.

Leah's motionless. "Where've you *been*, Yo?"

"Busy. Classes."

"You promised you'd look out for me."

Yolanda shifts her arm in one smooth motion. The ball zips forward so fast Leah can't react. *Pow!* She wobbles and steadies herself, palm cradling her reddening cheek.

"Look out for you? Okay, lesson one: remember to duck, sis!"

Unshed tears glisten in Leah's eyes. Two months at Peerless, worried sick about her sister—and this is what Yolanda does when they're finally together? I'm mad *for* Leah!

"Hey!" I scoop up the ball without thinking and hurl it. Yolanda dodges, but I just nick her leg.

"Ladies! You both out!" Maluchi barks.

"Better worry about yourself, first-year," a familiar voice calls. Another ball hisses through the air.

Pow!

I hit the floor in sections: shoulders, butt, heels. But when I can see straight again, I don't even care. It's Joey—completely okay, like nothing happened!

I walk right across the line and give him a hug.

"Hey, that's against the rules." He tenses, but eventually figures out it's not a trick and returns it.

"What…happened to you?"

"Professor Touré got me covered. I'm okay. Keep it hush, kid."

"Stay out of trouble, sis!" Yolanda hoots. "We'll get some time to hang after recital's over."

The third-years trickle out, high-fiving each other as they go. I have so many questions—what Joey saw, how he got away from the monster, what else Yo can tell us.

Leah's big mad. Nostrils flaring, fists clenched. I've never seen her like this, and she's been mad at me plenty. "I've been so freaking worried, and this is how she acts?"

"Maybe when we speak to her alone, away from, uh, dodgeballs—"

"Forget that! We don't need her for one drop of magic. We never did! You can put my name on that." She takes a deep breath. "This place changes people, Keynan. This school and its silly secrets. Don't change up on me."

The day just scribbled all over my already-busted plan. Yolanda? Not who we thought she would be. Joey isn't hurt, so now I feel guilty for giving Kinder and Touré the side-eye. I still have no good way to dig into magic in a hurry, and every minute I waste gives some storm a chance to take another chunk out of Bizzy Block.

We have open lab time in Physics, so I keep thinking through my next move. Is it bad to admit I'm kinda relieved? If Yo's not gonna help after all, learning magic falls back on me. A good poem is like uncovering something that was always there, and I'll bet magic feels like that, too. A whole lot better than someone just telling you what to do.

Oooh. That was nice!

"Hey, empty head." Dez waves at me from across our work pod. "How much longer you gonna scribble in that book?"

"My bad! Done."

"Good. I'm not doing all of this by myself. What's with you today?"

"Sorry. Peerless just…gets on my nerves."

"I heard that." He glances back at Professor Okoro and lowers his voice. "At least they let us build things in here."

"I heard second year will be better," I reply absently. "They're just weeding out anyone who isn't committed to Peerless."

He smirks. "So…are you?"

"Am I what?"

"Committed to Peerless?"

I check for Okoro before answering. "No doubt. There's stuff here that I'll never learn anywhere else."

The professor's eyes narrow on us suspiciously. We hunch over our wiring as he approaches. The class lights flicker overhead. I shudder. That fear never quite goes away, no matter how safe Peerless is supposed to be. Okoro grumbles loudly about Touré checking on his classroom last and returns to his desk.

Dez waits until Okoro's stabbing a message on his tablet. "Same. I don't get why Peerless is so empty. More parents must be sticking with *Build-A-Scholar* this year. Can't blame them, with the storms and all."

"But there's always been storms."

"I know it's hard to keep up since you pretty much stay in trouble, but anyone can see they're getting worse."

He's right. Blackouts do seem to be a regular thing since I opened that first Break, definitely more than on Bizzy Block. Maybe they feel small because Peerless is so big?

Dez licks his lips. "So… I heard the headmaster arguing with Touré last night."

"About storms?"

"About closing Peerless."

My jaw drops. "No way they would do that."

"What makes you so sure?"

"We…we just started!" Panic roils in my stomach like a ball of caterpillars. This can't be happening. Nope. "It would mess up everything to send us home now."

"I hope you're right." Dez eyes me. "You're not as bad as I thought. When you first got here—"

"That was…an awful night. You smashed my care package into crumbs."

"Sorry, I didn't know they were in there. I hate seeing good snacks wasted." He winks. "Almost as much as I hate seeing your line-up get worse every day."

My hand slips to my temple—I'm *way* overdue for a haircut. "Don't remind me. But…you're always clean. Does your roommate cut hair?"

"Nope. That's all me. My folks let me bring our clippers. Said they'd be fine without them." Dez grins. "I'll edge you up if you don't send Wiley Squad back to last place."

"Bet! That's a…" My voice dies as an obvious solution clobbers me. What did Leah say about her sister? *Yo's probably been stuck in more detention than you and I could be if we were trying.* How didn't I see this before? If Kinder and Touré taught Yo, what's stopping me from doing what she did? I can learn about magic today. Right this instant.

And Dez is gonna help make it happen.

"Sorry," I whisper. "I've got to do this."

"Do what?"

I reach across the table and dunk his circuit board in salt water.

His mouth falls open. "Hey! I've been working all week on that, you jerk!"

"Who you calling a jerk?" I make sure my voice is extra loud. "You probably did it wrong anyway!"

"Desmond!" Professor Okoro calls.

Dez grabs our tub of salt water, eyes flashing as he heaves it. Water goes everywhere. I trip over my chair, tumbling into another pod. Beakers scatter across the floor.

"Keynan Masters!" Professor Okoro is hot. "You just earned three days' worth of detention. If you weren't both in the same homeroom, I'd set your points back a whole month! Out!"

I grab my tablet and notebook and scurry for the door. Dez gives me a wounded look as he cleans up the mess. "I'll pay you back for this," he snarls under his breath. "Just you wait!"

I feel awful, but he wouldn't believe me if I told him the

truth. I vow to make this up to him somehow. He actually seems all right.

In the library, Professor Touré's head shoots up as I shut the door behind me. *"Today?"* She rubs her temples. "I've got things to do!"

"And two more days after this," I squeak.

She snaps her tablet up, eyebrows climbing as she reads. "Dez again? What is with you two?"

"He's fine." Here goes everything. Again. "I can't wait for second year, or even next semester or next week. I need to know right now."

"Know what?"

"What you did outside! With your rhymes, and the storm!"

Professor Touré laughs, a rumble that shudders up from her belly and echoes off the rafters. "Is there a secret record for fastest expulsion I don't know about?" she asks, wiping tears from her eyes. "You must love *Build-A-Scholar!*"

"I…I know about Breaks! And the Wars of Illusion! I know our art makes magic—that's what happened to me outside that night! That's where Joey ended up! He said it's a storm, but he's lying!"

Touré goes still. "How…what—"

"It doesn't matter. *I know.* I'm here to stay. To learn. Simple as that."

"Simple as that," Professor Touré repeats softly. "You're gonna stay here, all right. We'll take as long as we need to get the first rule through your head."

Finally! "What's the first rule?"

"First rule…ready? *You don't make the rules*. Now follow me."

Professor Touré sweeps out of the library and down the hall. I can't believe this worked! I manage to get in a skip when she's not looking. A heel click when she turns the corner. A shoulder shimmy when she fiddles with her ring of endless keys. I'll be running this place in a week! We'll need to upgrade my nickname! Maybe Magicmaster! I'll get my mama feeling good again! Scare storms away from Bizzy Block! Make snacks out of thin—

We stop before a familiar door. My excitement evaporates as Touré pulls out a mop and bucket. I already know her grin will give me bad dreams tonight. "Okay, Keymaster. Say hello to your two new best friends. Go to bed early tonight. You're going to need all the rest you can get."

CHAPTER TWENTY-FIVE

YOU DRAW IT, I'LL RHYME IT

Change my whole last name. Call me Keynan Disasters. I made an enemy out of Dez right when we were getting cool, and for what? Splinter palms I'm sure to get after mopping and sweeping. Raisin fingers from all the dishwater I'm about to be drenched in. I go to the courtyard. Smell the flowers. Touch some grass. Sit under the old oak. But nothing helps me see a way out of this mess.

Footsteps shuffle up behind me. "Uh-oh. What happened?"

Wordlessly, I hand Amari my tablet. He sits and scans my schedule, letting out a low whistle. "Wow. Kinder's going to keep you in detention until that's more than baby fluff on your chin. Touré found your light bulb, didn't she? I knew that would—"

"It wasn't that." I choke out my grand vision and how it all went sideways.

"She's got you all day. And extra homework...?" He sighs deeply. "Since this is your last night before you're stuck in the sunken place, we should just hang out for once. We can play bones instead of chess so you can actually—"

I straighten. "You're right. Tonight's my last night. I'll never get a better time."

"Exactly, and—wait. Time to do what?"

"Make some magic happen! What? Why are you staring at me like that?"

"Just memorizing your face. For the next time an idea this awful falls out of it!"

"I'll do something simple."

He shakes his head doggedly. "What does Leah call you again?"

"Keymaster?"

"The other one. Brick brain!"

"I..." A tight lump of frustration squeezes my throat. I don't want to go off on my own—again. But how do I get him to understand? "Look...no one will help us. Mendoza's scared. Touré's slow. You helped Leah with the hidden wing. I need you, too!"

His forehead wrinkles. "This is way different..."

I peer at my hands. Yeah...using Peerless Pact is kinda

shady, but I'm desperate. "Don't you want to see what we can do?"

"*We?*"

"We. Remember what Ian said, about combining art forms?"

"The part about not doing it, yes!"

"It'll go better with both of us. Come on! We'll make something small. Useful." Surrounded by the courtyard's greenery, a perfect idea springs to mind. "Pollinators! For the gardens."

Amari gawks at me. "Like what exactly? Magic bees? With magic stingers? *How* is that a good idea?"

"No one said anything about bees!" I tell him hastily. "But something. You draw it, I'll rhyme it to life."

A grin splits his face in half. "Draw it? Next time, say that part first. What about Leah, though?"

"Let's see if we can actually make it work first."

"Mmhmm. Before she can talk us out of it."

Amari said *us*—he's really in. A knot in my shoulders untangles itself. "We just got back to being friends, okay? I don't want her mad at me again. Especially after everything with Yo."

"Yeah, she deserves a few drama-free days." Amari nods thoughtfully. "My granny would call you two peas in a pod. Both dragging me into fresh problems."

"Not if you show out with your drawings. Let's go! There's no telling how much time we have."

I lead us to the school's main entrance and slip through the tall double doors. A tingle of anticipation flutters down my spine.

"Kinder will never look for us here," Amari says approvingly. "I haven't been back since day one. How'd you think of it?"

"Ian found a spot for my baba's bike." I jerk my thumb over my shoulder to the metal rack. The bike's still there, rust and all, tucked behind the main steps.

I offer Amari a few sheets of notebook paper while he digs some colored pencils out of his bag. He turns his back so I can't see his warm-up sketches. Sheesh. Artists are so sensitive.

While he draws, I nudge some rhymes around on the paper, clearing my throat loudly when Amari tries to peek. So *nosy*. I keep expecting Headmaster Kinder to pounce from behind a column, but the grounds are spider-silk quiet on every side. Somehow, I don't trust it. But I do trust my rhymes, and they're unfolding nicely.

"So…what's it gonna be?" Amari finally asks. "Besides not bees?"

We bat some ideas around. Bugs make the most sense, but we're both terrified of messing those up. We finally agree on a bird and a butterfly. "One spreads seeds, and the other pollinates. Win-win, right?"

"Still a bug, but a pretty bug," Amari concedes. I give up two more notebook sheets. His pencils whirl over the paper, outlining a beautiful monarch butterfly and a goldfinch. They shimmer on their pages, catching the late morning sunlight. He gets details right I'd never think to draw: antennae, and the talons. Amari's really amazing.

"I don't know why yellow feels so important," he murmurs to himself. "I hardly ever use it. Your turn."

Here goes. I take a deep breath and spit out my part, slapping a beat on the steps:

> *Here to rhyme new magic at my own pace*
> *Time to put old magic back in its old place*
> *Amari's gonna get us there with all haste*
> *keep us…out of harm's way*
> *So we can get our Peerless crew back in this race.*

He frowns when I finish. "That didn't feel right."

"What? That was perfect."

"But you didn't call out the bird or the butterfly. That rhyme could have been for anything!"

The papers glow, brilliant as golden sunflowers, and rise into the air.

"Look! Magic, see? It's fine."

Amari points past my shoulder, eyes widening. "Sure about that?"

I turn and spring to my feet. My baba's bike is floating straight for us. The metal is glowing the same bright yellow as Amari's drawings.

He's right. I messed this rhyme up bad!

CHAPTER TWENTY-SIX

A SHRIMP NAMED SLICKBACK

"You messed this up bad! Make it stop!"

"I'm working on it!"

"Proceed indoors immediately." The intercom wails like Peerless itself is snitching on us! I half expect Kinder's voice to call us by name. *"A storm is approaching the school grounds. This is not a drill."*

My bike bubbles like hot oatmeal. The frame and tires bend and fold around both drawings, swallowing them up in a glimmering yellow tornado. There's no way to stuff a rhyme back where it came from, but I try:

> *Let's go try this again uhh*
> *I need a bird to be my friend uhh*
> *And a butterfly too uhh*

Gotta complete the picture
Cook at a different temperature—

A charged, burning odor wrinkles my nose. Rancid buttery flashes swirl through the slag of my baba's bike.

"What was that?" Amari spluttered.

"Not helpful!"

The threads of sparkling magic pull away to reveal a dull, slug-like blob. The bird beside it is the complete opposite: an actual beak, feathers, and eyes take shape. The bird stretches its wings, clearly impressed with itself.

"Well, mine didn't turn out so bad," Amari says.

"Hold up! Who said that one's yours?"

"The lumpy one is your bike, so that's all you!"

The bird looks at us, cocks its head, and vanishes in a burst of sparks.

I groan. "Neither one made it. I should have started working on a piece sooner. Yesterday, or something."

"Sometimes my best drawings just…happen," Amari offers. "Maybe you should try that more. You know, freestyle."

"It's not that easy."

"There's this thing, bruh. Called practice?"

"Can we do this later?" I peer at my ruined bike, wondering how to hide the mess. I could try freestyling, but

I like my rhymes in front of me, where I can see them. Sometimes I get little nuggets, nice lines, but I've noticed other nights where the words just pour out. Like a forgotten language I'm starting to remember again. Is it really mine when that happens? Or is it magic, like Mendoza said? Hiding inside me?

Amari looks on anxiously. "You're not actually gonna touch that? It could be playing dead!"

The blob won't budge. It's cool and smooth to the touch. "Are you gonna help? This thing's heavy!"

"Well, it basically absorbed your bike, so it's extra dense."

"Dense?" a small voice erupts. "Y'all got nerve tossing out insults after this display of scrub sorcery!"

"It's talking," I croak, scrambling back.

"Oh look, a prodigy on our hands! Not that you actually made me some hands." Six nubs pop out of the griping lump of metal. Puffy little finger-toes unfurl from the new legs, one by one. "Much better. If you want it done right, do it yourself."

"What happened to the wings?" Amari hisses.

"I don't know!"

A head wriggles loose, with round, black-slitted eyes and hungry hollow cheeks. It looks back at itself and wriggles out a tail. "Gotta keep my balance. Now for some camouflage." The skin turns yellow with blue and black spots, glistening like fresh paint.

"What is it?"

"Maybe a gecko?" I whisper. "Except for that slick back."

"With six legs? More like if a salamander and a shrimp had a baby."

"I guess as my creators you get naming rights." The creature glares at us. "But a shrimp named Slickback? You best believe our creative directions will part ways from here. Now where is she? Where's my colleague?"

Light flashes behind us. The bird flutters cheerily by the entrance to Peerless, wings spinning like a hummingbird and shooting out fountains of color. "My bird," Amari breathes, relieved. I wish it had stayed gone. The thing glimmers like a Break with wings. How will we hide it?

"Just our luck to get conjured up on amateur night for sorcerers," Slickback observes. "This ain't finna go well for you, young blood."

"Who you calling young? *You're* five minutes old!" I fire back.

"Disco!" Slickback snaps his fingers, and the bird zips to his side. "Here's some free schooling—name everything you create, or someone else will steal it. Now, unless the two of you have snacks…" Slickback sighs when we stammer. "I shouldn't be surprised. Deuces!"

"Wait! I made you!" I cry. "That means…you gotta do what I say!"

"Then why didn't you spit that in your verse? It's better this way, believe me. We'll never be homies if you expect us to follow you around like pets."

Slickback scampers between us, pausing at the Peerless doors. He sinks his teeth into one of the metal hinges, and the door groans open. "Tasty," he proclaims. "I'm gonna like it here." He disappears inside, and Disco winks into nothingness.

"He just. Ate. The door." Amari clasps his hands to his face. "This is a disaster. How'd I let you talk me into this?"

"We'll be fine! We'll probably never see them again."

Only…it's not fine. At. All.

The next morning, my tablet wakes me with an early message from Professor Touré:

Detention is postponed. Go to your scheduled classes.

I eat breakfast with Ian, halfway expecting Touré to pop out of a locker with her mop and bucket. *Just another day*, I try to tell myself. Power is back and so are classes.

I nudge Ian. "Hey, you told me about combining art forms, remember?"

He gives me a blank look. "I did?"

I blink. "Yeah. You did. What's the worst that could happen?"

"Umm…losing cohort points, I guess? I dunno, Keynan. I'd remember saying something like that." He goes back to his homework. Ian! Doing homework! He's still not himself. I just let it go.

Amari catches up to me on the way to homeroom, bleary-eyed and munching a cinnamon bagel.

"Postponed?" he asks dubiously. "Sounds too good to be true."

A cluster of first-years blocks the hall outside of homeroom. We edge closer and gape along with everyone else. Lockers, ceiling, walls, and floors are all splashed with eye-searing colors, like two rainbows had a dance battle. Professor Wiley glares around suspiciously and settles on Amari.

"Tell me you brick heads didn't do this!" Leah cries as she glides over.

"First time seeing it," I say faintly.

In every class, everyone's buzzing over who painted the hallway, and what Kinder will do to them. Even Professor Mendoza teaches for the whole hour; she must be dreading a visit from the headmaster right along with the rest of us.

Amari is practically shaking when we meet up with Leah over grilled cheese and tomato sandwiches with Soup's Soup, some kind of spicy vegetable broth today. "Touré pulled me from Art. I've never seen her so tired. And scared."

A lump rises in my throat. "What did she say?"

"That she's never seen magic like this—and there's damage everywhere, teeth marks on the pipes! She was so mad! Said it's not like there's a hardware store around the corner."

"What's a hardware store?"

"That's what I said!" Amari darts a glance at me, then back to his tray. He hasn't touched his food. "But Touré cleaned it up. There's not one drop of color in that hall anymore."

"Something got out of the hidden wing, didn't it?" Leah squeezes her eyes shut. "This is on us. On me!"

Amari opens his mouth, but I cut in first. "Are you kidding? I'm surprised it doesn't happen every day. Something small probably did it." I can't meet Amari's eyes, and my face burns as I continue. "Two somethings, maybe. One for the metal and one for the makeover?"

Leah purses her lips. "What we need is a trap."

"Maybe a pile of old nails? For bait?" I suggest. "Along with our magic."

216

"Better get your rhymes right then," Amari mutters under his breath.

We finish and head back to the first-year dorms, talking through how a magic trap might work. Quiet snuffling halts us near the courtyard, so faint I'm sure I imagined it. We cut straight through the raised vegetable beds, over the stone bridge with its burbling creek, past the old oak, and weave under the smaller trees. The far walkway spreads out before us. The flawless slate is drowning in swathes of harsh orange, lopsided patterns of pukey green, hot pink, and weepy blue sprinkles.

In the middle of it all, Professor Touré scrubs furiously. Her hands are stained past the wrist. Multicolored smudges cover her cheeks just beneath her reddened eyes. An untouched sandwich sits on a tray near a dirty bucket and dirtier sponges.

"This will take her all night." Amari swallows. "I'm... I'm going to help."

"I will too—"

"No." Leah's urgent voice stops me. "We wouldn't be in this mess if I hadn't pushed you both about finding Yo. We need your rhymes to turn this around. Go, Keynan. We got this."

I almost spill everything right there—Slickback and Disco, messing with Dez for detention. I don't deserve friends this cool. I've been kinda terrible lately, and magic is still just outside my reach.

I linger as my friends head over. They all speak too low for me to hear. Professor Touré shakes her head sternly, eyebrows drawing down when Leah crosses her arms. Finally, the professor throws up her hands and points. Leah's extra pleased as she scoops up a sponge. Amari squeezes Touré in a hug. The professor bites her lip, trying to hold in a grateful smile. All while I skulk off alone, when I'm the one who started this mess in the first place.

I should be back there.

"Psst." Professor Mendoza's bun edges cautiously around the side of the old oak's trunk, followed by her searching, nervous eyes. "Why so guilty-looking?"

"What if I just told the headmaster I'm sorry?" I blubber out. "And it won't happen again?"

Mendoza pops a strawberry in her mouth and chews thoughtfully. "It's too late for that, Keynan. These latest problems are too big to ignore. I've heard whispers, and I'm afraid Kinder's mind is made up about closing the school."

"She won't do that! I could convince her if—"

"Doubtful. A flawless recital might turn the tide. A performance for the ages." Mendoza makes a face and spits out the strawberry's green top. "That's not really your style though, is it? Reciting, I mean."

"Of course I'll do my part! Even if it means putting everybody to sleep with these awful rhymes." Kinder's really going to do it. I never believed it, deep down—not even when Dez warned me. "But... Touré could fix all of this in a flash with magic."

"She won't. And now your magic is loose inside Peerless." The sky above the courtyard rumbles. I flinch, searching for clouds, anything that looks off, but there are only stars overhead. Mendoza's calmer than I've ever seen her, eyes hunting the night. "Going home might be what's best. Maybe we were all just lying to ourselves that this place could ever work."

CHAPTER TWENTY-SEVEN

BUCKLE DOWN

My detention starts forreal the next day, and I can't imagine a more perfect fit for how awful things are going. I don't know what's worse: mopping, wiping dusty old cobwebs from window panes, polishing door knobs until they gleam, oiling hinges until they open soundlessly. How does one building have so many doors? I'm no stranger to hard work, but my hands and feet are aching by the time Touré finally nods her approval. I'd swallow my tongue before complaining, though. The scrapes on her hands and circles under her eyes are all the proof I need that she finished ten times the cleanup last night.

Besides, I'm *still* not done.

I rearrange old books in alphabetical order, about everything from earth science to constellations and engineering. Then she changes her mind and makes me put them all back the way they were before. If I even think about cracking open a book to skim it—I swear Professor Touré knows before I do. Every time, she clears her throat and I scurry to work. More than once, I wonder nervously if magic can let someone flip through my thoughts like the pages of a book.

A little cheer escapes my throat when my tablet finally chirps on a study table. Classes are over, and my feet are throbbing through my soles. "Never thought I'd be grateful for homework," I mumble.

"Where do you think you're going?" Professor Touré's eyes dart up from her tablet.

"Class is over."

"For them it is. Not you."

The chores get worse. I organize the supply closet's old recycled nails based on size, then hammer out the ones that are crooked. "Waste not," Touré says, munching a sandwich.

But do I get lunch? Snacks? Nope! Maybe I'm supposed to eat the yellowing leaves I prune from vines in the courtyard instead of chopping them up for mulch. After that, I transplant berry bushes from a glasshouse tucked behind the main buildings—one sprout at a time.

"I could probably do all of this with one good rhyme," I mutter glumly.

"Finally." Touré closes the book she's reading with a snap. "Now…why didn't we?"

I hesitate, surprised at the first time she's mentioned magic the entire detention. "Because you're grouchy and really need a hug?"

"I swear on—" She stops herself, glowering at me. "Think, Keynan. It's easier to use magic, cut corners. That's where it tricks you. If you can't be patient, you can't be taught. Can you get that through your head?"

"Yes," I answer.

"Good. Wait here."

Touré stalks off before I can respond. A moment later, Soup pops into the library with a tray of suspicious, stale-looking crackers, water, and bruised apples.

It's all delicious.

"Really stepped in it this time, didn't I?" I ask around gulps of water.

"I've only seen one student get in Touré's doghouse like you. Stayed in trouble nonstop. In and out of detention for a whole semester. You might know her."

A little piece of me dies inside. "Yolanda?"

Soup nods sadly. "Should've thought this through before popping off at the mouth, kid. There's easier ways, you know. Slow cooking don't mean bad cooking. Simple recipes still make for good eats."

I piece together what he's hinting at. "Why is the recital

such a huge deal? I don't get how something so boring is all the headmaster cares about."

"That's above me." Soup shrugs. "Buckle down. Tomorrow's gonna be worse."

I stare at him, aghast. "Worse than this? How?"

"She told me that you're with me in the kitchen first thing. Don't bother with homeroom."

So...yeah, maybe I should have stuck with our plan to find Yolanda. Badgering Touré into teaching me about magic blew up in my face. I could've skipped all of this instead of just repeating Yo's mistakes. Instead I'm going to be shoulder-deep in dirty dishes tomorrow. My hands will stay wrinkled until the rest of me catches up!

I finish up my homework in the library. It's still dark outside the windows, but morning birds are singing by the time I finally trudge back to the dorms. A tray of cold dinner awaits in my room—I can't really express how tired I am of eating food left on my bed. Cheese and fruit and crackers.

Even Ian wouldn't touch it.

A whole semester of this? How, Yolanda? I'm ready to fold after day one, and I've still got two more to go. How am I supposed to be my amazing self if all I want to do is sleep? I'll have zero time left for rhymes. But that's the idea, isn't it? It took me a while to get them back after my first detention session. Touré's determined to outdo herself this time around. I replace the lid on my sad dinner.

A note flutters down from the tray. The handwriting is bold and slashing and fancy:

We see you, Keynan. Don't let them hold you down.

I can't help but smile. Exactly what I would expect Starbreaker to say. My friends got my back, and Touré won't change that.

The next day, she pours it on even worse. I finish random tasks and chores from sunrise to sundown. Tend the courtyard garden. Prepare meals under Soup's watchful eye. Clean every nook of Peerless—except the hidden wing. When that's done…homework. If this keeps up, I'm scared I'll forget my friends' faces! There's never a break in the day to see them, and everyone's asleep by the time I'm finished.

Two hours into my third day, the library door opens. Touré blinks as Leah peeks in. "Keynan's still in detention," the professor announces. "No friends allowed."

"I'm not here for him," Leah says. "I'm here for me. Detention for the rest of the week."

I could hug her right there. I'm hiding things from her, but she *so* has my back. It feels great and awful at the same time.

Professor Touré tries to burn holes through us both with

her glare. "So that's how it is?" she growls. "Okay then. Okay. You'll start with—"

"Sorry," Leah interrupts. "You might want to wait for..."

Amari enters with a shrug. "Sorry. Had to pee. Heard you don't do bathroom breaks."

"So y'all are staging a protest!" Professor Touré explodes. "Are Dez and Ian bringing snacks?"

"Just us," Amari says hastily.

"Professor, I heard your rhymes," I say. "I know I can do that. I'm not gonna be able to think about anything else until I do. What could be more important?"

Touré rubs her face in her palms. Her voice totters off into some muttering that it's probably best we don't hear. "I'll teach you. But *promise* me no more detention or picking fights with Dez." Her glare widens to include Leah and Amari. "No more exploring grounds after curfew, sneaking out to the third-year dorms, or messing with your tablet's source code. And when it's time for the recital? I need your absolute best."

Leah bites her lip and Amari's face flushes, but they both nod.

Touré's eyes narrow before she strides off. "You want to learn? Fine. You're gonna learn today."

CHAPTER TWENTY-EIGHT

THE BREATHING ORCHARD

We fall in behind Professor Touré. She didn't exactly admit that she'd lied to us, but she gave in. She's not treating us like little kids. I'm stunned. This is finally happening!

Amari's cheesing so hard, his gums squeak together. "You made this happen!" he says, squeezing my shoulder. "The first thing I'm gonna create is a magic box that's always full of your favorite snacks!"

He's so excited that Professor Touré stops to shush him. Leah's quieter than I've ever seen her, arms tucked tightly by her sides. I don't have a sister, but I can imagine how awful she must feel. When I've mastered magic, I'm going to sorcerize Yolanda into hugging her on sight. And if that doesn't work, I'll cook up a dodgeball for Leah, one that never misses.

Touré abruptly turns down a winding corridor that ends in some stairs, leading us to a room full of old metal water tanks, with little gauges next to them on touch pads. Pipes snake off in every direction on the ceiling.

Through yet another door, we're suddenly outside, blinking in the sunlight. Glancing around, I hold in a shiver, even though it's a warm day. We're beside the auditorium, but nowhere near the soccer field. Long, patchy grass surrounds a huge toolshed that reminds me of Bizzy Block's workshop. We cross the grass toward some thick undergrowth, where a sign reads,

PEERLESS ACADEMY GROUNDS
END HERE
PROCEED AT YOUR OWN RISK!

Professor Touré turns to face us.

"So. You think you know about magic. Did you stop to think of why no one's taught you yet?"

"It's busted," I offer.

"Dangerous," Leah adds.

"Stick figures," Amari says.

Huh?

Touré tilts her head. "Go on."

I tap a finger on my chin. If combining art brings out

the magic… "That's why Professor Mendoza's poems are so…well…"

"Basic?" Touré supplies.

"Yeah."

Leah frowns. "I don't get it."

"Simple arts can harness the world's magic…maybe even restore it," Touré explains. "But when arts are combined, or improvised…well, chaos breaks loose."

Amari grins. "Peerless actually makes sense now! Points to keep everyone in line. If we're in line, magic is in line."

"Exactly. And we *must* keep magic in line. That's why no one sings in your fields, throws block parties on your streets, or does any of the other stuff y'all should've grown up knowing. It's too dangerous. There's so much corrupt magic in the world now, most people think it's supposed to be there. Or they lie to themselves to hide what their own eyes are telling them."

"Forreal?" I shake my head doubtfully. "How could anyone miss it?"

"What's a block party?" Amari murmurs.

"Do y'all want to do this, or stand here and ask me questions all day?"

I share a glance with my friends. "Let's do this."

We follow a footpath through chunky shrubs with spots on their leaves. Touré turns in to a clearing that reminds me of the courtyard. Overgrown flower beds nestle under rows of crooked trees. This might have been an orchard once. "This will be our classroom: a pocket of corrupt magic, but not so much as to hurt us, if we're careful." The professor sighs when her tablet chirps. "This woman…sit tight."

"I don't like it here," Leah whispers while Touré is distracted.

"Me neither." My skin feels like a shirt that's two sizes too small. A breeze tickles the nape of my neck. The space is quiet and beautiful and somehow completely wrong. I peer at the one bush I recognize, behind Amari. "Blackberries! We make jam and turnovers from these back home. They're ripe, too."

"That sounds good. Especially since someone forgot about snacks." Amari side-eyes Professor Touré, still absorbed with her tablet. He's licking his lips.

Leah waggles a finger at him. "Be smart!" she hisses. "Look!"

The blackberry bush…vibrates. The ripe berries swell, then plop onto the ground before our eyes. I gasp as flowers bloom and wilt, only to be replaced by berries that go from light green to ripe all over again.

"Corrupt magic preys on your thoughts, uses them

against you," Professor Touré calls out behind us. "Reality itself will trick you if you're not paying attention."

"I was really hungry," Amari admits guiltily. "What would happen if we ate one?"

"Do you really want to find out?" Professor Touré asks. "Corrupt magic is difficult to purge—especially if you allow it inside."

She nods back at the bush. Small turnovers now grow where the berries used to be. They're even *steaming*, like they're fresh from the oven. The breeze pushes the delicious pastry aroma into my nose. It ebbs and flows across my face, like something breathing. "You said *prey*...that means a predator, right?" I ask. "Some extinct animals used bait to hunt. Lanternfish. Or pitcher plants."

"Look at you, Keynan. Perceptive." We all inch away from the blackberry bush.

Leah runs her fingers through her locs. "How are we supposed to know when magic tricks us?"

"Finally, the right question. You might have more brains in your head than these two put together. The battles that created the radiant waste were called the Wars of Illusion for a reason."

"But magic can't be all bad," I press, impatient. "We don't have any days to lose! We'll never know the good from the busted without taking chances."

Professor Touré skewers me with a look. "What do you think we're doing out here, if not taking chances?"

Amari's face goes slack. "Y'all. Look up." Beyond the breathing orchard's treetops, a slice of moon suddenly curls across the sky. Stars twinkle in the blue as though it were the dead of night. "There it goes again!"

We gawk as the moon zips above us, over and over. The sliver widens with each pass until it's full and bright. The entire sky vibrates like it can't decide between day and night.

"Are we a month older?" I squeal, touching my face. "Is this peach fuzz on my chin?"

Leah wobbles on her feet. "This isn't happening."

"Oh, it is. And this isn't even that messy," Professor Touré says faintly. "Remember what you said, Keynan? 'We don't have any days to lose.' That was the root of this corrupt magic."

"But we just—" I cut off in shock. Gray is creeping into Touré's hair at the temples. So the busted magic took my words and twisted them all up? I swallow. "Can we go back?"

"You wanted this. Leah?" Professor Touré's voice is still calm—how? The waning moon is down to a crescent! "Show me some moves."

Leah blinks. "You…want me to dance?"

"Isn't that why you've come to Peerless? Today, please. I'm not getting any younger."

Leah flinches and does a few measured steps, simple enough that even my two left feet might pull it off. Her foot squelches in a pile of blackberries. She yelps—but finds her rhythm again. The bush quivers like it's disappointed.

Touré kisses her teeth. "Lovely. Professor Kurosaki's homework. How would you dance if no one's watching?"

Leah hesitates, nibbling on her lip. She shifts into a cross step, then adds twists like wings sprouted from her feet. A pleased look blooms on her face. Amari and I burst into applause when she finishes. Around us things…shift. Ripe blackberries stop falling off the bushes. I can still see the too-bright stars, but the moon is fixed in the sky, like it's supposed to be. She shakes her head in wonder. "I felt… something."

Touré's eyes twinkle. "Through and through B-girl. Nice."

"A breaker?" Amari exclaims. "My granny talks about how much she misses them."

"We all do." Professor Touré nods. "Dance creates an… agreement. A shared *now*. Corrupt magic can't ignore rhythm. In the radiant waste, one breath can feel like an eternity. A clear sky can hypnotize, drown you in blue for fifty years. Gifted dancers can cut through that, can strengthen their crew's magic."

"Crew?" I repeat. "That part doesn't sound so scary."

Touré's voice softens as she beckons us back toward

Peerless. "Not everyone is built to deal with corrupt magic, especially at your age. That's why Peerless doesn't teach it openly. There can be no doubt."

"We're not going anywhere," I declare. Leah and Amari murmur their agreement.

"Good. Crews can tackle magic from all kinds of angles. Y'all got potential, I'll admit. A crew that trusts each other, creates together...who knows what's possible?"

Back inside Peerless, we double-check our tablets. Even Touré's relieved to discover a month didn't pass in the orchard.

"Imagine the homework," Amari tries to joke, but no one laughs. If busted magic can twist up time, a night's stroll in the wrong spot might mean being a hundred years old and not even graduated. And me? I just tossed together some magical creatures and set them loose inside Peerless.

"Y'all are quiet. Hopefully that means you're catching on." Professor Touré nods grimly. "Eat and rest. Today you've proven you've got sense. Barely. Tomorrow we'll see if you can level up."

CHAPTER TWENTY-NINE

LINE BY LINE

We take our breakfast to the courtyard the next morning, at Amari's suggestion. To our surprise, Professor Mendoza is there early with a basket of fresh-plucked strawberries. She pats the bark of the old oak tree as she glides past. "What a time to be alive! Tell me what you've learned."

Her face clouds as we recount the bizarre orchard. "My moves made everything around us move," Leah finishes. Her eyes are red, but her voice is excited. "It was amazing."

"That's your idea of amazing?" Mendoza murmurs. "Braver than I could ever be—"

The sky above the courtyard booms loud enough to make us flinch.

"First-years!"

A bunch of professors suddenly ring the courtyard walkway, gesturing to us—Wiley and Okoro and some others I don't know. "Head to the dorms," Wiley calls out. "Storm came out of nowhere. It's safer back in your rooms."

I gape up at the sky. Bright globs float through the languid gray clouds, like chunky fireflies. All except two points of crimson light. They are fixed in place while the others drift. I want to point, scream, warn my friends, anything—but I can't lift a finger.

The monster's staring right at us. At me. I feel hatred in that gaze. Rage turning my heartbeat to jelly. This is a hundred times worse than my bike ride to Peerless, like I should go hide in a basement and stay there. Like I don't deserve to see the sun again.

Lightning flashes, leaving an afterimage of the oak tree's branches across my vision. Mendoza gasps. "Come, children!"

"Thunder's supposed to come after lightning, not before," Amari says softly.

Leah's hand rests on the back of mine. "Hey. What's wrong?"

I can breathe again. The monster's eyes are gone. "I... I'm not sure."

We set out for the dorms. Mendoza tries to murmur encouragement, but she's shaken herself—clasping Wiley's arm for support. He scowls at her, like she should know better.

We finish breakfast in the common room. When our tablets chirp, I snatch mine up so fast, I almost spill my orange juice. "Touré added on detention after classes," I announce eagerly.

Leah blinks at her tablet over her scrambled eggs. "But she wants us inside Peerless."

"A lecture," Amari moans.

"Maybe," I say. "Better than stick figures, right?"

"About that…" Amari peers around, then fishes something from his backpack. "So yesterday got me thinking."

He slides a brick onto the table. The side is full of crumbly cavities, like an avocado going bad. "You pried this out of those old stairs!" Leah hisses.

"Before Touré made us promise not to explore!" he says hastily. "Anyway, I wanna see something. Keynan—can you read your poem for the recital?"

"You want me to put a brick to sleep?"

He squeezes his eyes shut. "Just. Do. It."

It's still memorized; I recite it easy. We all gape as some of the flakier bits meld back into the brick! It's not perfect, but definitely more solid than before. Amari nods in satisfaction. "Simple arts harness magic, like Touré said."

"It barely fixed the brick," Leah points out.

"But that's one poem from one student," he replies. "They must use all of our stuff for something bigger."

Okay, wow. This is what Mendoza meant. Those endless hours of dreary practice with the sleepy rhymes—and dance routines and artwork—are supposed to patch Peerless together. "So the recital isn't a complete waste of time," I admit grudgingly. "But it's still...slow. These storms aren't waiting around for it. Don't tell Touré about the brick, or she won't trust us with one more lesson."

"Listen to your friend, Amari." Leah smiles at me before she heads off to class. "He's looking out for us."

Her praise clenches my stomach. Some best friend I'm turning out to be—letting her think Slickback and Disco are her fault. If Peerless closes because I didn't catch those little beasties, I'm officially the worst ever.

Amari's brow draws down. "How can you stand this? Guilt is eating Leah up and it's not right. I can't with these lies, Keynan!"

"I know," I say miserably. "We'll tell her—promise—as soon as—"

Amari snorts. "I don't think that word means what you think it means."

"She doesn't need something else to worry about." I wince, remembering her red eyes earlier, but press on. "Just a little longer. Touré's lessons will make our magic unstoppable—catching Slickback and Disco will prove it! Once that's done, fixing the school will be cake."

He doesn't agree, but he doesn't say no, either.

It's all I can do to sit through classes. Geometry and Horticulture are agony. In Physics, I'm on my best behavior, since Dez and I are paired together on a new project—Headmaster Kinder's decision, not Professor Okoro's, he assures us. We power through without uttering a single word to each other. Fine by me. I've got more than Slickback and Disco to worry about. I don't want to scare my friends, but I was right. That monster in the radiant waste is hunting us. Hunting me.

Classes finally finish and I join the crush of students, quickly finding Amari and Leah. We follow our tablets' navigation, beelining into quieter Peerless halls. We arrive before a very old, very worn door. I remember it from detention because of the heavy lock. Professor Touré strides up a moment later, munching an apple as she fiddles with her keys. She pulls one off and extends it to Amari, shiny and silver. "You're up. Leah's proven herself, but I have my doubts about you."

Amari flings open the door and darts inside. We follow behind him. Dusty art supplies line the shelves from floor to ceiling; the room is big as me and Ian's dorm room. Buckets full of brushes, some new and some ancient, unopened paint. Amari runs his hands over stacked canvases, spray paint in colors I've never even thought of, chalk, markers, crayons. He spins around and embraces Touré. "I take back every salty thing I said about Peerless."

"It's like a rainbow barfed in here," Leah observes.

"Yeah," Amari says in a dreamy voice. "There's just enough room for a bed."

My friends are so strange.

"An artist is capable of—" Professor Touré blinks. "No, there will be no sleeping in the supply closet. Tuck your lip back in, Amari! Now…your creations will aid you if your vision is clear. But if fear guides your heart, you'll create nightmares and worse. Most of all, a good artist helps their crew imagine the future, without forgetting their roots."

"So, you're saying his drawings can, umm…come to life?" I ask carefully.

"In a manner of speaking."

Touré's gaze swivels to Amari, who is suddenly intent on studying his shoes. I press on quickly. "So things he's created…can he uncreate them?"

"Magic isn't a switch you can flick on and off." Professor Touré eyes each of us in turn. "Especially when art forms are combined."

My mouth dries. That's exactly what we found out with Slickback and Disco.

"But why does Peerless *teach* art, if it's so dangerous?" Leah asks.

"Our founders believed the arts will do more than help us use scraps of corrupt magic. They believed we can heal it." A distant, faraway look comes over her face. "Line by line. Step by step, stroke by stroke. That's what Peerless stands for."

"The recital," Amari says. "That magic can do more than keep Peerless going."

Touré nods approvingly. "I believe the art we create at this school will change everything."

I am definitely, *definitely* here for this. I remember the musty old brick that we made better with magic—that's only the beginning of fixing Peerless. "So when do—"

Touré cuts in irritably. "Did you already forget that word I've tried to get through your head, Keynan? Starts with a *P*?"

"Umm…posthaste? We need to learn magic post—"

"*Patience!*" Her fingers twitch and I edge out of reach, just to be safe. "So help me—"

"Look at what I made, y'all!" Amari holds up a black-and-white sketch of an apple, the kind of thing I've seen him draw a hundred times on his tablet. Only this one is on real paper. And he's holding it like a real apple. It's round in his hand, but still black and white, flat and curved at the same time. My eyes water, trying to make sense of it.

Professor Touré's face grays, like she gulped down some of those blackberries from yesterday. *"Give me that!"*

"I was only—" Amari flinches as she crumples the paper-apple in a trembling fist.

The blaring intercom makes us jump. *"Proceed indoors immediately. A storm—"*

Touré's fingers slash across her tablet, and Kinder's voice cuts off. "Never inside Peerless! I've no skill in art, so… please. Don't do anything foolish." She shakes her head when Amari hands back the key. "Keep it."

"So who is going to teach him?" I ask.

"Not Professor Cartwright," Amari blurts out. "He clapped over my sphere drawing yesterday just because it was round. No highlights…no shade."

"I see what you did there," I whisper. He daps me back, rolling his eyes.

Leah inhales sharply. "Not all the professors know about magic?"

"Correct, once again," Touré says. "Along with staff and other first-years." Leah and I share a worried look. No wonder Professor Mendoza got so jumpy in the courtyard—she's not supposed to know a single speck about magic, let alone help us.

Touré studies me. "No more questions, finally? Good. You've got next. Tomorrow you're going to open a Break."

CHAPTER THIRTY

THE MOST DANGEROUS GIFT

My turn. Finally. Saving the best for last. I can't sleep that night—can't shake my nervousness. When I finally drift off, I dream I'm on the biggest stage ever, and everyone I've ever known is gathered for my next poem—only I don't know my lines. Ian's snoring is right on cue. Amari and Leah are embarrassed and won't look at me. My baba and mama are right in the first row, disappointed.

The people who attend Peerless are the folks who make a difference. Maybe even figure out these storms one day. No reason that can't be a Masters.

I give up on sleep and wander. I don't see any new artwork or leaky pipes from Slickback and Disco. That probably means their next mess is going to be extra big if I don't stop them soon. After they're dealt with, I'll rebuild

Peerless so it's even stronger than before. Just a little more time is all I need, maybe even this one last lesson.

My feet lead me to the courtyard, and I settle into one of the hammocks, rocking and listening to the crickets chirp. It's always easier to think here, but I can't shake how scared I was the last time I opened a Break. What if something goes wrong?

Whispers drift toward my perch. I peek my head up and peer past the tulips. Amari gives me a little wave, and Leah's right behind him.

"Hey fam." She squeezes my shoulder and cuts her eyes at Amari. "He couldn't sleep, either. You okay?"

"I'm fine."

Which isn't quite all the way honest. Leah's eyebrows rise, but I know how to change the subject. "How are you doing, though? I mean, really. That dodgeball game was—"

Leah juts out her chin. "I'm over it."

Amari and I exchange a look. "That's not how the Peerless Pact is supposed to work," he says. Ouch. He's right, but ouch. "You're not fine. We've seen the red eyes. The extra grouchiness. The skipped meals."

Leah hesitates. "I just...wish I could help her, but it's not like Yo ever listened to me about anything. My parents always say she's...gifted."

"As gifted as you?" I ask. "Please! You're doing writing

and dancing in your first year. If she wants to ignore you, her loss."

A smile tugs at Leah's lips. "You're right. Forget her. I've got you two for family now."

Amari gives me a dirty look and sighs—why is he so loud? "When we get Yo's attitude right, the first thing I'm going to ask her is what gets on Touré's nerves the most," he growls.

"Besides us?" I ask.

"I just got him calm again," Leah groans. "Don't get him started."

Amari glowers in the general direction of the library. "She's so messed up for this." The key to the art supply room dangles from a cord around his neck. He fiddles with it nonstop.

"You're mad she won't let you sleep in the closet?"

"I'm mad she gave me this key!"

"But you wanted the supplies."

"Don't you get it? This is a test. Using what I love against me. It's savage!"

Leah and I bust out laughing. We talk Amari down. By the time he's nodding his head, I'm feeling pretty good about things, too. Because even if tomorrow is a hot mess, I'll be okay. My friends will be there.

Classes the next day do their best to rattle me. The

watermelon seeds we soaked in Horticulture play hide-and-seek with Professor LaRue the whole lesson. My desk in Physics is warm to the touch for no obvious reason. By the end of class, I feel like an omelet someone forgot to flip.

Magic is everywhere it shouldn't be.

Between classes, students gossip around the teacher's lounge. "Nothing to see here," Professor Guerrero says gruffly. "Off to class."

Professor Wiley's eyes twinkle when I ask him what's up. "Just the best headmaster ever," he croons. "Remodeling the teacher's lounge for us. A quick peek won't hurt."

Wiley cracks the door wide enough for me to slip inside. My mouth falls open immediately. The carpet underfoot squelches with every step. The lounge's glass wall and door collapsed outside. Shattered panes lie on the patio and grass. A jagged hole in the countertop is all that's left of the sink. The fridge is gone. All of the furniture is in shambles, like...

"Something ate all of the metal," I moan.

A couch cushion wriggles and Slickback emerges, gnawing on a coiled spring. "Young blood! Miss me?"

"You little—stop eating up my school!"

"Hunger's too powerful a thing to ignore," he says knowingly. "Don't worry, though. I'll make sure open mouths get fed around here. Believe that."

"I'll stop you," I growl.

"Little old you?" He cackles, wiping tears from his blue eyes. "Gonna need a crew for that. Ain't got one of those around here, do ya?"

"I do, actually!"

"Scared of you. How's your freestyle these days? Still hopscotch-simple? Patty-cake basic?" A shiver crawls down my back. Slickback's words sound way too familiar. His slitted eyes drill into mine mischievously. "Does your crew know? How you freeze up? How you can't rhyme without your—"

The door to the hall squeaks open. Slickback freezes. I spin around to see Wiley peeking in. I turn back to the couch, but Slickback's vanished. "Gonna be great when it's finished!"

"For sure," I manage. Headmaster Kinder's convinced him this isn't a disaster. How? How does she keep everyone so oblivious to what's really going on?

"Best school ever." My tablet chirps, and Wiley gives me a sly look. "Hustle! I'll cover you on points if you're late. This time."

When classes finally wrap, I'm just relieved to meet back up with Amari and Leah. My crew. I like the sound of that.

We're amazing together, no matter what that goofy gecko said about me or my rhymes.

Our tablets guide us outside for my lesson. My shoes suddenly weigh a thousand pounds when I realize where Touré's waiting for us: the soccer field, where this whole mess started. Not one blade of grass is out of place—even the bench is back where it was before. My breathing goes jaggy, like I swallowed a bee whole and my stomach's trying to kick it out without getting stung. I swear I hear Joey's scream before the Break gobbled him up.

"Setup for a comeback, remember?" Amari murmurs.

"You've got this, Keymaster," Leah whispers.

"A wordsmith speaks truth to life, Keynan." Professor Touré's voice is solemn. "You can sculpt corrupt magic. But your words also move ideas right in and out of people. That's the most dangerous gift of all. The Glories let magic saturate them—their words, their every waking thought. Most historians suspect their madness didn't begin with the Failing—it started when magic swallowed their dreams."

Their dreams? Yikes. Sudden nausea thickens around my excitement. How many times have I been inspired with incredible rhymes that come out of nowhere? Sometimes those random lines are ten times better than anything I could come up with in my notebook. My poems are still mine. Right?

"Professor Touré?" Leah says softly, watching me. "What are Glories?"

"You uncovered something of the Wars of Illusion." A muscle in Professor Touré's face coils before she smooths it again with another deep breath. But there's no mistaking what I saw: she hates who she's talking about. Hates them down to the bone. Double yikes. "They were the people on the other side. Sorcerers who bit off more magic than they could chew. They were known by many names. Brights. Defedates. Illumined Ones. Glories. They fought to keep magic for just themselves, and nearly destroyed everything and everyone. They still wander the radiant waste, hopelessly poisoned by broken magic."

Leah clasps her hands together so tight the tendons stand out. Amari tries to play it off, but I know he's worried. Professor Touré's trying to scare us, and it's working. What if I had opened up that Break in my dorm room instead of outside Peerless?

She slides her attention back to me. "Now. Run back the same beat from when you accidentally opened that first Break, please."

The three of us share an alarmed look.

"Can I at least write a rhyme down first?" I squeak.

"If that's what it takes." She folds her arms.

I set to scribbling. The last time I tried writing on the spot like this, we got Slickback and Disco. I hope this one's okay. "Welp." I sit back on the very same bench as before. "Here goes nothing."

Bump. SLAP. Bump BUMP.

My hands won't stop shaking.

"Let me help," Leah says.

I start the beat again, and she picks it up immediately with nothing but her feet and hands: *Stomp. Clap. Stomp stomp. Clap.*

The air flexes, like the whole world is waiting on me. But it's okay. Leah and Amari are here. So I let the words go:

> *Here with my crew and it's a special day,*
> *Learning 'bout magic with Professor Touré.*
> *Got my bestie Starbreaker keeping up the beat.*
> *Amari on my right, drawing on his sheet*
> *Of paper for the art, cuz we got things to do.*
> *Call me Keymaster—we're the Peerless crew.*
> *So get your shoes laced, pick up the pace,*
> *We're all about fixing up the radiant waste.*

"That...was...*amazing!*" Amari grabs my shoulders. "I knew it. I *knew* someone couldn't carry that notebook around all day and not have one good thing come out of it."

"Thanks! But what do you mean, not one good—"

A small point of light flashes to life in the air between us. Amari yelps and hides behind Professor Touré. I don't blame him…it's a Break. Only the edges aren't ragged snaggleteeth ready to gobble everything up. No wind pulls me inside. The light is warm, smooth as sunshine reflecting off a still pond.

"You really did that, Keynan," Leah says earnestly. "You've got skills, forreal."

Wow, my face is burning. I've always been good—I'm mostly, *probably* sure—but it's nice when other folks say it. Especially Leah, because I know she would tell me if my rhymes were busted.

Professor Touré's voice makes us all jump. "What are y'all waiting for? These were just warm-ups! The real lesson is about to go down."

CHAPTER THIRTY-ONE

THE MURAL

We step into the Break. A whirlpool of light bends and splits around us. When my eyes adjust to the glare, the bubbly pancake plains I expected aren't there.

My breath frosts in front of my lips. Strange, twisting spires as tall as Peerless bristle around us, with long branches that make me think of a beaver dam. Bulbous orange windows cover them, glowing bright. The ground is yellow and orange and gold, crunchy under our feet.

Leah's legs are tensed, ready to sprint. "Was it like this for you before, Keynan?"

I force myself to take a deep breath and stop looking every direction at once for the monster. "Not even a little bit."

"Ground under our feet. Landscape at least pretending

at natural laws." Professor Touré peers at her tablet. "This is good. I think we're in Loop Land. It's a place of seasons, cycles, repetitions."

"So how big is the radiant waste?" Amari asks.

"Concepts like *big* will just give you a headache," Touré warns.

"But if we're going to stop the storms—"

"Repairing the radiant waste will take work. Real. Messy. Work. If you can't be patient, corrupt magic will twist everything you care about. We need to find out why Keynan's rhyme brought us here, and then leave."

Amari looks doubtful, but for once I'm on Touré's side. This place feels immense, bigger than a city, like I could walk all day and still not reach the end. No wonder the storms that boil out of here keep causing such a mess.

"What's that over there?" Leah asks, pointing. Beyond the weird spires, crumbly sidewalks and streets lead to some old buildings with dusty brick sitting above glass-fronted shops. The buildings look like they should be taller, but something came along and lopped off their upper floors. Blue and purple glitter floats through the air around them.

I shiver. Why would my rhyme bring us to this? "People built that with tools, not magic. It doesn't fit in with the rest."

"You're right." Touré's gaze flickers to me. "Ruins from before the Wars of Illusion. Let's go see."

We creep past the spires. Beats thrum from inside them—music—thumping the ground beneath our feet. Caterpillar-shaped shadows flitter past the orange windows. "Uh-oh," Amari whispers. "Block party?" Whatever it is, I feel like the spires are ready to burst.

"Keep your heads on a swivel," Touré says. "Loop Land won't stay quiet forever."

We enter the nearest building through a glass door. A tiny bell at the entrance rings. Every surface is caked in dust: empty shelves, counters, and flooring. Amari points out footprints. "Someone else has been here."

We follow the footprints and find old, tattered blankets and a torn backpack with a canteen inside. The stuff all feels newer, and out of place. Touré taps her lip. "A place to hide from the worst of the radiant waste."

"Peerless students?" Leah wonders aloud.

Touré doesn't meet her eyes. "No, not students from Peerless. But there are other schools still open, I'm sure of it, even if I've never left ours. Storms make it difficult to communicate. Drones run into...problems."

I rub my arms, remembering Eli's belly, the glowing gashes. "Their crews would need places to rest. Camps."

She gives me an approving glance. "And your rhyme took us straight to one."

"We could find them!" I say. Other schools with talented students and different ways of doing things? Maybe they've already figured out how to beat the storms! If my rhymes had a reason for making a Break here, this must be it. "Maybe we can work with them?"

"This won't be a camp for much longer," Leah points out. Some of that strange blue glitter is inside, too. Everywhere it rests on a surface, turquoise ice spreads out. "Whatever kept this place safe from the waste is fading."

"There's gotta be something else." I hustle back outside. "Something we're missing!"

"Stay together!" Touré barks. We circle the buildings, but there's no more signs of other crews. Just an old wall that might fall over from a hard sneeze.

Amari's transfixed. "Are you seeing this?"

I squint. "Lots of dusty bricks?"

"No... I need some stuff." He kneels down and pries a chunk of concrete from the battered sidewalk, then rises and begins using it like a pencil, scratching a picture into the brick wall.

Touré goes rigid. "Is that a...*door*? Don't—"

The brick wall sizzles with magic. Touré lunges forward too late—Amari swings it wide and disappears inside! Before I can truly panic, he returns with his art supplies an instant later. "It's a shortcut back to Peerless," I marvel. "Amari *drew* a Break!"

He's not done, either. Touré seethes but allows Amari to crack open paint buckets and pop the tops of spray cans. He paints in such a frenzy that sweat breaks out on his brow despite the chilly air. Leah and I trot back and forth, grabbing fresh supplies, new brushes, even lugging out a ladder so he can keep going.

Finally Amari steps back with a satisfied sigh. "Not sure where that came from," he admits. "It just felt right. Anyone know what it is?"

The mural is mostly purple and blue swirls that slowly *flow* over the wall. Most of it revolves around a series of dull reddish-gray angles, the only object with corners in the whole painting. The colors constantly move and shimmer, tugging at my memory. A flare of orange that ripples and changes colors grabs my eye—I've seen it before. "This is a tree in the radiant waste. I'd bet my best rhyme on it."

Leah's eyes narrow. "Does this ugly red-and-gray square remind you of anything?"

"Ugly?" Amari splutters. "Hello? I'm standing right here!"

Leah crooks her head sideways. "If you could see it from the top down? That's the building we just explored."

"The bodega," Touré supplies, her face tightening un-happily.

Leah points at a bright square point. "Then wouldn't this be Amari's Break?"

"The supply closet," I murmur. It all falls into place. "And this other one is mine, that goes back to the soccer field." Little circular bubbles simmer in the weird pink sludge around the fiery tree—that has to be the pancake plains. "You made a map for us!"

"It's not finished," Amari says, sulking. "It's making me itch."

"How can we help?"

Professor Touré backpedals, taking it all in. "I never ex-pected anything like this. What if we—" She stumbles over an open bucket of paint. Gray splatters across the ground.

"Aww, I needed that!"

Touré stares past my shoulder. "Oh, *no*. We opened a Rip."

I spin around. Ten steps away, a glowing, silvery split wavers into existence, about as long as my forearm. The squirming strand of light snakes off through the spires before our eyes. "Time for us to slide out...!" Leah grabs the handle to Amari's door and turns.

"No...stop!" Touré cries.

A shiver creeps down my back as the Rip *quivers*. Leah

256

yelps and yanks the door shut. The quivering stops, but the split has grown. I swallow. "It's bigger!"

"I barely had the door open!" Leah says defensively. "How was I supposed to know that would make it worse?"

"The Breaks are tugging at each other. They're not close together here…but they are back at the school." Professor Touré scrubs a hand over her face. "That Rip can slice Peerless open if I don't seal it. Carefully."

"We can help—"

"*No*, Keynan! I can stitch it closed, but I need this Break—" she takes in Amari's door "—to stay exactly as it is. I need the three of you to guard It."

"You're…leaving us?" Amari squeals.

"I—" Touré sighs deeply. We all exchange worried looks, but her voice is cool, calm, and collected. "I…can't do this alone. And no, Leah, I know what you're about to say. If you all come with me, who will watch the door? Something else could get inside the school."

Her eyes touch mine for an instant, and my heart dropkicks itself. She doesn't know if she can do it. We'll be safer here, with a way straight back to Peerless, if things go bad. She just won't say the scary part out loud.

"But Amari can…make this one go away," Leah protests. "Paint over it or something!"

Amari's voice is queasy. "I don't think it works like that."

"No. That door is the only thing anchoring the Rip in place. If it's gone…" Professor Touré wets her lips. "We can't risk Peerless. But if anything happens, go back through Amari's door and find Headmaster Kinder."

I don't even want to think about that Rip stretching wide. It's bright like a Break—does it open up to somewhere, too? Who knows what might pop out? Touré strides to the nearest edge of the Rip. We all hold our breath. She whispers urgently—so I can't borrow her rhymes, how rude. The Rip wobbles, the part near us shrinking and dimming.

Touré's shoulders sag in relief. "Hold tight. Don't do anything reckless. I'm trusting y'all can handle yourselves—I *know* you can! I'll return through Amari's door when it's done."

She follows alongside the rest of the Rip, leaving the three of us standing there.

"I'll bet we could close it all at once if we did it together," I grumble.

Leah snorts. "You heard her say *carefully*, right?"

"Like that's been working out."

"What is your deal?" she demands. "We're supposed to do this together."

"That's literally what I just said!"

"But you meant all of us doing what *you* want. You can't rush everything!"

"Y'all?" Amari murmurs. "This is—"

"You better not take his side!" Leah growls. "Not after making a Break without asking anyone. You're both acting like you can do anything!"

"We're all here, aren't we?" I fire back. "Touré wouldn't have taught us at all if someone didn't step up!"

"Stepping up?" Leah glowers. "Which part do you mean, exactly? Getting sucked into the radiant waste? Or the storms you say keep following you around—"

"Don't forget who set us up to be chandeller snacks when—"

"This Pact is *busted,* if you keep—"

"Y'all!" Amari shouts. He points to the supply closet door. The handle is wriggling. "I think someone's trying to lock it from the other side."

Leah and I exchange a terrified look and spring forward. Her hand closes on the handle a second before mine. The door swings wide. Professor Mendoza's eyes nearly fall out at sight of us standing in the radiant waste. "Keynan! Leah? What…what is this?"

Leah and I crush her in a hug. Our explanations spill over each other while Professor Mendoza gapes at the spires behind us.

"Why are you here?" Amari asks nervously.

"I wish I wasn't! I just came down to borrow a splash of red for the cheekbones, and…" Her eyes flick to Amari's mural. "Busy little beetles, I see."

"Can you help us?" I ask hesitantly. "Professor Touré should have been back by now."

"So she can go tell my business to the headmaster? Chickadees, that's more than I signed up for!"

"But we could make it up to you!"

"How?"

"Berries! Cantaloupe! Sunflower seeds!"

"Please. A year's supply wouldn't scratch the surface."

"A favor! I'd owe you big. We all would!"

Professor Mendoza stops backing toward the door. "Well, now. That's different. Let's discuss it, back in the courtyard. Safety first."

"But my mural!" Amari protests. "The map!"

Leah shakes her head obstinately. "We can't leave. We're supposed to be guarding this door."

A distant roar pierces the air. It's terrifying and sweetly beautiful, all rolled up in one horrible sound. I know that roar. "Oh." Mendoza swallows. "Oh my. That changes things."

Leah turns in a slow circle, trying to look every direction at once. "That's the monster?"

The air squeezes my lungs with every breath. My voice barely shakes past my lips. "It is."

Amari shudders. "Ratchet."

The spires' orange windows wink out one by one. The steady beats inside them cease. Overhead, there's a strange whistling, like a distant flock of birds. A bright blue octagon shape, thin as a sheet of ice, plummets from the sky. It lodges in a spire with a hollow boom, nearly slicing it in half. "It's snowing," Professor Mendoza moans. "Seasons. I despise this place!"

More massive snowflakes descend on us, huge buzz saws of interlocking geometric patterns, each wide as a basketball court. We scatter, shouting. Dust and chunks of ice spray everywhere as they slam to the ground. One carves into the wall. Crumbly bricks and concrete fall off in ragged chunks. Little frosty bears leap down from the snowflakes' centers. Barely tall as my knees, they sniff the air, let out adorable battle cries, and trundle toward the spires.

"What are those?" Leah cries.

"Who cares? Let's get outta here!" I yell.

"The closet is blocked!" Mendoza wails. She holds her stomach, breathing in small gasps. "They collapsed the wall!"

"Keynan, rhyme us a way through!"

This is it. My time to shine. Mendoza is panicking. No telling when—or if—Touré is coming back. They're depending on me to get away from these things, to be safe, and I...freeze.

I can't think of the first thing to rhyme.

"Perfect." Leah turns away, peering toward Touré's path. The disappointment in her voice curdles in my stomach. "We can still follow her, right, Professor? Get back to our first Break?"

"More time in the waste?" Mendoza shivers. "I suppose we've no other choice."

"No way am I leaving my map behind!" Amari huffs. "It's not done!"

Professor Mendoza and I each grab an arm and drag until Amari's legs start churning. A baby-blue bear hops down from a snowflake with a cute snarl. I squeal. It's tiny—but the teeth on this thing! Little icicles! Mendoza inhales fearfully, ready to unleash a scream. She's more worthless for rhyming than me. Before her voice cracks the air, a snowball busts the frosty bear right in the forehead. It goes cartwheeling aside.

"Would y'all come on!" Leah shouts. She's already packing another snowball. We run straight through the spires for the Break. Pumpkin-headed creatures burst out of the structures, bouncing like centipedes made from a dozen basketballs strung together. Blue fire lights their eyes as they swarm toward the invading frosty bears.

Something is wrong. We don't see any signs of the Rip on the way, so Touré must have sealed it. But she's nowhere to be found. Another roar rumbles the ground as we reach the glowing circle of the Break and spill back onto the soccer field. "Where's Touré?" I cry.

"I'm sure she's fine!" Mendoza says. She's still standing on the other side of the Break. Why didn't she follow us through? "Time is strange in the waste. She's probably on her way to the closet door, unless…" She squeezes her eyes shut, leaving the worst unspoken. "But we must make sure that door is closed! Not a word to anyone that I was ever here!" She closes my Break with a breathless rhyme.

We just stand there for a moment, staring at the air where the Break used to be. It's well past dark outside as we trot back toward Peerless. "Mendoza in the radiant waste, by herself?" Amari murmurs. "I don't like this."

"I know." I can barely process what just happened.

"Why would Touré leave Keynan's Break open if—"

"I know!" I lick my lips. "Do you…think we should close Amari's, too?"

"Can you, though?" Leah asks softly.

The door to Peerless bangs open, and Professor Touré races out. "What happened! Are y'all okay?"

I speak up first. "Amari's Break got blocked by rubble when these giant snowflakes hit—we thought it was better to try for a sure thing instead of making another Break."

"Giant snowflakes…?" Touré rubs her temples. "You made the best of an awful choice."

"Professor, what happened?" Amari asks. "Why would you leave the Break open?"

"I didn't. It…wouldn't close." She frowns worriedly. "The waste is already unpredictable. The Rip must have changed things even more somehow. When I opened Amari's door, I didn't see any of you, so I sealed it and hoped you would make your way back here. This isn't how lessons are supposed to go. I… I'm sorry."

"It's okay," I say in a small voice. Touré? Apologizing? This is way weirder than anything we saw in the radiant waste. Leah's and Amari's eyes feel like hot coals pressed in my forehead, but they don't bring up Mendoza's help, either. "You were doing what you thought was best for Peerless."

"Same as you three," Touré admits grudgingly. "Amari, Leah—relax. You did well. And you can stop holding in that smile, Keynan. You made it."

We made it! We actually dipped into that nightmare space and came out without a scratch. "Did anyone get frostbit? Get it? Frost—"

All three of them groan.

264

"Any more jokes from you, and I'm taking points from Wiley Squad." Touré points us toward the courtyard. "I'll join you shortly. Sit right under the oak tree, it'll keep corrupt magic from sticking to you. I'll explain how it works later. It's the most important part of Peerless."

We nod innocently, pretending we didn't already know. Once we reach the courtyard, we plunk down on the bench in the tree's shadow. I'm grateful for the cool and quiet since my mind is racing. Touré doesn't know she closed Amari's door on Mendoza. What good is not snitching if she's stuck because we're keeping her secret?

"What's that?" Leah points out something I almost sat on. A piece of my notebook paper, some neat origami folds making it look like a stretching cat. I unfold it curiously to reveal a note:

If you're reading this, you're safe and I'm safe, too. But how can you trust a professor who left behind your crew?

"Mendoza!" I wheeze. "She's good! She got back out!"

Amari lets out a woot, and Leah slumps onto the trunk. We were all so close to snapping on each other in the waste, but we're okay again. We were just scared. The Peerless Pact is shaky but still holding on.

"Thanks, Leah." Amari stretches his arms wide for a hug. "You saved us. I'm sorry, y'all. That mural… I've never felt like that before. Like if I stopped painting, my heart might stop beating."

"It was worth it," Leah acknowledges after a moment. "We learned a whole bunch more stuff. Touré's right, about taking it slow."

"Slow? Actually—"

Professor Touré returns with a cart full of dinner, so I swallow my clapback for now, even though Leah's wrong. We're all starving. Soup's Soup, served in a still-hot bread bowl, makes my stomach rumble. "That could've gone better," Touré declares. "But it could have gone a whole lot worse. I've never been in Loop Land for a season change, and I hear spring is even worse than the winter you experienced. Hang out here until lights out, so we can be sure any corruption is purged."

"Shouldn't you stay here with us?" I ask worriedly.

"I've got a few places to do the same, believe me." She hesitates. "It's a shame we lost your map, Amari. The area was completely destroyed." Professor Touré reaches behind her back, then flicks her arm forward. Blue flashes through the air. *Thwock!* A snowflake throwing star is half buried in the oak tree's bark above our heads. "Nasty little things. We're lucky their skirmish didn't spill into Peerless.

You handled yourselves, but I'll need to prep before your next…lesson. And fall break is just two weeks away. The recital is coming up quick. The magic that protects Peerless is under more strain than ever before. The recital will be essential to replenishing it."

Amari gives us a smug look. "If we're in line, magic is in line."

"Exactly. I need all of you at your very best for the recital—Peerless needs you. So finish your homework. No more detention sit-ins. And not a word to your friends."

I wait until she's nice and far off. "She's supposed to be the teacher, but she's just as shook as we were."

"Careful and scared ain't the same," Leah snaps. "*I'm* shook, and I haven't even seen the monster yet."

Amari shudders. "How'd you get away last time, Keynan?"

"I didn't. Y'all pulled me out, remember?"

We finish our dinner in silence. The courtyard lamps dim, revealing a wonder: filaments of light snuggled in our brown skin, pores glowing faintly like someone sprinkled us with stardust. Corrupt magic. We're drenched in the stuff. The motes rise steadily toward the oak tree, turning the air green and purple and gold. Even the blue throwing star dissolves into a sparkling mist.

"It's so pretty," Leah breathes.

By the time we find hammocks and wrap up homework, the light show's over. Leah's exhausted and still a little salty, while Amari is moping over his lost map, so I don't bring up Touré. But Professor Mendoza's warning won't stop scampering around my brain. When Leah mentioned other schools while we were in Loop Land, Touré changed the subject quickly—why? Worse than that... I think she knocked over Amari's paint on purpose. Something on that map scared her, something Amari was going to finish. And Touré didn't want us to see it.

CHAPTER THIRTY-TWO

NOT A WHISPER

After that first lesson, I gobble up every free moment between classes to write new rhymes. Poems about frosty bears minding their business, hibernating in winter instead of leading snowflake air strikes. About finding other schools and even other crews. Making Breaks that open easy as Amari's door. Cleansing corrupt magic from the radiant waste, like the oak tree does for us.

And most of all?

Poems about catching Slickback and Disco, before they ruin anything else. They're too smart to practice on—my trap for them needs to be perfect on the *first* try. I spend time in the courtyard whenever I can. I've already seen too much of what busted magic can do. I don't want it anywhere near my rhymes.

In the dining hall one morning, I even get an idea for how to fight the monster. I finish refilling my orange juice and hurry back to jot it down. Only...my notebook won't open. The pages are stuck together! Sticky sweetness tickles my nose.

It's unreadable. Ruined. My stomach clenches like I'm about to throw up.

There's an ugly snicker behind me. Dez. "At least now you'll never lose it again!"

I try opening to a page, any page. It rips before I can make out a single word. Hot tears sting my eyes. "All of my best rhymes...they're gone!"

He flinches. The dining hall stills—I didn't realize I was shouting. "Keynan?" Professor Mendoza calls out sharply from the oatmeal bar.

"Maybe now you won't mess with other people's grades like it's a joke!" Dez sneers. "Now we're even."

Those rhymes were more than just new magic. Those were poems my parents clapped over, stories from around Bizzy Block. I'm so mad I could shake him. Or pop that smirk off his gloating face! Wait. Can I actually fight? My baba showed me how to throw a punch, but this is different. And part of me is afraid to admit Dez isn't wrong. I got so caught up with magic and rhymes, I didn't even bother apologizing to him.

Still…no one touches the notebook and lives to brag about it! I snatch Dez's water bottle and dump it on his head. Water splashes his tablet. The screen flickers heroically for a few seconds and then winks completely off.

We both gape at it. Dez's voice goes shrill. "You *didn't*."

Students yank out tablets on every side of us to record. *"Fight, fight, fight!"*

This is really going down. We both stand, but Professor Mendoza elbows through the crowd to plant herself between us, juggling a bowl of fruit and her usual giant mug of tea. "Oh, no. I've been waiting a month for Soup to put out honeydew. You two are *not* about to mess up my breakfast! Not today!" she huffs. *"Silence and manners, best do what I say, not a whisper of violence for the rest of the day!"*

Mendoza's rhyme tingles on my skin like peppery sunshine. Actually? Things will be fine. Dez can go bother someone else. *My* tablet isn't soaked, at least. So why not do some extra homework? I even study at lunch, where Soup makes those burritos with the yummy salsa again, and Amari and Leah wave their hands back and forth across my face. Rude. Ian does the same thing before we go to sleep.

The next morning, Slickback gnaws on one of the sink's faucets while I brush my teeth. "Whoo, boy! She did a number on you, young blood!" He wiggles his tail right in my face. Rude. "Magic ain't going so great, is it? I told you. Bet you wish you could grab me right now, huh? Shake me like a salt shaker?"

"That would be mean," I hear myself say.

"We didn't start off so hot, but I can't lie. You growing on me. It's too bad, too. Me and Disco been chopping it up with one of your other friends. You know the one. Big, scary thing. Unforgettable claws? All that anguished roaring? Turns out we all agree this little school of yours needs a makeover. If you thought that teacher lounge was a mess, just you wait!"

Breakfast in the courtyard sounds nice. After that I'll—

Wait a minute. I glance around me. When did I get in Writing class? My notebook is still ruined. Shouldn't I be mad about that? A nudge in the ribs turns me to Leah, her face scrunched up in worry. "Are you finally done sleep-walking? You scared the mess out of us! What's with your clothes? Did you sleep in them?"

I open my mouth to argue and stop. My clothes are wrinkled and I smell...oof. I need a shower. The last thing I really remember is—

My eyes snap to the front of the room. Beyond the students laughing and chattering, Professor Mendoza smiles at me over her mug. I swallow and approach her desk. "Such good behavior since I saw you last."

"You...you used..."

She puts a finger to her lips. "Oh, shush. Better if that silly boy ruined all of your progress, got you back in trouble? Hmm? What do you think would've happened if *she* had found out? Or Touré?"

"Nothing good," I admit.

"Exactly. Now, more importantly. That night, after our... field trip. What happened at the oak tree?"

"It was just like you said!" Her eyebrows rise, and I bring my voice back down to a whisper. "We saw the corrupt magic floating right...right out of us. We didn't leave until it stopped."

"That's good. Very, very good." Mendoza looks relieved. "If you three aren't safe and—" She cuts off with a strangled sound.

A hush falls over the class. Headmaster Kinder strides in. Her eyes latch on to me. "Professor."

"Headmaster."

"Is Keynan causing problems today?"

"None so far." Professor Mendoza's fingers are laced so tightly together, I'm surprised her knuckles don't pop. "Anything I need to worry about?"

"We'll see soon enough. Keynan, come with me."

I gather up my tablet, exchanging a panicked look with Leah before following Kinder into the hallway. The headmaster's eyes are bloodshot, like she's been taking long walks in a dust storm or got tricked into taking a bath in lemon juice. Her clothes are as fancy as usual, but almost as rumpled as mine.

"You've had a rocky start," she says abruptly. "I'm glad Professor Touré's steered you in the right direction."

"Glad enough for me to come back next year?"

Her eyes narrow. Why? Why did I allow those words to fall out of my face?

"Don't get ahead of yourself. Everything depends on your performance in the all-school recital. Are you prepared?"

"I am! I just don't want to let anyone down."

"Then prove it. The recital is just a week away. Fall short and you'll be back in *Build-A-Scholar* for good."

Our tablets chirp for lunch, and I'm grateful that she marches off without another word. I hurry to the dining hall. I'm so confused. If she knew about Slickback and Disco, I'd be home right now. Leah shakes her head when I share the whole encounter with her and Amari.

"She's trying to scare you," Amari declares. "But we know why everyone's so pressed about the recital. My professors make it sound like the only thing keeping Peerless together."

"After Keynan's poem and that brick, we know they're not lying," Leah observes. "She didn't mention magic once?"

"Nope. And she won't have to for a while," I say glumly. "I'll need weeks to remember all of those lost rhymes."

"Longer than that if you have another day like yesterday," Amari observes. "We thought you needed to move in under the oak tree."

"I...I might." Their eyes widen when I tell them about Mendoza's rhyme. "I know how it sounds. But I was *so mad* at Dez. She got my mind right. Really."

The two share a long, doubtful look. "If you say so," Amari relents reluctantly. "What if you hadn't snapped out of it?"

"I did. That's the whole point. But y'all... I still think Kinder might keep Peerless open. Show her what my magic can do, and I'll bet she will!"

Leah gives me an unreadable look. "*Your* magic?"

"*Our* magic," I say sheepishly. The silence stretches until Amari mutters something under his breath. We're definitely not okay. She's still mad about the waste, but I wasn't wrong—we need to learn faster.

"Anyway. I just wish those frozen teddy bears hadn't ruined the wall." Leah grimaces. "We lost the map."

"Did we?" Amari grins and digs in his backpack, pulling

out a smaller version of the map on a little canvas! "Not a perfect copy, but…"

"Are you kidding me?" I exclaim. "It's exactly how I remember!"

"Well, I've got a pretty good memory. I didn't get into Peerless just because I'm cute. I only wish I could remember the parts I didn't finish."

The colors shift and change before our eyes, just like his mural—almost like it's updating itself. We pore over it excitedly. There's more little squares like the bodega, and we're convinced that means more camps.

Amari's eyes narrow. "Keynan. I know that look."

I stop tapping my lip. "What?"

"Whatever you're thinking, stop thinking it."

"But also say it out loud," Leah adds. "So we can tell you what a bad idea it is."

"Okay, fine. I think we need to go in the radiant waste by ourselves." I tell them about my suspicion, that Touré knocked over the paints on purpose. "They're hiding magic from us, trying to keep us safe. But there's more to it, somehow."

"What I want to know is—" Leah gives me her best stink eye "—can you go more than one day without causing new problems? Why can't you just wait for the recital? Slow down, for once?"

"Last time didn't go so well," Amari points out. "Even with *two* professors helping us."

"The professors are never gonna help us forreal with Kinder hanging over their heads. We can do this, y'all! I know you're salty with me, Leah, but when will we see each other again if they take away Peerless? If we're gonna be a crew, it's up to us to make it real."

CHAPTER THIRTY-THREE

WITHOUT A SCRATCH

We dive so hard into planning, I spend more time in the courtyard than my actual dorm room. They needed serious convincing, especially Leah, and I worry we're just wasting time. Sure, I can write rhymes that stop frosty bears from nuzzling us to death. Amari can draw stuff that gets us across the radiant waste faster. And Leah's moves can do slight work—I guess—little things like bending time and space. I'm glad she's on Team Keynan—she's probably ready to level up after Yo was so mean to her in PE. I don't think she's as sad about her sister anymore, and that's good for us because we've got bigger problems to fix. For Bizzy Block, and all of our homes. There's no ignoring the truth anymore. Storms are getting worse.

But for each bit of weirdness my crew can sidestep,

there's a hundred more things waiting to happen in the radiant waste—and we won't know until we see them. I can't write that fast. So memorized rhymes will have to do—because I can't be the one to let down the crew.

"I miss my bed," I grumble, pushing peas around my lunch tray.

"This was your idea," Leah replies halfheartedly. Amari grunts what might be agreement.

I spot Ian just leaving the food line. He looks odd talking and joking with other first-years, practically himself again. Our eyes meet. I gesture to our table, inviting him, but he gives his head a tiny shake and goes the opposite way. Like he's looking for a table that's furthest from ours. We're still friends—I think. But magic made it all messy.

Ian suddenly trips. His bowl of Soup's Soup goes sailing and splatters across the floor.

"Where are your tears, child? Wasting my masterpiece like that!" Soup fusses so loud over his mop that we hear him clear across the dining hall.

"Y'all. *The floor*," Leah whispers. Broth, bits of noodle, carrots, and celery sink through the tile like a secret drain sucked it away. Soup's mopping turns frantic. I shiver, realizing he's afraid of sinking through the floor, too.

"Y'all hear that?" Amari asks. Leah and I share a con-

279

fused glance. "Exactly. Nothing. No headmaster on the intercom."

He's right. Magic is burrowing even deeper into Peerless. Students eat all around us, clueless, just like Touré warned. *There's so much corrupt magic in the world now, most people think it's supposed to be there. Or they lie to themselves to hide what their own eyes are telling them.*

And it's my fault. Slickback and Disco are breaking down our school from the inside out. Soup's finished cleaning before I can offer to help. As he hurries off, holding the mop at arm's length like it might bite him, inspiration smacks me in the face. "That's what we're missing," I breathe. Amari and Leah lean in curiously. "The radiant waste is, what? Big as a city, at least? Busted magic, in every brick or blade of grass. We need to fix the magic itself—not the things it's messed up."

Amari nods. "You're right. It could take us our whole lives to restore that one old building."

"And it could go back the way it was, soon as we leave," Leah adds reluctantly. "So we're going to fix the whole thing? Just like that?"

"If it were that easy, someone would have done it already. Let me think on it some more."

Leah shakes her head. "Shouldn't we worry about catching those little monsters from the hidden wing first? They wrecked my dance studio this morning—ate the metal off our barres! Maybe it's time to tell Touré. If I hadn't been so obsessed with finding Yolanda…"

"Not yet," I mumble. "We can still catch them ourselves! Imagine Kinder's face when she finally sees what our crew can do? We'll be like honorary professors after that, watch."

Amari glares at me, but our tablets signal the end of lunch, so we finish off our buttery rolls on the way to class. Leah eyes me before we go our separate ways, and she doesn't sound like someone's dragging her words out when she speaks. "You still get on my nerves, but you're not half bad at this stuff."

"What stuff?"

"Moving people around with your words. Keep it up, Keymaster."

If only it were that easy. Ever since my talk with Headmaster Kinder, all of Peerless has shifted to a new level. More lessons. More homework. More group projects—I'm not paired with Dez again, thank goodness. Everyone is focused on throwing as much work at us as possible to prepare for the recital, so the three of us barely get a moment to ourselves. I can't even complain, not when the fate of Peerless hangs on the recital repairing some of the broken magic. Unless we can figure out something better.

Whenever I get half a second with Leah and Amari, in

the halls between classes or brushing our teeth before bed, they've got the same frazzled look I see in the mirror. Even my reflection is too tired to prank me.

Professor Touré preaches patience whenever we cross paths. "I've been working on something special for y'all. Just keep doing what you're doing."

"But we could help with the power outages!"

She shares one of her tired smiles. "I've no doubt you would, Keynan. Be patient!"

I always smile back, but it's hard to ignore the worry hiding behind her eyes. I don't blame her, either. Blackouts hit Peerless almost every other day now. Guilt tangles my stomach up like old fishing line every single time because my magical creatures are to blame. How much more of this can Peerless take? The storm sirens are tested nonstop, with Kinder's voice droning about safety over the intercom once the drills are over.

One night after dinner, Amari pulls out his redrawn map in the dining hall. He insisted we all eat the same thing, black-eyed peas and rice. "My granny says they're lucky," he explains. "It's not a new year, but we need all the help we can get."

I go along with it. "So, what's up? I've got rhymes to write."

"The waste is changing." He points to an indistinct blob.

"Remember where the mural was? That camp we found by it is gone. Like someone smudged it with an eraser."

Leah nods. "Another one is, too. I remember because it was furthest away from Keynan's Break. Who would do that?"

We pore over it tensely for more changes. "That burning tree I saw the first time isn't where it used to be, either."

Amari gives a sheepish laugh. "I don't know if it's a live stream, y'all. But isn't it weird?"

Leah and I touch eyes. No doubt she remembers Amari's drawing of Kinder as much as I do. "I found the tree," she says, pointing. "You were looking in the wrong place. That thing is something else." She's right—my smudge of light is no tree, and it starts sliding around on the canvas like butter on a hot skillet.

I blink. "Am I the only one who saw that thing move?"

Amari licks his lips. "Nope."

Before our eyes, the smudge of light sharpens. It meanders around the canvas, from the Pancake Plains to Loop Land. I recognize more details. The turquoise-and-violet gleam. That loping prowl, like a hunting cat. Three lashing tails. "Y'all!" I exclaim. "Those black-eyed peas actually worked! Now the monster can never sneak up on us." They both give me a blank look. "Don't you see it? We can keep eyes on it now!"

"Ratchet?" Amari asks in disbelief.

Abruptly, the monster shape on the map stops and tilts its head. Two glaring green eyes appear. "I think it heard you," Leah breathes.

The monster becomes bigger and bigger, as if prowling toward us, like it could pounce off the page. "Do something!" Leah shrieks.

It suddenly swipes out a paw. Six slashes tear across the canvas before the whole thing bursts into flame! We leap back with a shout. Amari flings his water on the canvas, and Leah dumps the rest of her peas on it for good measure. The bowl settles and stills, upside down.

We wait, holding our breath. Nothing emerges from beneath.

The lights wink out, and I squeal.

"Proceed indoors immediately. A storm is approaching the school grounds. This is not a drill."

"Maybe...wait before drawing another one," Leah ventures.

"You think?" Amari says dryly. "I can't believe I'm saying this, but Keynan is right. We can't just mop away the busted magic. It won't last."

That night I dream of the monster clawing into Peerless while I cower under the oak tree and write horrible rhymes. *Me and Disco been chopping it up with one of your other friends.* Slickback perches in the branches, jawing at me as Ratchet stalks closer. *Turns out we all agree this little school of yours needs a makeover.*

Grouchy and exhausted, I wake up to my tablet's chirping, and insistent knocking on my door. The tablet alerts me that the power's still out and classes are canceled again.

Amari's at the door, wide-eyed. "Are you okay? I was about to get Touré!"

"What? I'm fine."

"But that sound…!"

"Oh. Ian snores."

Amari grimaces. "Sorry. Come straight down to breakfast when you're ready. I can't stop thinking about those camps in the waste. I've got to show y'all something."

After a quick breakfast, I join up with Leah and Amari. We slip through dim Peerless halls to emerge outside, near Touré's supply sheds. This time, we don't go anywhere near the fence and the breathing orchard. Instead, we skirt the wall to another nook that holds dozens of saplings, most of them taller than me. Their planters are spaced in neat rows.

"You don't want to find camps in the waste," I say slowly. "You want to make one!"

Amari glances at us nervously. "I know it's last minute, but the time just feels right."

I barely keep from rolling my eyes. This sounds exactly like Leah's argument for going to the hidden wing! But everyone gets salty when I'm the one improvising?

"Who knows how much of a difference this will actually make?" Leah asks. "The oak tree is huge, and old."

"There's a tree across the street at home that still has my old treehouse," Amari acknowledges. "I'll bet it keeps magic out of my whole neighborhood!"

"We've got an orange tree," I muse. "And all kinds of smaller ones and shrubs around Bizzy Block."

"Palm trees ring our apartments." Leah purses her lips.

"But these trees are basically babies," I point out.

"We won't take them all."

"I say we go for it," Leah declares. "Let's make *something* good happen for once. All we need now is the right rhyme."

Okay, so, yikes. No pressure. I set to writing in the new notebook Amari found for me in the art supply closet. He and Leah load shovels and the saplings and loose soil into the old wheelbarrows he's hunted down. He slings art supplies over his shoulder, and Leah loops a hose over hers. We wheel toward the fence, away from school grounds. Writing on my tablet feels clunky, but I get something ready:

We need a place to remake with style and grace
Gotta stay on Earth not outer space
gonna keep it real so done with the fake
no time to waste, so give me a Break!

A rippling hole of blues and pinks shivers open. I swallow. We're doing this without Professor Touré; she's going to be disappointed. But exhausted as she's been, maybe it's time someone has her back, too.

Leah marches right through. She still believes in me. "Come on, Keymaster," Amari says, disappearing after her.

I heft my wheelbarrow but hesitate when I notice a metallic glint on the ground. The trinket Leah found, Yolanda's necklace. Probably slipped from her pocket. I scoop it up, and a noise makes me twist around, causing my wheelbarrow to tip. I steady it before the saplings tumble, spinning back in time to see the door to Peerless closing shut.

Someone saw us.

Worse, they saw the Break.

CHAPTER THIRTY-FOUR

TI ESREVER DNA TI PILF

I barrel into the crush of light. "Y'all, we've got a problem! Someone saw the Break!"

I spoke too soon. We've got problems. Plural. Amari and Leah are running…away from me. But they're *facing* me, and their arms and legs are pumping the wrong way. Slow and jerky, like they're swimming backward through jelly.

"!kcab yats, NanyeK" Leah shouts.

Umm. Huh? How am I supposed to rhyme if the radiant waste is jacking up our words? I fight down a moment of panic. The Break brought us inside a building with gleaming white walls and tall windows. Four jagged bronze statues stand atop pillars on the other side of the long room. But these statues are *moving*, prancing in tight circles, beckoning Amari and Leah to them with shining claws. One pretends at a fishing line, reeling them closer.

I race forward to grab them, but the walls flash a brilliant rainbow of colors. Amari and Leah change direction and run toward me at full speed! "Stay back, Keynan!" Leah shouts.

"We need Professor Touré!" Amari hollers. "It's some kind of trap!"

The walls flash again. My friends slide back toward those creepy statues.

"!part fo dnik emos s'tI" Amari hollers. "!éruoT rossef-orP deen eW"

"!kcab yats, nanyeK" Leah shouts.

They're...stuck! But every time the magic rewinds them, they get a little closer to the statues' waiting talons. I've got to rhyme something fast!

Leave my friends alone, we're just trying to get along
We don't need you clawing—

Nothing happens. The building walls ripple—it's laughing at me! *"Where's this Keymaster I've heard so much about, hmm?"* A musical voice comes from everywhere and nowhere at once. *"I thought you'd be back in this piece, doing thangs I ain't never seen!"*

"I'm right here! Can you maybe not eat my friends?"

One of the statues' claws grasps Amari's sleeve. He screams. Bronze seeps over his arm and swallows him up. No, no, no! He's turning into a statue!

The walls flash—now my friends are running forward, and Amari's arm is unharmed. "We need Professor Touré! It's some kind of trap!"

I've got to fix this! My brain feels like it's folding in half, but I try another rhyme:

> *Forwards or backwards, I'm running out of patience so*
> *No invitations to my parties if you don't let my friends go!*

Nothing, again! Why are my rhymes trash? The walls flash. Amari slides backward. Leah's not far behind. Their eyes are fixed on mine, begging. They're right. We need help. I turn back to the Break, but long-legged figures in top hats and neon suits slide in front of it, wagging their fingers, with gleaming eyes full of midnight stars.

"That's it? I heard you could spit!" the walls tease.

The statues smile, like they already know my rhymes are going to fall short. I'm scared of the fear and doubt

I see in my friends' eyes. Something cracks open inside me, a whisper that reminds me: I'm Keynan Masters and I'm made of strong stuff.

> *Why you lurking in the shadows?*
> *Stop circling the battle!*
> *Or I'll put my rhyme down, flip it and reverse it.*
> *.ti esrever dna ti pilf ,nwod emyhr ym tup ll'I rO*

The statues let out a delighted howl and disappear in puffs of rainbow smoke. Leah and Amari stagger forward, and I catch them awkwardly. "No one's hurt? Yes! Group hug!"

"I was so scared!" Leah cries, pulling away from me. "Where were you? You should've been with us!"

Amari shudders, panting and wide-eyed. "It felt like we were underwater for days. I couldn't move!"

"I'm so sorry, y'all, I saw—"

The musical voice bubbles out of the walls again, fading. "We'll meet again, Peerless Crew. Don't you have work to do? You better do it! Do it do it do it—"

Rainbow shimmers outline a door into the next room. We snatch up our wheelbarrows and hurry for it. I slow, and Leah bumps into me. "What's with you? Move! We need to get out of here."

"Look at all this cool stuff!" I say.

Along the walls, there are stands full of instruments I've only seen in pictures: rusty trombones and trumpets, a purple guitar caked in dust, and more. One holds a device wide as a lunch tray, with two plate-sized circles on top. Something about those tickles my memory. Buttons and knobs cover the rest. Amari's eyes won't leave it. "I think we need that. Don't ask me why!" he says.

"It feels important to me, too," I admit.

Leah's ready to shake us both. "Are you serious right now?"

We hurry on reluctantly. The radiant waste outside the museum is flat ground blanketed in fog thick as pink-and-purple cotton candy. Leah stops short just past the doors, tugging on our hose. "This is as far as it will go."

Amari wipes his face. "We better get started."

We set to digging while Leah looks out. They're both scared after the museum. The ground is spongy, but every so often my shovel sparks blue in the hole. Amari tries to fish out one of the rocks and yelps when it leaps out of his hand, rolling off into the haze.

"Nope." He slides two steps back. "Why are we wasting time on this when you can rhyme us some holes?"

"It's not like I have a notebook page dedicated to digging holes! Why don't you *draw* us some holes?"

"One of y'all do *something*," Leah growls.

Touré's lecture rumbles in my head. *Repairing the radi-*

ant waste will take work. Real. Messy. Work. If you can't be patient, corrupt magic will twist everything you care about. But my friends are depending on me. I won't risk them getting hurt again because I waited. Better get used to rhyming on the spot.

I can do this. Leah starts out a beat before I even ask. I get a feel for it and throw out some words:

> I need this ground to open up with a quickness.
> Just enough for these trees to set the stage for the realness.
> My crew, my school, we hail from the Peerless.
> Here to set things right, got no time for deftness.
> So please step left—you see these sleeves rolled up!
> Give us a semester—maybe less—we'll get this magic sewed up—

The ground rumbles. Six neat holes form a circle around us, perfectly spaced to allow room for trees to grow. Amari and Leah stare at each other, then back at me.

"I know, not my best," I say defensively, "but I got the job done, okay?"

"It's not even like that," Amari says. "I think you're just scratching the surface."

"We need to thank Dez," Leah adds. "Losing that notebook might be the best thing to ever happen to you. You were talking to magic like an old friend, instead of just making it do what you want."

Amari and I grab our first sapling and set it in the ground. "There's nothing in our textbooks about talking to plants, but the tomatoes my mama hums around taste a little better in the salsa," I say. "I think we're the ones who make magic good or bad. Even if the Glories broke it here in the radiant waste, that's not what it really is."

Leah nods thoughtfully. "Just because the Glories screwed up doesn't mean we will."

"Right!"

We finish transplanting, taking turns holding the sapling trunks upright while the others shovel in soil. We have just enough. Leah gives them all a good soaking.

Shimmering points of light drift out of the haze and into the saplings, just like the oak tree in the courtyard. We gasp. The ground beneath our feet blurs, too. Dirt and chunks of asphalt replace the spongy honeycomb.

"See?" I can't help but grin. "This was so worth coming here!"

"But how much busted magic can they handle?" Leah asks worriedly. "What if it makes the trees sick?"

"Then we'll just have to bring more. Lots more." Amari

sketches on his tablet, mesmerized by the trees. They're bright enough to catch fire.

Will they need extra water, I wonder? The haze around us is thinning, revealing more gray-and-brown ground beneath it. "This is definitely the *waste* part of the radiant—"

A roar snaps our heads around. Red lightning sizzles through the distant fog. I see a familiar loping animal shape, moving scary fast, right for us.

"We should have left when we had the chance!" Leah wails.

I push them both back toward the museum and our Break. "We gotta go, y'all!"

Amari hesitates. "But our stuff—"

"Leave it!"

"No, brick brain! The hose will lead Ratchet straight to Peerless!"

"Not if we close the Break first. Come on!"

We sprint for the museum. We're not even halfway there before Ratchet is on us. I gotta do something, but rhymes won't come! We scream in terror—we're all the way caught—but the monster doesn't pounce. It ignores us completely, so we race into the museum.

Inside I risk a look back. Amari stops, too. "It's like a big crystal gargoyle," he whispers.

Golden footprints boil around our saplings as Ratchet

stalks angrily, sniffing and growling. The monster abruptly rips a sapling out of the ground with a snarl and spray of dirt, swallowing it whole. Spongy material replaces the shattered concrete and asphalt as the monster bites at more trees.

"All of our work," I groan. "Why did it do that?"

Leah tugs at us. "*Please*, before it sees us." Tears wet the corner of her eyes. We steal back through the museum, following the hose to our Break. We're back on Peerless grounds, but the knot in my shoulders doesn't loosen as Leah starts looping the hose through.

She gives it one last jerk and the rest of the hose flops around her feet, but shimmering golden flakes are melted into the rubber. Amari whistles. I close the Break with a quick rhyme, trying not to shiver. The gold is the same shade as Ratchet's footprints.

Amari swallows. "It was right there! Right on the other side!"

Leah wags a finger under my nose. "I told you Ratchet would follow us! Can't listen to anybody, and for what? Our trees are gone."

"Why is this all my fault?" My voice crackles with anger, and I throw Leah's glower right back at her. "This whole thing was Amari's idea, and I don't remember you saying one word against it! It's not my fault Ratchet showed up. We have more trees. We can try again! With better rhymes—"

"That's what you don't get. You can't magic away every problem, Keynan!"

"Again with the arguing?" Amari groans.

"Magic got us into the waste. Twice! My rhymes saved your skin and got those trees in the ground!"

"Your rhymes are about as good as—"

"I think," Amari cuts in loudly, "that the monster is a Glory."

I can't believe what Leah was about to say. This is Star-breaker. My BFF, my homie, my ace beaucoup! But my brain caves in around Amari's words.

Same for Leah, by the shock on her face. "Don't be ridiculous!" she huffs as our footsteps echo through the halls. The power's still out. "There's nothing human about it. The Wars of Illusion happened a long time ago."

"Time is messy there, we know this," Amari says. "No telling how the Glories might look now."

Leah scowls, but clamps her mouth shut. A Glory. What did Professor Touré call them? Sorcerers. Elites. Amari's waiting for me to say something. "It's a monster. We've seen talking buildings and attack teddy bears. This is just more of the same weird."

He flashes me a frustrated look. "Remember how much magic stuck in us after an hour? Imagine *years*. A lifetime."

297

That gets us hurrying to the courtyard a little faster. We plop down under the old oak. I keep expecting a student to holler out when they spot the corrupt magic floating out of our skin, but no one is around.

"At least now we know the radiant waste doesn't like trees," I offer after some time. "When I have a better rhyme ready—"

Leah snorts. "What do you think Touré's gonna do when she finds out about the lost saplings, or her wheelbarrows? We're lucky we made it out ourselves."

"But we're *fine*," I insist. "We learned so much. And Amari can draw us some new wheelbarrows, just like he drew—" I swallow the words, too late.

Leah's eyes narrow. "Drew. What?"

"Slickback and Disco," I mumble, face flaming.

"Am I supposed to know what that means?"

"The creatures chewing up the school," Amari says reluctantly. "We kinda made them."

"You *what*?" Leah's mouth falls open. "So the water leaks...the color bombs Touré cleans every night...the blackouts? I can't even with you two!"

"We should've told you." Amari's gaze stays glued to the ground.

"I can still fix it, Leah!" I clasp her hands in mine. "Especially now that I—"

"Do you hear yourself? It's not all about you!"

"I know, I know. Peerless Pact. I'm just saying—"

"There is no Peerless Pact!" Leah explodes, yanking her hands away. "Had me thinking the school falling apart was my fault! You lit one little lightbulb and think you can do everything yourself. And you know what? We'll let you!"

She abruptly stands and stomps off. Amari gets to his feet too, shoulders drooping as he hesitates.

"Come on, don't look at me like that," I rasp.

"That was foul," he says quietly. "We shouldn't have lied to her, Keynan."

"But—"

"You can't even admit we were wrong! I'm done. Try not to do anything brick-headed. I won't be there to pull you out."

He hurries after Leah. Unbelievable! Hot tears sting my eyes. Our first time into the radiant waste alone and we came out safe—scared, sure, but not a scratch on us. But the whole thing is a big steaming failure pie? Somehow, it's supposed to be my fault? Nah.

Leah got one thing right: Peerless Pact is broken...and that's fine with me. I'm better off on my own.

CHAPTER THIRTY-FIVE

THE UTTER GALL

Classes blur by after breakfast the next morning. My next rhyme needs to be flawless. The stuff of legends. Because I'm finally gonna take care of Slickback and Disco. If I can't handle these two little wannabe beasties, what chance do I have against Ratchet? It's not only Peerless on the line anymore. I've got to show my friends that my way is right.

I'm such a jumble of nerves and excitement, it barely registers when Mendoza takes us to the auditorium for practice, up on the big stage. The recital is finally about to happen. It's hard to believe. Leah doesn't look at me once. Whatever. I've got bigger problems.

On the way to Professor Okoro's class, I accidentally jostle my favorite person, and my tablet goes skittering across the tile.

"Watch where you're going!" Dez growls.

"My bad!" I scoop up my tablet and sweep past him. Nope. I ain't got time today. Professor Okoro gives me an approving nod from his desk. "Glad to see your behavior improving, Keynan. I knew Kinder was wrong to think you were behind these pranks. Not your style."

Who knew a compliment could make you feel good and awful at the same time?

Finally the day ends. Amari and Leah ghost me for dinner. I eat with Ian instead, chili and cornbread. He's done after just one bowl. Afterwards I dig into Touré's supply closet for the first part of my plan: bait. I wrap a cloth rag around a handful of old nails—Slickback will come running for those.

I set up my trap in one of the weird glass study rooms. Once Slickback shows up, I'm going to rhyme a net around him. Short and sweet. A reading nook around the corner gives me the perfect place to hide and wait.

"See? I told you!" I whirl around to find Amari and Leah scowling at me. Sneaking up on folks! "He couldn't last one day."

"Why are you bothering me?" I snap. "My rhymes are good as garbage to you, right?"

"I didn't say that," Leah stammers.

"You were about to."

"We're worried about you is all," Amari says. "We were in the waste a long time. Busted magic could be messing with our heads."

"I'm good. Never been better. Just about to trap Slickback."

Leah folds her arms, peering past my shoulder. "Don't Slickback and Disco run together?"

"We don't know that," I say defensively.

"But Keynan—"

"Snacks!" A familiar, annoying voice echoes through the halls. "I can smell them. It's so good to be loved! Adored!"

Amari hides a smile behind his hand. "Wonder who he got that from?" Slickback's polka-dotted little backside wiggles down a wall and into the glass box. "You made him, no question."

"I should've been there for that," Leah murmurs. "He's kinda cute."

"He's an absolute pain," I mutter, peering around the corner.

"No question," Amari repeats.

"Say that," Leah chimes in. "Big mouth, brick head—"

"Can y'all be quiet? I'm trying to focus."

"Nope, we're getting Touré!"

I shrug off Leah's hand on my shoulder. "No! If he sees you, he'll never fall for this again."

"But what good is grub with no company?" Slickback wails, burying his face in those weird, grabby nub-fingers. "A creature this fine should never dine alone."

The air flashes and Disco appears! She flies merrily to Slickback's side.

"Now it's a party!" Slickback pops a nail into his mouth. "Light it up for us, bird!"

I'm frozen. I practiced for the lizard—not both!

But this is my one chance to trap them and show my friends I was right. I stand up and take a deep breath.

"Keynan, don't—"

Two targets with one shot, one chance
To clean up a failed plot before the last dance
For this lizard talking slick,
and the bird who's too quick
We've got a cage for you, and a net aimed true
Not gonna hurt our two, but you're overdue!

Slickback howls as a cage of splinters leaps up from the table, slapping shut around him. Disco disappears—only to flash back into existence, trapped in a gleaming silver net! Bursts of color shoot from her wings, but the net absorbs them all. She flops around, tweeting furiously.

"Busters! Impostors!" Slickback splutters. "The audacity. The utter gall!"

"This…actually worked!" Amari looks ready to cartwheel.

"Told you!"

"Not bad." Leah gives me an appraising look. "I'm still mad at you, though. Now what?"

"Umm…" So… I kind of didn't think past the trap.

"You didn't think past the trap?" She groans, reading my mind. "This is exactly why—"

"The radiant waste," I blurt out. "We'll take them there."

"Sure. Open another Break so that monster can tear up Peerless."

"The art supply closet has a lock," Amari suggests. "Until we figure something out."

"What are you smiling at?" Leah growls at me.

"He said *we*." It's hard to admit how much I miss my crew. A whole day hasn't even passed yet! Going it alone is, well, lonely.

"Fancy institution should have a meal plan that fits my dietary needs," Slickback bellows.

I jab a finger at the creature. "We could've hooked you up if you'd listened to us!"

"Listen? To you?" Gecko tears leak from his eyes. Disco's red and orange flashes pass for deep belly laughs. "Word on the street is you got bigger troubles knocking on your door. Not my fault for getting one last plate or two before the cookout's through! If you young bloods have one lick of sense—"

His ranting washes over me—I stop listening. I can breathe again. That's another rhyme down with no notebook. One more example of magic behaving. And my rhymes? I'm getting good, no lie. If I can keep this up, nothing in the radiant waste can stop me. Not even Ratchet.

The lights suddenly flicker. Around us, Peerless rumbles.

"What was that?" Leah squeaks. "Did Keynan do that?"

No way I'm letting another storm steal my moment. "The lights didn't even go off. Don't worry!"

Amari moans. "Too bad…look."

Dez stands at the far end of the study lounge. Spilled milk spreads from the cup he dropped by his slippers. My heart drops into my stomach. He's seen everything.

CHAPTER THIRTY-SIX

NOW HE LEARNS

Dez inches backward. "How…what…"

"Great going. Another brick head who's seen magic." Leah gives me a surly look.

There's only one way out. Tell him everything. "Dez," I call. "Headmaster Kinder already knows."

He stops but keeps his distance. "I saw a hole of light swallow you outside," he says cautiously. "Thought I was losing my mind. There's no way she's okay with that."

"Come to the library at lunch tomorrow," I say. "Professor Touré will catch you up. What do you think we've really been doing in detention?"

"Was that smart?" Amari asks after Dez disappears around a corner.

"The answer," Slickback declares, "is no."

Leah glares at me. "I can't believe you're making me agree with a lizard."

"The truth will set you free, boo." Slickback says. "We ain't know him!"

"We barely know *you*!" I snap. She's really on Team Slickback? "Let's get these two hidden before anyone else shows up."

Leah still won't say more than two words to me, but Amari convinces her to go along with it. Slickback and Disco are caught! What more does she want?

Professor Touré smiles when we file into the library the next day. "To what do I owe the…" Her smile slips when Dez scoots in after us. "Oh no. You didn't."

"It…it was totally an accident. I was trapping the creatures—"

Professor Touré makes a choking noise. "The *what* now?"

I tell her everything, from creating Slickback and Disco in the first place, to the talking museum and our latest brush with Ratchet. Leah's happy to chime in and point out wherever I didn't listen to her and Amari.

I only leave out Mendoza—it's not right to snitch after how much she's helped us. Amari and Leah at least respect that. I've never made someone's eye twitch, but

307

Professor Touré's eyelid is fluttering like Disco's wings by the time I finish.

"I don't have time for this foolishness." Touré rounds on Amari and Leah. "And you two just stood by? Crews look out for each other!"

"Who said we're a crew?" Leah mutters crossly. "Crews *listen.*"

Touré searches my face. I cross my arms and scowl. She sighs and turns to Dez. "One whisper of this to anyone, and Jocelyn will drag you home by your ears. Am I clear?"

"Yes, Professor," he squeaks.

"Good. Now show me these…creatures." We shuffle for the door. Professor Touré barks at Dez, who was heading the opposite way. "Where are you going? You're in this now."

"*What?*" Leah and I say at the same time.

"He's seen magic, so now he learns, too. No arguing—not a word, Leah! It'll be a miracle if Kinder doesn't skin us all."

Dez falls in beside us. I cannot believe it. He's part of our crew, just like that? How is that even fair? But it's happening. He's still right here when Amari unlocks the closet to reveal Slickback and Disco.

Slickback squints in the sudden light. "If you're the one

teaching these kids manners, I need to speak to your manager."

Professor Touré gives us a long look. "I'll…deal with this. You four get to class."

My heart sinks and Amari's face wilts. Even if these two caused a mess…well, they're ours. "You won't hurt them, will you?" he asks.

"No longer your concern," she declares. Dez runs his hands along one of the shelves, and Touré snaps at him, too. "Don't touch that. Don't touch anything!"

Dez backpedals out of the closet to stand with the rest of us. Disco's pastel glimmer feels…nervous. Slickback gazes up at me, lip quivering. "You gonna let her do us like—"

Touré slams the door shut.

"Professor, I caught them," I say. Leah snorts and Amari kisses his teeth, but forget them. They didn't help! "If they're not messing things up anymore, the headmaster won't close Peerless, right?"

Touré holds my eyes for a long time. "I honestly don't know, Keynan. I'm sorry. Dez, come straight to the library after classes." Our tablets chirp that lunch is over. "What are y'all staring at me for? Go!"

We scramble off to classes, weaving through other hurrying students. Great. From the look on Touré's face, a flawless recital is our last hope of convincing Kinder. Without that, there's no more learning magic. No more fixing storms. And the frosting on this disaster cake? We're stuck with Dez through the end! He'll probably stir up trouble just to get back at me.

I reach a hall that splits off to Horticulture. Leah hesitates like she's about to say how amazing my magic turned out—or stick out her tongue. We might be broken for good.

I glance at Dez, who is murmuring with Amari. Are they friends? When did that happen?

"Keynan Masters!" Headmaster Kinder bursts out of the staff lounge and strides toward us. "What are you doing?"

"Oh, hi! We were, uh, just playing Why Our Headmaster Is Bomb. Weren't we, y'all?"

"Drills?" Dez blurts out, running with it. "I always know what to do if a storm comes. Hide under a desk. Try not to pee myself."

"Cute outfits," Leah adds. "Especially shoes."

"You took mine," Amari grumbles.

Kinder's mouth twitches. "I'm not here for you today, Keynan, but keep tempting me. Amari." He freezes as her gaze swivels to him. "Yes, you. That blotch of color by the auditorium stage? I know you're behind it—start talking!"

Amari's lips move but no words come out.

"It was me."

Headmaster Kinder's jaw nearly slaps the floor as she turns to Dez. "What did you say?"

"It was me," Dez repeats. "I wanted to make recital signs, but I spilled the paint." He holds his hands up apologetically—they're stained with colors. "Amari...he tried to help me fix it."

"And I still will," Amari adds shakily. "We just need primer."

Kinder studies us one by one. I get why Mendoza's so scared of her. If she ever used magic on us...yikes.

"I'm pleased to see you all taking the recital seriously," she finally says. "That's exactly what Peerless needs right now." She flicks at her tablet. "I'll forgo a point deduction, so long as it's cleaned up." She abruptly marches off.

"I can't believe that worked," Leah breathes.

"I know, right?" Dez shrugs uncertainly.

"Sit with us at lunch, Dez," Leah offers. "We'll help you stay out of trouble."

The three of them sweep off down another hall, whispering in a tight knot. Without me. A lump rises in my throat. Just like that, they're cool with someone who doesn't know our jokes or dap or even play Mirror Maze Castle? The same someone who ruined my notebook? This is so messed up! I caught Slickback and Disco, with a freestyle, by myself. I saved the day and it didn't even matter.

CHAPTER THIRTY-SEVEN

EXTRA CREDIT

The night before our recital, I should be happy, but I've never felt so alone. Ian still won't talk about anything but snacks or Mirror Maze Castle. My friends sit together for breakfast, lunch, and dinner with Dez. I'm not invited. Peerless Pact is in shambles. Our recital is the only thing stopping Kinder from closing Peerless—and I have no idea how it will turn out.

The courtyard is my only real happy place. Professor Mendoza talks with me sometimes, whenever she's looking for fruit. She's actually really cool outside of class, not so nervous. I'm extra glad she's here tonight. "It's so unfair," I say, pawing around the brambles of a raspberry bush. "With enough practice, I could clean up storms. I know I could! Maybe for good."

"Not that one." I move my hand around until Mendoza nods. "Yes, that one's perfectly ripe. What if your storms are just how things are now?" A memory pops in my head, my mama staring at a blank wall. A thorn jabs my thumb and I let out a yelp. "Careful, Keynan!"

I drop the just-plucked raspberry into her waiting palm with the rest. "You don't really believe that, do you?" I say, sucking my thumb.

Mendoza takes a moment to choose her words—or she could just be counting her raspberries. "Kinder believes it, and that's what matters." She offers me a pinched smile. "Anyway. I'd planned to give this to you after fall break. But since there…ah…might not be any Peerless left, you might as well have it now."

Mendoza rummages in her jacket and extends an actual paperbound book with crisp edges and a blank white cover. The first page reads, *Collected Poems from the Lost Century*. "Extra credit, as promised. Your bribes weren't earth-shattering, but you did bleed for me a little bit."

"New poems!" I exclaim.

"More than that. These explore magic. Best not recite them out loud. And keep it to yourself."

"Oh I will, believe me." The cover tingles in my hands. I've already picked out a place for it on my bookcase back home. "Why don't we ever talk about the Wars of Illusion?"

"You and your questions. That's…complicated." Professor Mendoza stills. "So many people don't even believe they happened, or *can't* believe it. Most people choose the path of least resistance when it comes to accepting reality. I trust you're not like most people."

"I'm not."

"Good. You know just enough to stay safe. Don't stop your poems, Keynan." She pats the oak tree fondly. "Not for the headmaster, your friends, or anyone who tries to make you feel small."

I thank her profusely and rush straight to my room to stash her gift. When Ian finally starts snoring, I eagerly pore over the pages. Some of it is heavy and a little hard to understand, but it's *new* and challenges my brain. The rhymes still whisper in my head long after I fall asleep.

Headmaster Kinder's voice rings through the intercom as we're getting dressed the next morning. "First-years, I hope you're ready for the big day. All of Peerless is eager to see what you're capable of."

"I cannot wait to get this over with," Ian mumbles from his bed. "Can you believe we're going home tomorrow?"

"I know, right?" Wow. Fall break is finally here. I miss Bizzy Block terribly. Everything's been such a mess, I haven't spared a thought for what happens *after* our recital is over.

"What's the first thing you'll do back home? My auntie bakes this apple pie that will make you cry real tears. Better than Soup's. Maybe I'll save you a slice."

"To make up for all of my snacks you ate up?" I tease.

"I was thinking more of a trade. Bizzy Block turnovers versus Trap Street pie."

"I can work with that!"

"But seriously, what are you going to do?"

"Same thing I do every day." I can't hold in my smile. "Write down the best words to say."

Ian chucks a pillow at me. "Because you rhyme all the time."

"Ian! You're a poet and you don't know it."

"How do you stand being you?"

"Might as well ask the sky if it likes being blue! Could I be anything but true?"

His next pillow hits me in the face, but I'm laughing too hard to care. After everything that's happened, I'm just happy to share one more fun moment with Ian.

We meet up with our homerooms and stream toward the auditorium. After getting through Breaks, Ratchet, and the bizarre museum, a recital should be cake. So why am I nervous? I'm ready. More than ready. Is everyone else, though?

I practice my lines out of habit. I don't even notice Professor Mendoza gliding beside me until she clears her throat. "Big day. Remember...regurgitate. Exactly as they've told you. *Exactly*. Good luck." We're seated by homerooms in the auditorium, and it's just my luck that Professor Wiley plops me between Amari and Dez. Awkward. I'm actually grateful when Headmaster Kinder takes the podium, addressing us.

"Welcome, first-years. This exercise is a small demonstration of all you've learned in our short time together. Follow your professors' directions."

Five minutes in, I get what Professor Mendoza meant: good luck...*staying awake*.

The movement showcase kicks everything off. First-years file onto the stage one at a time, each performing the exact same routine, the exact same way. Knees bending, a few twists side to side, some swaying around, all topped off with a stiff bow. Lacretia beams the entire time, while Leah finishes her movements off with a stony face. I raise my hands to clap so she at least knows she's seen— friends or not, no one deserves this.

Professor Wiley shushes me before I can cheer, though. "Don't disrupt the performance!"

Dez, Amari, and I exchange a horrified look, before we remember we're not friends and are supposed to be ignoring each other.

Movement mercifully ends. Composition is next. I gather backstage with my classmates. Anxious energy clings to most of them.

I stride out to the stage when my name is called. Flawless recital, Peerless itself on the line. I've got this. But my knees are suddenly shaking for no reason. It's not like I've ever forgotten rhymes before when it mattered most... not the Keymaster. Nope! Two spotlights fix on me, so bright I can't see any faces. I take a deep breath...

A shadow flickers up high across one of the spotlights. I catch a flash of color on the ceiling that shouldn't be there. My whole body goes numb as I follow a polka dot figure creeping along, so small I shouldn't be able to see it, except for small flashes of eye-bending light, like fireflies that can't decide on a color.

Slickback and Disco!

CHAPTER THIRTY-EIGHT

THEY CALLED IT BEATBOXING

No one else has spotted them yet—except Leah, standing offstage with her hands clasped to her face in horror. I hear Professor Mendoza's desperate hiss from the first row. "You're making me look bad! Go!"

"Keynan Masters!" Headmaster Kinder thunders. "What is the meaning of this?"

I barely push the recital lines through my teeth. The faintest flash comes from the ceiling—Disco's still up there.

"Bravo!" Slickback's voice shatters the silence once I finish. "You did good. But now it's payback time, young blood! You stingy, and selfish. So we gonna teach you today. Teach you how to share!"

This isn't happening! First-years rumble across the auditorium with professors calling loudly for quiet. At the edge of the ruckus, I can just make out the quietest rhythm.

Stomp slap stomp stomp slap

Leah! She gestures at me urgently. It's now or never to throw a rhyme out there:

> *Can't keep me quiet for long, can't keep ignoring my sound.*
> *Get a peek while you can, before I shut this place down!*

The spotlights wink out!

First-years hoot and bang their chairs in the sudden wash of darkness. "Everyone remain calm. I'm sure this is only temporary!" Professor Wiley's voice rings out. I see one last flash of blue-pink at the back door of the auditorium and hop off the stage to race after it.

Dez grabs me halfway up the aisle. "That's the bird and the gecko, isn't it?"

"I've gotta stop them!"

I shrug him off. Before I reach the exit doors, Headmaster Kinder plants herself in my path. "I saw those...*things*," she shouts. "You allowed them into Peerless."

"I kinda...made them."

"You *what?*"

"I had it handled! I don't know how they got out. But I can fix this if we hurry."

Touré marches up with Amari, Leah, and Dez behind her. "Headmaster, these three—"

There's no time for this! I dance around Kinder and fling open the door. A nauseating glare assaults my eyes. The walkway and garden outside the auditorium are overrun with garish colors. Pumpkin-headed creatures with glowing green eyes bounce around the multicolored ground, smaller gourds snaking behind them like centipedes. Smoke pours from their orange-fanged mouths. Professor Touré lets out a yelp as one sets fire to the tulips. They burn pink and white.

A tiny frosty bear zips past Dez's ankles, ignoring his shriek as it scales the building's bricks with its little blue claws. Brilliant flashes light the sky—Disco, bright enough to be a storm.

"Look!" Leah hisses. "Those things from the museum!" A dozen of the long-legged figures with the brilliant neon top hats are peering into the windows, perched on huge snowballs half-buried in the Peerless brick.

"They'll never leave if they get inside!" Kinder buries her face in her hands. "A pinch of their magic will ruin everything!"

"A masterpiece!" Slickback roars. "A party to end all parties, and wait until you meet the guest of honor!"

"Block party," Amari moans.

Rhymes spin in and out of my brain faster than my tongue can catch them. Even if they were perfect, it still wouldn't be enough. Every creature we've ever brushed past in the radiant waste—somehow, Slickback's drawn them here as surely as if they had received a letter with a shiny golden seal. *Guest of honor* can only mean one thing. Ratchet.

I sink to my knees, staring down at my palms. I've messed up everything. "I...I can't do this by myself."

A hand rests on my shoulder, then another. "That's all I've been needing you to understand," Leah murmurs. Together, she and Amari yank me up.

Kinder's scowl deepens as Dez slides in beside us. "You foolish children, you don't even know what you've done. This will take years to repair!"

"We don't have years," Touré shouts. "We never did!"

Leah squeezes my hand as the grown-ups argue. Everything's falling apart, but I squeeze back. "Peerless Pact?" I whisper hoarsely.

"Peerless Pact," my friends answer. A knot in my chest unravels.

Dez blinks. "Umm, what they said. Now what?"

I take a deep breath and reach for my words.

Headmaster Kinder, we're here to assist,
Don't know all the magic, but we get the gist.
Take the tinder from this fire, I must insist to start.
Can we all work together, and use each other's art?

The pink-and-white fire boiling over the tulip blossoms winks out. They're a little wilted, but okay for the most part! Kinder's mouth falls open. Touré's eyes twinkle. "I tried to tell you," she murmurs to Kinder. "They can handle it."

Headmaster Kinder meets my eyes. "I can't do this alone, either," she finally says. For the first time since I arrived at Peerless, I think we understand each other.

A gang of frosty bears trundles from around a corner, brandishing icy battle axes. Kinder straightens, staring them down. They shimmy right on back out of sight. "Three squads," she pronounces. "A rhymer with each. Amari, Professor Touré? Round up all of those creatures and send them through a Break." Her voice softens. "Leah? I worked with your sister, and I'd work with you too if you're willing."

Leah nods uncertainly. "She could help us, but I don't know—"

"Students are still locked down," Touré interrupts quietly. "It's better this way."

"Okay, then. Let's go."

"Good. We'll repair any damage to the school itself," Kinder says.

Finally, Kinder and Touré turn to face me and Dez. My heart thrums faster. "You two find those creations. Subdue them."

"But my trap didn't hold."

"You created them—you share a link. You may be the only one who can stop them."

"Shouldn't I go with them?" Amari asks worriedly.

Kinder shakes her head. "No one goes alone, and I need you with Touré. Leah?"

Starbreaker raises her chin. "Let's do this." They march off around the corner.

"I'm going to regret this." Touré glances down at Amari. "Try to keep up."

The two of them hunch over Amari's tablet. The air begins shimmering around them.

I exchange a sheepish look with Dez. "I guess we better get moving."

"Guess so. Let's make this better than Physics."

We fling open the doors to Peerless. Lockers are floating off the wall in the hallway. Floor tiles are changing colors. This is bad. Worse than all the other magic leaks I've seen in Peerless put together. Weird hoots and howls and whistles fizzle from behind every door. Icicles stretch from ceiling to floor. A massive rumble-roar shakes me to my core.

"What was that?" Dez cries.

"Nothing nice! Come on!"

The trail of busted magic hooks around a corner to the left just ahead. I motion Dez to slow.

"How did I miss this feast?" Slickback's voice rings out. A brilliant flash is Disco's reply.

"Trophy room," I whisper. "Snacks. They're distracted."

"Then what are you waiting for?"

"I need Leah! My beats aren't enough to hold down my rhymes—hers are better."

Dez licks his lips nervously. "Beats? I'm new to all of this!"

I turn back to the trophy room, hiding my disappointment. What was Kinder thinking? I'll have to make this trap on my own. "Be ready to run if this goes left, okay?"

I can't do the same lines over again—they didn't work the first time anyway. Then I hear something:

poom poom click

poom poompoom click

I whirl in amazement. Dez gives me an awkward shrug. He doesn't slap or clap or stomp. He makes a beat with his tongue and lips! "How did—never mind. Do that again!" I nod along as he keeps it up. "Yes! Are you ready for this?"

He gives me a wide-eyed thumbs-up. We rush into the trophy room together.

Disco and Slickback freeze over a half-eaten plaque.

"Hold up!" Slickback barks. "Y'all couldn't stand each other! Now you homies?"

No time to practice or think ahead. I need a better trap, and that's the only thing on my mind:

> We ain't finna argue, we need a change of pace,
> Can't stay in Peerless, won't dump you in the strange place.
> You need your own world your own time your own safe space,
> Fresh start, way apart from me and mine's face!

Light bursts through the trophy room. Dez screams in panic. He stopped the beat! Wind whips around us and I back away in fright. Cases crash and topple, scattering glass shards across the floor. Gold flashes swirl in the air as trophies get swept up by the gusts.

A Break is forming...inside of Peerless.

"You may have whupped me this time, young blood!" Slickback's howl peals through the light. "But it's gonna cost you your *whole school*!" He scuttles away, knocking over more trophies, but a loop of magic snags him and drags him into a blue sphere of light. Disco dives in after him. The gathering wind stills. The magic we just created hangs in the air like a glistening, watermelon-sized raindrop.

Beside it, the new Break quivers. But instead of vanishing, it pulses out of the trophy room, humming down the main hall, swelling against lockers and ceiling lights.

"But we stopped them!" I croak. If they aren't opening the Break… Oh no. Slickback wasn't just bragging about bringing Ratchet to Peerless. He followed through.

"Dez? I need you." He's burrowed into a corner, half-buried under a shattered trophy case. A slice mars his shirt, the sleeve is stained red. "You're hurt! Can you get up?"

"You…you're going after that thing?"

"Not without you. Come on." I extend a hand and he takes it, wobbling to his feet.

"Shouldn't we get Kinder?"

I hesitate, then shake my head. "She's trusting me, and I'm trusting you. Let's go!"

We race down the hall toward the courtyard. The Break darkens as a silhouette pushes through—a shadow with red eyes. Ratchet is massive, bigger than I remember—crystalline, translucent scales bristle over murky layers of turquoise and violet. The monster's powerful shoulders brush the lower branches of the oak tree, and those three tails lash around furiously like scorpion stingers. The smell of a lightning strike chokes the air. Dez and I skid to a stop, holding each other up. Those jaws are big enough to swallow a wheelbarrow whole! The monster peers around, snarling like it's expecting a trick. It's now or never.

Go home, take a nap, why you messing up
our spot?
Leave our trees be if—Dez I need you!

Ratchet roars and lashes out. The oak tree tremors with the shock. Falling leaves fill the air on every side. Diamond-sharp claws gash the bark deep, and the air around us vibrates. Cracks shoot through the Peerless walls surrounding the courtyard.

This is my home away from home,
my forever friends zone.
We gotta make amends, we gotta set the tone.
Our professors pass the test, I see that now.
Amari draws so crisp, much wow,
Dez drops fresh beats, ain't seen his best yet.
Leah moves the world with her feet,
every time she'll get my bet—

I cut off—what am I rhyming? A menu of monster snacks? Dez hasn't even tried a beat, he's just staring at me. Ratchet rounds on me and shudders. Fine cracks spread along its powerful neck. It twists its head, and glittering dust fills the courtyard. For the first time, actual alarm appears in the monster's red eyes. It rips at the garden's dirt before pouncing back into the Break!

Ratchet's three tails lash through the hole, and then the Break vanishes completely. Falling leaves spin and loop on every side as I find Dez. "You did it," he rasps.

"I didn't do anything," I admit, still stunned. The monster was…cracking apart. The glittering residue in the air trickles toward the old oak. "I know when my poetry hits. I started off trying to trap it, but that rhyme wasn't anywhere close."

"Fair. It did feel like you were trying to talk to it," Dez agrees. "But it worked. For a second there, I thought it wanted to say something to you. And you still did more than me! I just froze."

"Listen, we've all screwed up. My first trap for—" I cut off with a groan. "We gotta make sure it worked!"

We race back to the trophy room. The teardrop is still where we left it. Reflections of Slickback and Disco float on the surface. Wait, no. They're stuck *inside* a miniature version of the trophy room.

"They own magic blew up in they faces," Slickback hoots. "Good riddance! You ate those party decorations up! Wanna find some more trouble?"

Disco flashes in response.

"Fine. Good trouble it is." Slickback strolls off down school halls within the teardrop as we watch.

Dez peers at the thing curiously. "You made some kind of fishbowl."

"*We* made. You've got skills!"

"Thanks. Some friends back home taught me how, before..." Loss shadows his face, the same sadness I've seen in my mama's eyes. A storm must have got to his friends. "Anyway...they called it beatboxing."

"You couldn't have picked a better thing to be good at. Look at them. They don't even know they're trapped! Professor Touré's gonna be happy and mad at the same time."

Dez lets out a big belly laugh. "How did you all stand her anyway? All that detention?"

"We had each other. Come on, we better see who else needs help."

The school halls heal around us as we make our way back. Floating lockers settle into place and lights flicker back on. We emerge into the sun just as Touré punts a frosty bear through an open Break. Amari seals it up with a can of spray paint. "Keynan!" He trots over, eyeing us both anxiously. "You're okay? What happened?"

"We caught them."

"And Keynan pushed the monster back through a Break."

"*What*?" Touré exclaims. "Tell me everything!"

I talk through it all in a daze. Dez helps. Honestly? I'm

not sure how I stood up to Ratchet, but the professor nods thoughtfully when I try to explain my rhyme. It's about time some luck happened for us. Touré exhales in relief once we finish. "Thank goodness. I'm...sorry for this. I don't know how they got out. We'll step up your lessons after fall break. You have my word." I really think she means it. My heart does a somersault—Peerless isn't closing, then. Right? "Just keep the magic quiet— imagine the damage these creatures would do at your homes."

"No one saw us, either, if you're worried about that," Dez adds. "Everyone must still be in the auditorium."

"Where's Leah?" I ask anxiously.

"Right here!"

We whirl around to see the headmaster and Leah emerge from Peerless. Leah calls out, "Whatever you did was right on time. I thought the whole school was going to collapse!"

Kinder and Touré touch eyes. "We were very lucky," Kinder says, then abruptly clears her throat. "I suppose there's the rest of the school to look after."

"I couldn't be prouder of the four of you. I'll deal with this." Professor Touré gingerly takes the bubble trap from my hands.

"It's sound?" Kinder asks.

"It is," I say firmly. "We made it together."

Amari gasps as he looks into the bubble trap, where Slickback is munching on a bathroom door hinge. "They don't even know it's fake?"

"For the moment," Professor Touré says softly. "Living things can't be imprisoned in magic forever. It's part of their nature to see through the illusion."

Kinder watches her go, shaking her head.

"So…" I clear my throat. "Be a shame to close Peerless, after going through all of that drama to save it, right?"

Headmaster Kinder hesitates. I exchange nervous glances with my friends. "A shame," she says finally. Somehow, she scowls and smiles at the same time. "The work's far from finished, I'll admit that. Now get in there before I change my mind."

"Yes, Headmaster!"

We scamper into the auditorium, filing into an open row in the back. Professor Wiley and Professor Mendoza both look us up and down nervously but say nothing. We did this. We really did this.

"Y'all…" I murmur. "Sorry for getting a big head back there. My bad."

Amari grins. "We won't let it happen again."

"Nice work, Keymaster," Leah whispers.

"Not so bad yourself, Starbreaker."

"I guess I'm just going to come up with my own nick-name," Amari grumbles.

"We get nicknames?" Dez asks eagerly.

"Later," Leah says. "Tell me everything that happened."

We trade whispers about our challenges, how Dez can beatbox, how Touré and Kinder used rhymes more incredible than anything Amari and Leah had ever imagined to help fix Peerless, brick by brick. I wish I could have seen that.

Scattered clapping echoes through the auditorium when the lights flicker back on. Headmaster Kinder stands at the podium as if she had never left, gazing imperiously over the first-years.

"You've all performed admirably. I've observed all I need to of this class. The recital is complete." A surprised cheer ripples through the first-years. Her eyes rest on the four of us. "Get some rest, but get ready. I believe you'll be the best first-year class Peerless has ever seen."

CHAPTER THIRTY-NINE

REVEAL THE REALNESS

We chatter excitedly on our way to the dining hall. All of Peerless feels electric somehow, with the recital and quizzes over. The four of us have more reason to breathe easier.

Dez demonstrates his beatboxing at lunch. Amari and Leah are so impressed they clap. Which is fine, I guess, but they've never clapped after one of my poems.

"We're not going to see each other again for a whole week," Leah comments on our way to the dorms. "Y'all make me want to pull my locs out, but I'm actually gonna miss you."

"Me too." I really am.

"Even you, Dez," Amari adds, and we all laugh. He's right. Instead of going to bed, we spend the whole night eating snacks that Soup set aside for us after dinner. Leah helps Dez get into Mirror Maze Castle. We play dominoes, which goes much better once Amari understands the rules. Dez brings out his clippers for me and Amari. We laugh and joke and clown, only stopping when the first rays of dawn split the sky.

When I wake up, Ian's already gone. Well, dang. We didn't even get to say goodbye. I stuff my clothes, my tablet, and Professor Mendoza's poetry book into my bag and hurry to the entrance. Amari and I trade dap before he gets on his shuttle. I pile into mine with Dez and Leah.

Joselyn nods approvingly. "You sure did turn it around, kid. Good stuff!"

"No Yolanda?" I ask Leah.

She snorts. "She got permission to stay with a friend again. I'm over it."

We're the only ones chattering away. The rest of the first-years are quiet, like they're sad we're all leaving the school and won't know what to do with themselves over fall break.

We pull up on Bizzy Block first. I hate leaving my friends but am overjoyed at seeing home again.

Dez and I bump fists. Leah drapes me in a crushing hug. "I'll look for you online," she whispers. "Stay out of trouble, brick brain."

"I'll do my best."

I step off. I don't stop waving until I can't see the shuttle anymore. I'll miss them, but I'm back on Bizzy Block. Home! I can't wait to tell my folks everything about Peerless.

Well, almost everything.

The air tastes just how I remember it: clean and citrusy. My parents don't meet me outside, but I'm in too good of a mood to be salty over that. I open the front door nice and quiet before belting out, "Guess who's back from school?"

My mama's head pops out from inside the office. "Keynan! I missed you so much!"

"I missed you, too!"

She squeezes me in a monster hug, then examines me from head to toe. "Tell me everything about Peerless! Favorite classes, all of it. Is your roommate cool? And clean?"

"Ian's the best." Something tickles my memory. Something funny. Something wrong. "He doesn't smell like feet. He thinks his folks' snacks top ours, though."

She rests her knuckles on her hips. "We'll see about that. Did you meet anyone special? I know you love poetry, but it's important to meet new folks your age."

A cold feeling settles in my stomach. My mama's happy and so am I. But this conversation is off. I just can't pin down what's wrong. "Yeah… Leah from virtual goes to Peerless, too. Still my best friend, hands down."

Mama claps her hands delightedly. "That's what I'm talking about. Let's track down your dad. We weren't expecting you until later. We'll want to hear *everything*."

"Sounds good. And Mama? I'm glad you're feeling better."

She cuffs my arm and smiles. "How else would I be feeling? My baby boy is home."

She hurries out while I lug my bags into my room. It's exactly the same, from the old cream lampshade on my nightstand, to the red, yellow, and green quilt that's topped my bed forever. Just looking at it gives me warm and cozy fuzzies. But it feels small, too, like outgrown shoes that are pinching my toes. The whole house feels that way. And my mama acts like herself, but her smile sets my teeth on edge.

I barely start unpacking before the back door bangs open. "Where's this almost grown child of mine?" my baba's voice booms out.

I dash for the kitchen and vault into him. He spins me around, laughing the whole time. "Whoa! Your mama wasn't lying, you did get bigger. Can't tell you how much we missed you. Everyone did."

"Really?"

"You know Bizzy Block would run through fire for you. Welcome home, son."

I want to tell them *everything*. Busted magic, the radiant waste, and how our art creates magic. Everything. But we've barely started cooking when a whole parade of folks come through, like a potluck caravan. So many dishes get dropped off, our kitchen table sags in the middle. There's barely room for my mama's jambalaya.

My heart is even fuller than my stomach, though. Yua squeezes me in a hug and makes me promise to come by the shop. Her granny pinches my nose like I'm their puppy, Buster. The Chandlers and all of our neighbors visit. These are my people forreal.

"Why are you so surprised?" Yua laughs as she sets down her granny's blackberry cobbler. "You're the whole neighborhood's little brother or nephew. When you rise, we rise."

Later that evening, I even manage to steal a win against Old Zeph in dominoes, which never happens. "Prolly all that schooling!" he chuckles, sauntering out with a plate of food. "Scared of you!"

When the sun goes down and the last of the neighbors leave, I chatter on about Peerless, my favorite professors, and how the food compares. But there's so much I can't say. They smile faintly, nodding in all the right places. But I can't shake the suspicion that they're waiting for more. I'm just not sure what. Do they know about magic already? What if they're scared of it? Would they keep me home from Peerless? That can't happen.

My dreams that night are the worst I've ever had. Leah and I lost in the radiant waste, searching for each other, but every time I find her, that monster chases me off. I spend another dream running from it while Slickback laughs at me. It's so scary, I go sit by our orange tree as soon as I wake up. Corrupt magic doesn't leak out of my pores, even though I feel like it should.

I check Mirror Maze Castle right after. If the game's castle gryphons catch us, we get sent to the dungeon, and prisoners can scratch messages on the stone walls. I don't see anything new, though. I write:

hope y'all break is going okay. talk to me
—keymaster

All morning, I can't shake off the funky feeling. My baba peers at me over his coffee while I pick at breakfast. "What's up?"

"Just worried about my friends."

"Y'all got close?"

"Yeah. It felt good, you know? Folks my age. I didn't know how much I needed that."

A muscle in his face pinches. "I wish we could've done more for you, but we can only control so much. Anyway, listen. I've got chores that need more than two hands. How about spending some time with your old man? You know, bonding."

I manage a smile. "I don't think that word means what you think it means!"

We solder circuit boards for Yua and dig up a leaky irrigation hose in the community garden. The old routines feel empty though, and there's never a good time to talk about my rhymes and magic.

I'm ready to rest when Mama hollers from the patio to come eat lunch. But the best of our leftovers still isn't what I'm hungry for.

It's only been a day, but—I miss rhymes!

I want—*need*—to share them with my parents. We don't lie to each other, not ever, and I can't imagine a bigger lie than this. If magic scares them, Professor Touré will convince them it's okay. I know it.

They'll be all in once they see what I can do. Just a little something. Small, like my first bit of magic with the light bulb. I work out the beat I remember from Dez's beatboxing. I even add in a pencil, tapping it on my nightstand:

Stomp
Slap
Stomp stompstomp
Slap
Clickclickclick
Slap

That's *niiiiiice!* Now what to rhyme with it? A safe, snack-sized demonstration of magic:

> *I'm Peerless, fearless, with important things to do.*
> *Gotta show my parents not to fear this when I know it's right and true—*
> *and real—like the laws of physics, like light and air.*
> *Reveal the realness of this magic if I'm really being fair!*

A point of light flutters into existence above my palm. Perfect. The orb glows yellow and white, not bright enough to be too scary.

My pencil wiggles off the desk, dissolving into a puff of sparks that gets sucked into the orb.

Umm…that shouldn't have happened.

So why did it?

I silently replay the rhyme over in my head. It's all about showing that magic is real. Revealing realness. It's probably the clearest rhyme I've done yet. The orb crackles again. I stand up in alarm as it hovers over my desk. The wood shivers into bright sparks that swirl into the light, vanishing completely.

"Think, Keynan!" I'm trying not to panic. *Reveal the realness of this magic if I'm really being fair.* Not a word out of place. So why is a rhyme about revealing magic tearing up my bedroom?

"Keynan?" my mama calls sharply from the kitchen. "Everything okay in there?"

"Fine!"

The floor beneath my disappeared desk shudders apart and floats into my orb. Carpet, wood, nails and concrete. Something spongey and familiar lies beneath it. Cold sweat breaks out on my back. It reminds me of the ground in the radiant waste.

Reveal the realness of this magic. My room, *my house*, down to the foundation, is made of magic! That's why my orb is swallowing it up and ignoring me.

"It doesn't sound fine—" My mama strides in, toweling off her hands. She cuts off with a gasp, eyes widening at the faintly glowing orb. It wobbles and drifts toward her.

She shrieks as the towel disintegrates in her hands, sweeping into the orb.

"It won't hurt us, don't worry!"

"Keynan!"

"I can fix this!"

Tiny motes of rainbow dust drift from her fingers, same as when we sit under the oak tree to cleanse ourselves of corrupt magic. But my orb isn't purging her. My mama is *unraveling*.

I grab the orb with a shout and hurl it at the open window. It freezes just inside the frame. Curtains unthread. The window frame flakes into the light. Pounding boots thunder behind us.

"Son?" My baba bursts inside, face twisting to make sense of what he's seeing. He snatches my quilt from the bed. "Fire! Get the neighbors! Go!"

"Heck, stop!" my mama screams. "Stay away from it!"

"Baba, no!"

We throw ourselves at him, but he's too strong. He shrugs us off. Squares of fabric split apart and pinwheel into the light as he flails, trying to smother flames that aren't flames. He stumbles back, gaping at his hands. His fingers are glowing, coming apart, glittering like dust in a shaft of sunlight. He sees my mother's hands and lets out a frightened cry. My parents sink to their knees, arms clasped around each other, trying to squeeze each other together.

Tears stream down my cheeks. I couldn't rhyme if I tried. My baba reaches out to me, his fingers flaking away. "Keynan what...did you..."

I stagger backward. I can't look at them. I can't think. I can't breathe. My heel catches on a splintered piece of wood in the disintegrating wall. Spongy ground catches my fall, and colors ripple away from my elbows. More radiant waste.

My house is not my home. It's an illusion.

And my parents are not my parents.

They are made of magic.

★ ★ ★ ★ ★

ACKNOWLEDGMENTS

So many people poured into Keynan Masters, directly and indirectly, and I'm so blessed by every hand that took part in shaping this project. For anyone I've left out…charge it to my head and not my heart.

For my agent, Mary C. Moore, your dedication in making this story shine and believing in my vision means the world to me. I couldn't dream of a better home than our Inkyard team. To Claire Stetzer, I'm so thankful for your all-in enthusiasm and intentional approach. Bess Braswell, your communication and energy have been invaluable. Jennifer Stimson, I appreciate your keen eye and care in getting the details right. Stephanie Cohen, thank you for seeing the potential in Keynan. Godwin Akpan, I'm beyond fortunate the world will see this story through your artistry.

Where would I be without my village: Nia, Brent, Eboni, Veronica, Eden, and Andre. Nia, thank you for your insight and willingness to iron out revisions and plot when I'm spinning out, you're an absolute godsend. Brent, your infectious energy and enthusiasm always remind me to seek the positive. Eboni, thank you for your rock-solid critique and incisive eye for story. Veronica, I can't imagine this journey without you in my corner—thank you for your insight and perspective. Eden, I'm constantly in awe of your acumen and thoughtfulness, you've left a lasting influence on my work. Andre, thank you for helping me to conceptualize this story and make it real. Shout out to all of the NSS crew who helped with a beta read, encouraging word, and good energy!

Maurice, thank you for sharing your time and perspective, your mentorship is priceless. Alechia, sheesh. I still don't understand why you chose to gather me under your wing, but this project never sees the light of day without your guidance.

Kwame Mbalia, I'm forever honored that you chose me—the opportunity you shared vaulted me forward. #BlackBoyJoy squad forever. Dhonielle Clayton and Zoraida Córdova, so much of your discourse directly impacted my process, and I'm deeply grateful for your willingness to send the elevator back down.

Tremaine Jasper and AJ Jones, you gave a very green writer the opportunities to keep fueling a very distant dream, and I'm indebted to you both. Neil, Sharla, Ian, Jealool, Chris, y'all are my bedrock from way back—thank you for supporting my passion.

The Phoenix poetry scene influenced me in more ways than I could ever do justice. All of the performers, venues, and family that nurtured my voice throughout so many years have my evergreen gratitude. Writing this book was a full-circle moment, and felt like coming home.

For my family… Azure and Dakari, you both inspire me to be the best version of myself every day. I'm so proud you chose me. You are my light. Tamlka, you have believed in me since day one, and it means everything after all of your faith and encouragement and patience that I get to share this joy with you. Love you to the sun and back!